"You are a single woman raising a child, running a business, and concealing a murder, Josie Pigeon. You certainly don't have time to moon around over the new man in town!" she lectured herself aloud as she circled the house, making sure all the materials stored outside were covered securely for the night. "You've been acting like an adolescent asshole," she was still muttering as she stomped up the stairs. She tripped on the top step, landing flat on the floor. It had been a long day; she was confused, frightened, and tired. She burst into tears.

"Are you all right?"

Jos[illegible]ream reverberated about the stairwell.

"T[illegible]s just me. Sam Richardson. The guy at t[illegible]or store."

[illegible]" she began, wondering if he could hear [illegible]oudly her heart was beating, "are you [illegible] up here?"

[illegible]oking for y[illegible]

By Valerie Wolzien
Published by Fawcett Books:

Susan Henshaw mysteries:
MURDER AT THE PTA LUNCHEON
THE FORTIETH BIRTHDAY BODY
WE WISH YOU A MERRY MURDER
ALL HALLOWS' EVIL
A STAR-SPANGLED MURDER
AN OLD FAITHFUL MURDER
A GOOD YEAR FOR A CORPSE
'TIS THE SEASON TO BE MURDERED
REMODELED TO DEATH

Josie Pigeon mysteries:
SHORE TO DIE

SHORE TO DIE

Valerie Wolzien

FAWCETT GOLD MEDAL • NEW YORK

A Fawcett Gold Medal Book
Published by Ballantine Books
 Published in the United States by Ballantine Books, a division of Random House, Inc., New York, and simultaneously in Canada by Random House of Canada Limited, Toronto.

Library of Congress Catalog Card Number: 95-90697

ISBN 0-449-14958-7

Manufactured in the United States of America

First Edition: February 1996

10 9 8 7 6 5 4 3 2 1

This one is for my brother, Tom Shelley

PROLOGUE

THE MAN WORE heavy Italian hiking boots which he used to kick through the rubble covering the floor. He waved his flashlight back and forth in long arcs. It might be here somewhere. And, if it was, he had to find it before one of those women did.

If only he were sure exactly what he was looking for. A ticket stub perhaps, although what were the chances of a tiny piece of cardboard still existing after all these years? A mouse scurrying nearby made him smile. A ticket hidden in a wall would make a fluffy and warm rodent bed if gnawed into tiny pieces. Maybe a cold mouse had done him a big favor.

If only he could be sure of that, he thought, picking up a rusted pipe and directing the beam of light inside. Was that lump at the bottom some sort of Indian tribal thing or a piece of fancy drug paraphernalia? Excited, he shook it and a chunk of black soot fell on the floor. Angrily tossing the pipe aside, the man leaned back against the wall and lit a cigarette.

Which he crushed out immediately as a beam from a passing car swept through the room.

"Damn!" He stooped down, now furious with himself. He was being careless. *Getting caught could be fatal.*

It was his last thought. And it was correct.

ONE

"It's simple. We either finish this job on time and under budget or I kill each and every one of you. Am I making myself absolutely clear?"

Josie Pigeon scowled at the group gathered around her. Propped up on sawhorses, leaning against studs nailed precariously to ceilings and floors, sprawled on the subflooring among open toolboxes and piles of lumber, four women looked at her expectantly. No one seemed the least bit concerned by the threat. Josie pushed her flaming red hair up off her forehead in a gesture they all recognized and added, "I mean it, ladies. If anyone screws up, they're dead meat."

"This is your idea of sensitive motivational management?" Chris Kelly asked, taking off her safety goggles and rubbing the deep lines they had etched in her chubby cheeks.

"So much for things being different when women rule the world," Betty Patrick said, tucking her hammer in the tool belt that hung around hips covered only by a pink gingham bikini, before jumping off the sawhorse where she had been perched.

"Well, the dress code will change—at least in your case. Isn't it a little cool for that getup?" Chris suggested. "After all, it's barely April."

"I'm working on my tan as I work on the house. Carpenters can't afford winter vacations in the Caribbean," Betty answered, running her fingers through her short brown curly hair. "Besides, what difference does it make to you?"

"How will we ever be taken seriously when you dress like that?" Chris argued.

"Are you suggesting that a carpenter can't be pretty?

That I can't be competent as well as sexy? Isn't that a little sexist of you?" Betty asked.

Their two silent coworkers exchanged knowing looks, having heard all this before.

"I think—" Chris began.

"I think we'd better get back to work if we're going to finish framing in the rooms down here by the end of the week," Josie interrupted loudly. "Remember, the Firbanks are planning on visiting the site next weekend. We want to have something concrete to show them."

"Not that they'll like it," Chris said, getting up from the floor where she had been sitting propped against a huge toolbox.

"Not Mrs. Cornell Connaley Firbank the Third, that's for sure," Betty agreed. " 'This is my kitchen?' " she continued in an exaggerated falsetto voice. " 'This is going to be too, too small! Where is the space for my miles of handmade cherry cabinets? Where is the butler's pantry for my famous collection of eighteenth-century silver fish knives? Where are the silk-lined drawers for my Limoges porcelain? Where are my imported appliances going to go? And where's the phone so I can call for takeout?' "

Josie giggled along with her crew and then, remembering that she was management now, worked unsuccessfully to turn her grin into a frown.

Chris grabbed her boss's arm and tugged her away from the group. "Some good influence you are. Keep up the fooling around and we'll be finishing this job on Labor Day," she whispered in Josie's ear when they were alone in the next room.

"Don't say that!" Josie wailed dramatically.

"Hey, I didn't mean to panic you. We've worked together before. Have we ever messed up a job?"

"No, but—" Josie began.

"Have we ever missed a deadline?"

"No, but—"

"Are we one of the best contracting companies on the island?"

"Well, I think so, but—"

"Then what are you worried about?"

Josie frowned. "I'm worried about screwing up. I'm

worried that we'll make a mistake so big it destroys the business that Noel spent years and years building up. I'm worried that no one will hire an all-female contracting company. I'm worried that we'll all be out of work when and if this job ends. I'm worried about everything!" Josie's red hair flew about as she spoke.

"Hang in there, kid," Chris said quietly, putting an arm around her friend's shoulders. "We're all afraid of failure. We won't let you down—you know that. Besides, you're the boss now. If anyone on the crew screws up, you can fire them."

A crinkled grin appeared on Josie's face. "Not a good idea. We can't afford to lose anyone if we're going to finish this job on time. Besides, we're all friends."

"And friends don't let their friends down. So you can stop worrying."

They heard a crash followed by curses coming from the room they had just left. "I'd better get back to work. And you were on your way to the office, weren't you? You did say something about picking up our paychecks," Chris added. "We're friends, but we do like to eat, you know."

"I'll be back in half an hour or so," Josie assured her, feeling around in the many pockets of her overalls for the keys to her truck.

"Sometime you must tell me why you don't put your keys in the same pocket every time. Then you wouldn't have to go through this over and over," Chris suggested, starting to leave the room.

"That would make life too easy," Josie answered, tossing the key chain she'd just found up in the air and catching it. "See you in thirty," she called out, leaving the house. Long planks had been balanced between the porch and the ground to replace rotting steps, but Josie ignored them, leaping into the beach grass that surrounded the house and jogging to the road.

Two vans and a pickup, the entire automotive fleet of Island Contracting, were parked in a neat line in front of the large shingle-style cottage. Josie hopped into the cab of her 1966 cherry-red Chevrolet truck and felt the tension leave her shoulders as the engine growled to life. She loved this truck. But she wouldn't be able to afford the new tires it needed if she didn't get going, she reminded herself, shifting into first, pressing down the accelerator, and steering down the street.

The Firbank house was perched on a dune at the north end of an island that jutted out into the Atlantic Ocean. Island Contracting's headquarters was at the other end of the seven-mile strip of land. Josie drove down the road with her windows open. The truck had no radio, so she hummed an old Beatles tune her son had played constantly when he was home for spring break two weeks ago.

Remembering Tyler Clay's sweet thirteen-year-old face (which could be found by anyone willing to take the time to peek underneath his too-long hair) made her feel warm and snugly—and relieved. After years of worry, the money for his education was in place, thanks to Noel's generosity.

And that thought brought tears to her eyes.

Noel Roberts had been the owner of Island Contracting. He had begun it with a small legacy left him by a buddy who died in the Vietnam War and it had become one of the most important parts of his life—the other being his involvement in various liberal causes. Having been rejected by his family when he returned from Vietnam less gung ho than when he enlisted, his employees had become a substitute family. And his political beliefs had caused him to hire women who were having a tough time entering a field usually reserved for men.

Josie began working for Noel before her son was born. She had enjoyed her job and was proud of the skills she had learned over the years. Noel's sudden death six months before had left a large hole in her life. But she had been astounded and deeply touched when his will was read and she was named the new owner of Island Contracting. Noel had also created a trust fund that would enable Tyler to attend boarding school and then pay for four years of college. The remainder of his cash was willed to various political organizations. He had left the continued success of Island Contracting up to Josie.

Sad about her loss, but grateful for the inheritance; thrilled that her bright son was attending an excellent school, but missing him daily; happy to be running her own business when she wasn't overwhelmed by the responsibility, Josie was on an emotional roller coaster that she was finding more than a little exhausting. She turned the corner, leaving the wide boulevard near the ocean and heading toward the bay.

She inhaled deeply, filling her lungs with the sharp scent of the salt marsh. Josie remembered Noel saying that life was created from rot in an estuary—and that it was a good lesson to remember. Josie remembered, but she didn't understand. She loved the marshy smell because it reminded her of childhood vacations, precious weeks spent barefoot on the beach. Fourteen years ago, estranged from her family, she had fled back to this comfortable environment. Her son, Tyler, had been born here and knew no other home.

She turned left and drove slowly down the last block to the tiny building that housed the office of Island Contracting. She parked next to the curb and hopped from the truck, peering over the hood at the front windows. She was rewarded by the glance of a cat or two—or four, she thought, remembering her latest acquisition.

Island Contracting was located at the southern end of the island, near the old creaky drawbridge that most of the locals crossed to reach the mainland. The other bridge, at the northern tip, was new, sleek and modern. The differences in the bridges mirrored the differences in the neighborhoods.

Island Contracting's building had started life as a one-room fishing shack built out over the water on a dock that tilted south. Since then, it hadn't come all that far. Enough plumbing had been added for a tiny half bath that stuck out at right angles to the one room. Two-twenty wiring made it possible for Noel to work on his computer; Josie was planning on taking a course to learn to run it herself—someday. Twin skylights had been cut into a new forest-green tiled roof. The exterior had been painted burnt sienna with warm cream trim. The color choices had been Josie's and she was proud of the result. An expensive crane had been hired to prop up the structure on new wooden pilings. It now tilted north—slightly.

Josie admired the sign that spelled out the name of the company in gilt letters as she fitted the key in the lock. There had been some discussion among the crew about whether or not a name change was in order. Suggestions such as Broads That Build, Built Broads, Women Who

Work, Working Women, and Cleopatra's Contractors flew around during the crew's weekly Friday-night meetings, but Josie preferred the dignity of Island Contracting. Besides, she was beginning to realize that a lot of people preferred men working on their homes—that they had hired Noel, not his crew—and it wasn't an encouraging thought.

But she didn't have time to mull it over. Six kittens flung themselves at her ankles as she opened the door. Six? Had she miscounted last night? She bent down to check and spied a little calico making a dash for the open door. She grabbed for the tiny escapee and, tucking it under her chin, headed across the room to the answering machine on her desk. It was off.

"Damn! Which one of you little buggers has been walking on the phone again?" Josie asked the assembled animals. One of the smaller mysteries of her life had been answered a week ago when, working late, she had watched as one of her strays leaped onto her desk, over the books she was trying so desperately hard to balance, then wandered across the answering machine, depressing the on-off button with a delicate paw pat.

Knowing it was an example of closing the barn door after the cow had left, Josie pushed the on button and settled down to record the paychecks in her account book.

It took only a few minutes, but it wore her out.

"I think," Josie commented to the feline population of the room, "that I have a math block or something. How many other people in their midthirties can't add and subtract accurately?"

The kittens apparently could have cared less. They swirled around her, rubbing on whatever part of her body was available. A tiny black-and-white female climbed Josie's shoulder and tried to find a nest in her unruly red hair. Josie stood up, delicately knocked the cat off her shoulder, stretched, and walked out the back door of her office to the porch cantilevered over the water. She leaned on the railing and waved to a passing fisherman in a worn dinghy. That's where she'd like to be, out on the water with a fishing pole in her hand. She thought about it while she pulled up the large commercial crab trap dangling from the porch railing. Only a couple of crabs and plenty of moss bunker, so she dropped it back into the water. It was too early in the year, but Josie couldn't resist trying to catch a full meal. Blue crab was delicious and, when you caught it yourself, cheap.

The thought of money forced her to start back to the job site. A good day's work deserved a good day's pay and her crew worked hard. A public success on this large and very visible job would lead to others, and every one of the women knew it. After a short search for her keys, she locked the front door and headed for her vehicle.

A massive lumber truck was parked before the Firbank house, but instead of busily unloading their lumber, the driver and his assistant were leaning against a large wheel with their arms folded across their chests, apparently enjoying the blue sky on this unseasonably warm day. At least that's what Josie thought until she realized that Betty had finally gotten around to examining the chimney flashings—still clad in her tiny bikini. Josie walked up behind the men and cleared her throat loudly.

Neither of them jumped.

"Yeah, what do you want?" the tallest man growled.

"I want my lumber stacked over there by the side of the house." Josie pointed.

"We're only paid to deliver to the site," the other man insisted. Neither of them had removed their gazes from the roof.

"Unloaded," Josie insisted. "That's the reason there's a crane on your truck," she added, trying to keep the anger out of her voice. Technically these men were right, but it wasn't the way business was usually done on the island. And it would take her crew the rest of the day—at least—to move, sort, stack, and cover this order. And that would put them a day behind.

Another day behind, Josie reminded herself, pausing to glare at the men before she stomped up the path to the house.

"Ladies!" she yelled, letting the massive front door slam behind her.

Chris was coming down the wide stairway. "You sound pissed. Does paying your loyal employees hurt so much?"

"No, spending time with those bastards outside does."

Josie pointed back over her shoulder. "They refuse to stack the lumber," she explained further.

Chris peered through the window next to the door. "What are they looking—oh, Betty's on the roof, isn't she? That damn bikini does it every time."

"I do think about telling her to wear more appropriate clothing," Josie said, "but she's a great carpenter and how she dresses is her own business. Besides, if I had a body like that, I'd probably show it off as much as possible, too." She glanced down at her plump thighs and frowned. "Not that that's ever going to be a problem for me."

Chris was silent.

"Thanks for all the support," Josie teased her.

"Why don't I go out and talk to those men?" Chris offered. "And you better get Betty off the roof if you want them to do anything at all."

"I'm not on the roof anymore." The announcement came from the top of the stairs. "And if it's the delivery from the lumber company that you're talking about, you better get outside now. It looked to me like it was being unloaded on the front lawn of the house next door."

"Shit!" Josie was out of the house in a flash.

"What's wrong?" Betty asked, mystified.

"You know how Josie feels about keeping construction mess from spilling off the job site."

"She doesn't have to worry about the people next door. No one's home over there. I would have noticed when I was up on the roof if there was. Everything's battened down. I don't think anyone told them the hurricane season ends in December," Betty said, looking out the window at the building next door. A massive white house composed of six intersecting rectangles, each and every one of the many windows was sealed behind closed metal shutters.

"If it's as fabulous inside as it is outside, maybe they have good reason to want to protect it," Chris suggested. "But someone over there put out garbage cans yesterday morning, so we should be real careful with our equipment and supplies."

Betty just nodded. "Think we should go help Josie?" she asked, changing the subject.

"I'll go. You'd just be a distraction," Chris said.

"I was going to put on jeans and a T-shirt first. It's getting cooler."

"Give Evelyn and Melissa a yell, too," Chris insisted, referring to Melissa Wright and Evelyn Boyd, the two other employees of Island Contracting. "I think they're still tearing down the wall between the kitchen and the pantry. Tell them they're needed outside. We want to stow away that lumber before nightfall." Chris followed her boss's path out the front door.

But Betty stared at the house next door for a few more minutes before leaving on her errand. And she wiped tears from her eyes as she went.

TWO

THANK GOD FOR daylight saving time. Even with the extra light, it was almost dark by the time the wood was stacked and protected under a large blue tarp. Betty had filled her thermos with strong coffee at lunchtime and that helped keep everyone going, but four very tired women drove off as Josie walked back into the house, flashlight in hand, to make sure that the building was locked up tight for the night.

She knew that children, boys in particular, adore construction sites. There's so much to do, so many fascinating things to play with, so many different ways to get hurt. The lumber had to stay outside, but Josie always assured herself that no one could climb in an open window and fall down unfinished stairs.

The Firbanks' house was called a cottage in the vernacular of East Coast seaside resort communities. It was, in fact, a mansion. It had been built in 1873 by a man who had made a fortune selling contaminated sulfa drugs to the armies on both sides of the Civil War. The summer after he moved in with his family and a phalanx of servants, his only son had drowned swimming in the bay. The man had left, refusing to return. His wife had remained, claiming that she was closer to the spirit of her dead offspring in this location. For the next thirty-two years anyone claiming a personal acquaintance with the spirit world could find a bed in one of the eleven bedrooms, and the island kept itself entertained with tales of spiritual searches through the dunes.

The woman died during a killer hurricane at the turn of the century. Completely mad by that time and convinced that the howling wind was the cry of her lost child, she was swept out to sea by a wall of water that also destroyed two of the dunes that had protected the property from the sea. It also removed the cottage's shingled roof, three of its nine chimneys, and the servants' wing. What was left lay abandoned for over a decade until it was bought and converted into a small hotel in 1920.

Summer visitors came to the island by train in those days and the less affluent ones drifted toward this hotel, where the decor and the food were equally sandy. Then the economy began to change, and as cars became popular second homes within hours of New York City increased in value. But this building was so large and in need of so much work that it was once again abandoned, the surrounding property sold off to millionaires who started putting up the massive modern structures that now dotted this end of the island. Every few years someone would write letters to the editor of the town's weekly paper complaining about the property, claiming it attracted undesirables. In the early seventies, hippies had turned it into a flophouse. Nearby neighbors, who summered on the island to escape the crime prevalent in their urban neighborhoods, formed committees and petitioned police to provide more constant vigilance. Nothing came of their efforts. Teenagers in the neighborhood continued to use it as a hangout when they could no longer tolerate the confines of their parents' luxurious homes, but it was more an annoyance than a danger to anyone. Nothing changed until a group of college kids had gone off to a rock concert, returning home hours later with one member missing. The brouhaha that surrounded the search for the lost boy drew attention to the activities in the abandoned home, and the town decided, rather late, that it could tolerate such gatherings no longer. The house was sealed and police patrols increased. And that's the way things stayed until the Firbanks bought the property and hired Island Contracting to renovate the hulk.

The Firbanks were, in some ways, an unlikely couple to buy such a place. Josie found them almost completely lacking in imagination, wanting to turn this magnificent seaside home into an imitation English country estate. She remembered Noel explaining that the property had been bought at the insistence of the Firbanks' money manager, who appreciated profit if not charm, and followed the philosophy buy cheap, sell high. The Firbanks, Mr. and Mrs., had one rule: If it didn't show, don't spend money on it.

She walked through the house, kicking aside rubble with the toes of her worn work boots. The wall separating the industrial kitchen from the remains of a butler's pantry had been torn down, but the resulting mess worried her. The other problem with working for people like the Firbanks is that they can't visualize anything. She couldn't just point to a spot on the floor and describe what it would look like after hours of hard work and expect any response other than "When will it be done?" or "Why is it costing so much?"

Josie continued through the house, wondering what Island Contracting could accomplish in the next four days that would knock the imported cashmere socks off the Firbanks when they arrived to inspect their property Friday night. Her own inclination would be to finish the new pantry that was being created between the kitchen and the aboveground wine cellar (there being no basements in houses built on pilings rammed into sand dunes), but that would be used mostly by the Firbanks' employees and she suspected that they would find it insignificant. She knew exactly what would appeal to the Firbanks: a sybarite's bathroom full of mirrors, marble, and a Jacuzzi as deep as a swimming pool, or a weight room where an expensive personal trainer would make them sweat just enough to make them feel they were accomplishing something without doing any real work.

She recognized where her mind was going and called a

halt to it. The Firbanks were her employers and it wouldn't be any easier to work for them if she spent her spare time throwing evil thoughts in their direction. They liked bathrooms—she'd give them a bathroom, she decided, pacing out the space between the dining room and the front hall. A half bath was to be put in here. If she could get deliveries in the next twenty-four hours, she'd have something other than demolition to show the Firbanks. She wondered if there was time to call her plumbing supplier. . . .

Glancing down at her wrist, she realized she had left her watch at home this morning. Besides that, Island Contracting's cellular phone, not scheduled for replacement anytime soon, was only working intermittently.

She glanced at the wide stairway. Betty had been the last person up there. Beauty and brains did coexist, and Josie knew she could rely on Betty to have closed all the windows. She hurried out of the house, pausing only to fasten the padlock on the door behind her.

The island's largest shopping area began only a few blocks south. Not surprisingly, the closest offering was a liquor store. Since it stocked mainly imported products—wine, beer, and the hard stuff—Josie patronized the store at the other end of the island. It usually could be counted on to have a sale on boxed wine from California. But right now speed mattered. It was just possible someone was still around at her suppliers'. And a liquor store that made deliveries was bound to have a phone.

She was there in minutes. She pulled her truck into one of the dozen available parking spaces, noting that a classic MGB was the only other car around. So she wasn't a bit surprised to discover that there was only one person in the store: a man whose good looks were rarer than his car.

"May I help you find something?" The golden hair, touched with silver, blue eyes, and tall tanned body spoke in a cultured tone of voice. Josie was reminded of a history professor she had during her one and only semester of college.

"The phone."

"On the wall by the cash register. Help yourself."

Good looks and kindness, Josie decided, moving around a large display of Chianti.

"It's not a long-distance call, is it?"

"Excuse me?" Josie paused.

"It's okay if it is," he added quickly. "You just have to dial seven-nine-nine first to get into my system."

"It's local."

When he smiled, the skin around his eyes crinkled up in an appealing manner. Josie dialed and glanced back in his direction. While she waited for an answer she wondered if he was single or if he just didn't believe in wearing a wedding band. But her supplier was working late, and by the time she turned back to the salesman, she had seen her reflection in the refrigerated ale case and was wondering how she could get out of here and into a dark corner before meeting any more attractive men.

"Can I help you with something else?"

"I . . . No, thank you," Josie insisted, anxious to leave before she made a lasting, and filthy, impression. "Thank you for letting me use the phone, though."

"Anytime. You're working up at that mansion in the dunes, aren't you?"

"Yes," she answered briefly, surprised that he was following her out the door.

"Anytime you need to use the phone, feel free to stop in," he added as they arrived at her truck.

"I . . . Thanks." She just wanted to get away and comb her hair.

"Did you lose something?" he asked.

"Just my keys," she explained, sticking her hands down in the pockets of her pants. "They're here somewhere," she assured him, knowing that the black stain across her nose just seemed to be getting larger by the second. "Here they are," she cried a little too loudly, and climbed up into the seat of her truck. "Thanks for letting me use the phone," she repeated, jamming the key in the ignition and turning it. Ever reliable, the motor roared to life. "Thanks again," she repeated idiotically, and backed out into the street.

She was still blushing as she climbed the stairway to her apartment.

Being a year-round renter in a resort community had unique problems and Josie knew she had been lucky to find a landlady who didn't either double her rent during the summer or throw her out and make an even larger profit from someone else. And she reminded herself of that fact every single time she unlocked the door to her apartment.

The mail had been slipped through a slot cut in her door, and Josie picked the pile up, hoping to discover a communiqué from her son. But, once again, a missive from Tyler was not among the bills and mailers on the floor.

Urchin, the short-haired chocolate brown stray that Tyler had adopted over a year ago, appeared and rubbed up against her ankle. Josie imagined that the cat was missing her son as well. "Nothing today, Urch," she announced, pulling offers for credit cards and ads for items that she couldn't afford to charge on them from the pile and tossing them in the garbage. "If credit companies know so much about everyone, how come they keep offering me credit?" she asked the cat.

"Are you talking with that animal again?" The voice of her landlady floated through the still-open doorway. "It's not right that you should only have a mangy cat for company. When I was your age, I had more lovers than fingers." Risa D'Amico appeared in the usual swirl of brilliant silk that covered her from her shoulder-length gray hair to the tops of her well-polished Italian boots.

"Come on in, Risa. Would you like a cup of tea or maybe a glass of wine?" Josie was in no mood to listen to stories of her landlady's amorous past. The contrast with her own life would only depress her.

"Wine!" The other woman's voice was full of scorn. "What you call wine wouldn't even be fed to the donkeys in the village where I grew up! Not even to the swine!"

Josie, who had never understood how such a strong-minded woman had decided to follow a lover across the ocean and then, apparently abandoned, stay in a country that she found so "barbarian," repeated her offer of hospitality as she headed across the living room to the messy kitchen.

"If my uncle Bepe, the winemaker, knew what you offer me to drink, he would turn over in his grave. He made a Vernaccia they still speak of with reverence in San Gimignano."

Josie headed to the refrigerator and pulled out a jug of

cheap chardonnay without asking any more questions. She glanced at the pile of dishes in her sink, pulled out two mismatched stemmed glasses, and after a quick rinse, filled the glasses with wine.

She had almost finished hers when she noticed that Risa was staring at her untouched glass. "Is anything wrong?"

"No, I'm merely surprised. You've never offered me anything like this before. This is very beautiful. Very generous to the eye." She took a sip. "Venetian crystal even improves this swill," she added.

" 'Venetian crystal'? Is that what it is?" Josie asked, pouring herself another glassful. She knew that her landlady had had more than a passing acquaintance with such things.

Risa gently tapped the rim of her glass with an elegant scarlet fingernail. "Don't tell me you picked this up at one of those flea markets you're so fond of. This can't be one of your fifty-cent finds."

"No. It was free. There are six more around here somewhere." Josie glanced about the room as she spoke. "I found eight of them in the trash pile behind the house Island Contracting is renovating. You know, that job is really beginning to get me down," she added, scratching the cat's little head.

But Risa was sticking to the point. "Around here? Where around here?"

"I don't know. Wherever I've been drinking something . . ." Josie didn't bother to finish. Her landlady was on the prowl around her tiny home.

Josie was rummaging around her cupboards, searching for dinner, when Risa reappeared, glasses tinkling as they hung from her fingers. "The product of hundreds of years of the glassmaker's art was being used to hold Snickers' wrappers on the floor next to your bed. What my uncle Giovanni would say, I don't know."

"I—"

"And what is that you are eating?" Risa's question ended in a shriek.

Josie looked down at the sandwich in her hand. "Peanut butter and banana with mayo . . . on whole wheat," she added virtuously.

"You work hard all day, then you come home and eat

that. It's a wonder you aren't dead. Just wait one minute." Risa rushed out into the hallway, boots tapping on the bare wood floor, and returned in seconds, a steaming casserole in her hand. "I made you a beautiful risotto.

"You just thank me and then have your dinner. I," Risa continued, "am going to take these glasses downstairs, wash them, and then do a little checking around to see what they are worth. Good night."

Josie didn't have the energy to argue. And besides, the food smelled wonderful. She'd eat the rice and then finish her sandwich for dessert. She thanked her landlady and flopped down on the couch in front of the television.

As usual, her remote had vanished, and too tired and hungry to get up, she found herself watching a rerun while she piled her landlady's food into her mouth.

THREE

A STRONG ARM pulled Josie tightly against his chest. Tropical air drifted through open shutters, gently ruffling the sheer mosquito netting draped around the large bed and bringing with it a potent scent of musky blossoms. The man by her side looked down at her. She glanced up and, recognizing the combination of admiration and lust in his eyes, sighed deeply—and inhaled dust and feathers leaking from her aging quilt.

Damn. She'd sneezed away her dream. She slowly stretched out her aching legs and felt the big toe on her left foot enlarge the tiny tear she'd noticed when putting sheets on her bed a few weeks ago. She was going to have either to shop for sheets she couldn't afford or to spend some of her precious free time sewing, which she hated. What a lousy way to start the day, she thought, putting her feet on the cold bare floor and propelling herself to the bathroom.

She had to move the second half of last night's sandwich from the edge of the sink before brushing her teeth, and the litter box in the corner was beginning to smell, but these things were normal, nothing to be worried about. Josie was out of her apartment in less than fifteen minutes. Risa, sipping a steaming cappuccino on her glassed-in front porch, waved at her, but Josie, a confirmed morning person once the shock of awakening wore off, hurried on to her truck. She wanted to get to the building site as quickly as possible.

Once busy working, maybe she would be able to stop thinking about the fact that her dream lover had looked a lot like the salesman at the liquor store yesterday.

She noticed that there were lights on in the liquor store as she passed by. And the MGB was parked before it. He sure got to work early. . . .

"You are acting like an adolescent," Josie lectured herself aloud. "You don't even know his name. Or whether he's married . . . he could have a wife and seven children. . . . Although that's not exactly the type of car a family man would drive . . . and he was very helpful. . . ."

Fortunately, she arrived at the Firbank house before she remembered those places where romantic relationships had led her in the past. No need to start the day depressed.

The sight before her eyes cheered her immensely. Everything shipshape. The tarp over the lumber was taut, revealing the outline of the materials hidden underneath. A large Dumpster tucked beside the huge gray house was almost full, ready to be carted away by a truck due to arrive before noon. The wooden slide leading from the second-floor window into the Dumpster had been pulled into the house and all windows seemed secure. The rising sun glinted off the large brass padlock securing the front door.

Josie hopped down from her truck and started up the walk to the house, slightly disappointed. Chris was nowhere in sight and it was her week to bring the coffee—and doughnuts. Josie was starving and she had been looking forward to anything with pink frosting from Dunkin' Donuts.

Oh well. She was searching through the pockets of her overalls for the key to the lock when a car pulled up and Chris jumped out, a thermos and a distinctive pink, orange, and white box in her hands.

"Hi! I used a 'two for the price of one' coupon. Twenty-four doughnuts for five people," Chris called out, waving enthusiastically, heading toward the house. "That makes six for each of us—if Betty is still on that weird diet."

Josie had discovered the key in a pocket she had filled with tissues this morning and was removing the lock from the door. "Is it grapefruit or mangoes this time?"

"Chocolate bars of some sort. Eat four and they provide you with all the nutrition you need to climb Mount Everest apparently," Chris explained, following her boss into the house.

"Mount Everest doesn't interest me. It's the roof I worry about. I've only had one conversation with Noel's insurance agent, but he scares me to death. I sure don't want to have to report that a worker fainted on the job and broke her leg."

"You don't have to worry about that," Chris assured her. "The problem that needs Betty's immediate attention is at the back of the house. If she falls, she'll land on the stone patio—and kill herself."

"You are such a comfort." Josie laughed, grabbing the doughnut box. "I don't know what I'd do without you."

"Starve to death," Chris replied, watching Josie struggle to open the box with one hand while holding it with the other. "Don't spill those."

"Only into my mouth," Josie said. "Why don't we dump all this on the table saw in the kitchen and then figure out exactly where we're going to work today? I'll feel a lot better when we have something dramatic to show the Firbanks this weekend."

"You don't think fifty or sixty miles of the best-looking copper piping in the state will do it?"

"They'll only ask why we're not using plastic," Josie muttered, stuffing half a cream doughnut in her mouth.

"Because it's not code for the supply system," Chris answered, licking sprinkles from the top of a frosted cruller.

"And why are we using extra-fine materials on this job? Is Island Contracting absorbing the difference in cost?"

"There won't be an Island Contracting if this job doesn't go well," Josie insisted. "It's not just our jobs I'm trying to save, it's the company."

"We're all doing the best we can. . . ."

"I know. Believe me, I know," Josie said. "Why don't we go upstairs and check out an idea I had in the middle of the night?"

"Coffee first," Chris insisted, filling two mugs from her thermos.

"We'll take it with us," Josie said.

"You're really getting into this management thing, aren't you?" Chris kidded.

"Is she hogging the best doughnuts again?" Melissa asked, appearing in the doorway, a hammer swinging back and forth in her hand.

"There are plenty left for you," Josie answered. "What are you doing with that thing? You look like you're ready to kill someone."

"I found it outside on the ground. Someone must have dropped it yesterday. I wouldn't mind using it to kill my husband, though," Melissa admitted. "The man is driving me crazy. He stays up all night with his books and then complains when I get up in the morning that I'm disturbing him."

Josie started toward the stairs. Melissa was very open about the problems in her marriage, but Josie didn't have time to stand around and listen to all the gory details. "I just want to check out the second floor and then I'll be back down."

"Do you want me to finish laying subflooring in the kitchen?" Melissa asked. "I should be done by lunchtime if I get right on it. And Evelyn finished up the plumbing in there."

"Fine, you complete the subflooring and tell Evelyn to start laying the pipe for the half bath that's going in right next to the kitchen. We're going to make sure that room is finished by Friday—even the tile work. Then we'll have something completed to show the Firbanks this weekend."

"Not a bad idea," Chris said.

"Anyone who has a better one should speak up," Josie responded. "I'm willing to listen to any and all ideas, believe me. I'm just trying to show the Firbanks that we're making good progress—outside of the walls," she added when Melissa opened her mouth to speak.

"It's true that they didn't seem terribly impressed with all the demolition," Evelyn said, appearing in the doorway.

"Yeah, I loved the crack that friend they brought along with them made—" Melissa began.

"What?" Chris asked, passing around the box of doughnuts.

"I think it was something like 'I don't understand why you pay people to do this type of thing. . . . Couldn't you just wait around until the next hurricane and open all the doors and windows?' "

The women all groaned.

"At least it wasn't sexist," Josie muttered.

"I think someone did make a comment about understanding why they name hurricanes after women," Evelyn said.

"Hey, it's been years since only women's names were used," Melissa cried.

"Only proof that these men aren't living in the twentieth century," Evelyn answered, taking a big bite from a jelly doughnut. "What can you do?" she asked rhetorically, licking a glob of stridently purple jelly from her top lip.

"Get to work," Josie said. "We have four days to get ready for the Firbanks."

Melissa hopped up from her seat on the floor and, grabbing a couple more doughnuts, sauntered from the room. Evelyn, equally equipped, followed her, chatting. "Ever wonder how these rich guys got so rich? Doesn't seem like they're all that smart, does it?"

"What I wonder is why I don't meet them when they're single," Melissa called out through a mouthful of fried dough. Josie and Chris exchanged looks. "You said something about work on the second floor," Chris reminded her boss.

"It occurred to me that you and I might be able to finish framing in the new master bedroom suite."

Chris nodded. "If we work night and day we could do it in a couple of days."

"And install the large window, too," Josie added. A master bedroom was being created from three smaller rooms in the middle of the house and would take up a full third of the second floor. The large bedroom was bordered by a bathroom (two sinks, Jacuzzi, toilet, bidet, shower, steam room, and sauna—Josie thought the Firbanks were going to be the cleanest people on the East Coast) on one side and three walk-in closets, a dressing room, and a small study on the other. Josie suspected that the Firbanks didn't own enough books to fill the study's one built-in shelf. But the focal point of the entire area was a huge, multipaned window that was to cover much of the bedroom wall. It was a custom job that had been waiting on the wraparound porch for the past few weeks.

"Jos . . . You're kidding. We'll not only have a difficult time getting a crane on this short notice, but we don't know yet if the dunes here will support the weight of a big piece of equipment like that."

"I know. I've had visions of three tons of metal sinking into the sand since I got up," Josie confessed, not admitting to the dream that was haunting her as well. "But it would impress the hell out of the Firbanks. And the window will show over the scrub pine. People driving down the road will see it. More and more home owners are around these days, checking to make sure there wasn't any storm damage to their houses over the winter. Some of them are probably thinking about additions or remodeling. That window would be a wonderful ad for the company."

"Then we'd better put our sign back up out front. The truck that delivered the lumber yesterday must have knocked it over."

"Then you think we can do it."

"I think we can give it a try. We've got to deal with that window sooner or later. It may as well be sooner," Chris said.

Josie grinned. "I was hoping you'd see it that way." She paused before continuing. "Didn't you once date someone who worked at the large equipment rental place out on the highway?"

"We broke up last winter," Chris said shortly.

"I remember. . . . Did you part amicably?" Josie asked, hoping she was using the correct word.

"Depends on who you are. I wasn't all that happy about it. I assume he was. I heard he got married three days after our last date."

"Three . . ." Josie started, and then decided there was nothing to gain by pursuing that topic. "Then maybe he feels that he owes you something."

"If you're embarrassed to suggest that I call the asshole and beg for a piece of equipment that has probably been reserved for months, go ahead," Chris suggested.

"You'll do it?"

"Why not? What do I have to lose? Maybe I'll find out he's miserable in his marriage and regretting dumping me. It could perk up my whole day."

"You're great," Josie exclaimed.

"On the other hand, his wife could have just given birth to twins. . . . Or maybe he won the lottery and they're on a trip around the world. . . . Or maybe he won't even remember my name."

"Could you call him as soon as possible?" Josie suggested before Chris could talk herself out of the idea. "I hate to waste time working up here if we're not going to be able to get that window in." She opened the door to the bedroom as she spoke.

The walls had been torn down during the general demolition of the interior, wires and pipes jutted up through gaps in the floor, and there were holes in the ceiling where air-conditioning vents were scheduled to appear. Debris was everywhere, and a particularly large pile under the spot where the window was to be installed was covered with a blue tarp. A few of the windows were cracked or broken and the space was chilly.

"How many days do we have to do this?" Chris asked.

"If you get that crane and we set our minds to the job . . ."

"And if we give up eating and sleeping . . . Okay. Fine, I think I'd better make that call. If no one is in the office, I'll just leave a message. They must have a machine," Chris said, heading toward the door.

"Where are you going?"

"Phone's downstairs," Chris muttered, vanishing back out onto the landing toward the stairs.

Josie, left alone in the room, walked over to the window and looked out. Betty had arrived on the job, strolling around the pile of wood that now marked the boundary between the modern edifice next door and the Firbanks' home. Josie frowned, noticing that Betty had parked Island Contracting's van in front of the other house. Neighbors frequently preferred that construction crews and equipment stay away from their houses, and they were often vocal about these preferences. She was surprised that Betty had forgotten. Despite her flamboyant dress, Betty was usually as levelheaded as they come.

Josie tripped over the pile of refuse under the window on her way toward the door. It was a big room and she was halfway across it when she realized that an arm had slipped from under the dropcloth.

FOUR

SHE STOOD STILL, hoping that she had imagined it, knowing that she hadn't. She forced her reluctant legs to walk to the door, which she closed carefully before returning to the pile of rubble. Praying that she had been mistaken, she bent down and lifted the blue plastic.

It was a body, all right, and not so right, he was dead.

Josie took a deep breath, vaguely surprised that she hadn't fainted. She dropped to her knees, pushed her hair over her shoulders, and lifted the cover higher for a closer look. The man was lying on his side in a fetal position with his face turned away from Josie. The back of his head had been smashed in, but taking a deep breath, Josie peered across the mass of splintered skull, bloody hair, and tissue that she didn't care to identify to look at his face.

She didn't know the man. That fact didn't bring her much relief. She stared at him for minutes until she heard footsteps in the hallway. Then she gently lay the cover back over the body, tucking it in as well as she could without actually touching him, and she turned slowly and stood up.

"We've got it!" Chris announced, joyfully entering the room. "And he's getting a divorce!"

"Who is?" Josie's mind was still on the person lying on the floor behind her.

"Jason, damn it! Who else would I be talking about? He says his marriage was a mistake. This is going to be my day," Chris exulted. "Not only are we getting the crane early today, but Jason is going to take the afternoon off and operate it for us—for nothing!"

"For nothing?"

"I mean we're not going to have to pay him anything. He'll do it as a personal favor."

Josie couldn't think of anything to say. In fact, she was discovering that she couldn't think very well at all. "That's nice," she managed through clenched teeth.

But Chris apparently didn't require a more enthusiastic response. "I told him I'd call back with an exact time. Do you think we'll be ready by ten, or is eleven o'clock more realistic?"

Josie suddenly realized that she was going to have to tell Chris about her discovery or else move the body before they started work. But she couldn't seem to think beyond the immediate question. "Eleven o'clock," she muttered, only knowing that the choice gave her an extra hour to do . . . whatever she decided to do.

"Great! I'll call him back." Chris whipped a portable phone from her back pocket.

Josie didn't know what to do. She wanted to be alone. She needed to be alone.

"Damn!" Chris frowned at the phone. "What is wrong with this thing? First it works and then it doesn't. Where the hell is the nearest phone?"

"Probably the liquor store," Josie muttered.

"It wouldn't be open this early."

"Yes." Josie knew she'd spoken too loudly. "He . . . they are. I noticed as I was driving by this morning. There's a very nice man there who let me use the phone yesterday. Just knock on the door. He'll let you in, and the phone is hanging on the wall."

"Are you okay?"

"Fine. Just a little keyed up at the thought of all we need to get done this week."

"Then I'd better make that phone call right away."

Josie just nodded, waiting until she was alone again to lean against the wall for much-needed support.

Her mind was beginning to focus. She had to save Island Contracting. A man had been killed on Island Contracting's building site. The business couldn't possibly survive being connected with murder at this point. They might have to stop working on this project and they couldn't start another. How would they survive without working? The company was too vulnerable. The women on her crew were too vulnerable. She was too vulnerable. She didn't know what to do—except make sure that no one knew about this until she had time to think. She opened the door carefully and looked out into the hallway. She was alone.

She couldn't leave the man here. She and Chris would tear out the wall where the window was to go, but as soon as that was done, the pile of trash would be removed. She had to move the body before that happened.

Better yet, she should move the body now, this minute, she decided, taking a deep breath and tugging the tarpaulin back again. (He had been a big man, but years of hard work had put muscles underneath her layer of fat.) Still, it would be difficult to lift him by herself. Josie ran from the room, knowing that no one would check if she made noise. Theirs was noisy work. Silence only meant a break.

All the rooms had been stripped of their furniture as soon as Island Contracting arrived on the job a few weeks ago, but a pile of T-shirts and ragged beach towels found in an abandoned linen closet had been saved. Rags were always useful. Josie just hadn't realized then exactly what they were going to be useful for. She pulled the largest towels from the shelf and, stuffing a T-shirt printed with exotic leaves and the assertion IF YOU'RE NOT WASTED, THE DAY IS back in place, hurried to the bedroom.

It took her longer to overcome her fear of touching a dead body than it took to roll it over onto the towels and drag it from the room.

At the end of the hallway and under the stairs to the third floor (which had once been the sleeping quarters for the boardinghouse staff and was to be converted into a luxury gymnasium for the Firbanks) was a small room lined with cedar planks that had begun growing mold in the damp ocean air. The future of the space was as yet undecided, but Josie thought it would make a fine temporary morgue. She shoved the body in and closed the door. There was no reason for anyone to go in there.

She ran back to the bedroom, her heart beating wildly. No one would notice the streaks in the dust on the hallway floor. There wouldn't be order in this mess for a couple of days—if then.

Betty was trotting up the stairs, a gray sweatshirt and holey jeans her costume of choice this morning. She carried a shocking-pink gym bag and a large thermos. "Hi!" she called out. "Chris is on her way to make a phone call or something—but she said you might need me up here."

"Did you finish putting the flashing around the chimney? And that cracked gutter is still up out back, isn't it?"

"I finished the gutter yesterday. And I'm putting down a layer of that new polyfiber seal under the metal flashing—as soon as it arrives. It's temporarily covered with plastic." She dumped the gym bag on the floor with a loud clunk. "Shit. I hope nothing broke."

"Want a doughnut?" Josie offered, looking longingly at the two crullers remaining from her share of breakfast.

Betty reacted with horror as though a vampire had wandered into the room looking for a snack. "Are you kidding? Do you know what's in those things?"

"I don't want to," Josie insisted.

"Fat, sugar, fat, sugar, and fat. Completely empty calories. I brought my own food," she added, unzipping her bag and pulling out assorted plastic tubs and boxes.

"Chris did mention that you were on another diet," Josie said, quickly biting into the next-to-last cruller in case Betty came to her senses. Being nervous always made her hungry.

"Oh, that. I read the ingredients in those Skinny Maid chocolate bars. If you added a vitamin pill to the fried junk that you're always stuffing in your mouth, you'd have a Skinny Maid Diet Bar. Gross. I'm going macrobiotic."

"That involves eating a lot of brown rice, right?"

Betty opened her mouth to protest such a simplistic view of her new way of life and apparently remembered that her coworker was now her boss. "Sort of," was all she said, continuing to unload her bag.

"How long is it going to take for you to eat all that?" Josie asked, staring down at the pile of food.

"It's not healthy to bolt your food . . . but I'm just going to have a snack now," Betty added quickly.

"Good. Chris should be back soon, so—"

"Chris is back." Chris announced her own arrival from the doorway.

"Where were you?" Betty asked, pouring dark brown liquid over a selection of steamed carrots, broccoli, and chunks of yellow squash.

"Liquor store."

"Oh. Did you see the hunk that works there? He's kind of old, but—"

"His name is Sam. And he doesn't work there. Well, he does work there, but he owns the place. He just bought it. He's an interesting guy," Chris said.

Josie was completely distracted for the first time since finding the dead man. Chris, her laid-back, unemotional friend, was actually stumbling over her words. Josie glanced at her, but Chris had just noticed Betty's food.

"And what the hell is that crap?"

" 'That crap' is my midmorning snack. And it is certainly more nutritious than your usual dreck. And I'll live longer—"

"Ha! It will just seem longer!" Chris cackled.

"Old joke," Betty muttered, swallowing loudly.

"We'd better get to work," Josie insisted.

One of the advantages of being the boss was that her suggestions became orders. Betty popped a clump of broccoli in her mouth and snapped the top back on the food.

Chris headed over to the crowbar leaning against the wall and looked at Josie. "Do you want to rip that frame off or shall I?"

The working day had begun.

For the next three hours all five women were busy. Evelyn came upstairs to report that she and Melissa had completed their other jobs and were working together on the first-floor bathroom. Three deliveries of materials were inventoried and accepted, the trash company picked up the full Dumpster and left an identical one in its place. The women working upstairs had removed the wall where the new window was to be installed, cleared the space of all litter and trash, and nailed jack studs and headers in place.

"Crane's here," Chris announced, looking out the window. "I was hoping we'd be able to get some lunch first," she added, glancing at her watch.

"Aren't you going down to see Jason?" Josie asked. She had become more relaxed as the morning continued and she got into the routine of work. But now that they had paused, she felt her panic returning.

"Maybe Betty should," Chris answered, her back to the other two women.

"No, you should," Josie insisted, becoming irritated. "If you've decided that you're more interested in that man at the liquor store, you can just wait until we have this window in to let your former heartthrob know about it."

Chris had a scowl on her face as she left the room.

"Maybe you should offer to go pick up lunch for everyone," Josie suggested to Betty.

"You want me to go into that greasy spoon again?" Betty asked.

"It won't leach into your body. You have to eat it for it to kill you," Josie insisted. "Be sure to ask Jason or whatever his name is if you can pick up anything for him. Lunch is the very least that Island Contracting owes him."

"I—"

"Could you do it right now?"

"I—"

"Right now. Please," she added, knowing she was being uncharacteristically abrupt.

Betty also wore an angry expression as she left the room,

but Josie didn't care about the feelings of her employees at that moment. She was almost sure she'd heard the squeaky latch on the hall-closet door immediately after Chris had departed. Josie ran to the hole in the wall and stared down at the ground. She watched the scene until Betty and Chris had joined the group and, once she was ensured some privacy, ran out into the hallway and pulled open the closet door.

The space was empty.

Josie took a deep breath, forced herself to move, and walked into the closet, yanking the door shut behind her. There was a light around here somewhere. . . .

She waved her arms around until she brushed against the soft string that hung from the naked bulb on the ceiling. She pulled and discovered that the light was only a few inches from her head.

She blinked her stunned eyes and peered around. No body. For a few seconds she doubted her own sanity. Was it possible that she had imagined the whole thing? Had the strain of owning her own company driven her crazy?

Josie shook her head and a bit of her old sanity returned. Of course she hadn't made up the whole thing. The man had been here and now he was gone. Just like he had been in the bedroom . . .

The answer was simple. Someone had moved him. Again.

FIVE

SHE LOOKED AROUND the closet, trying to ignore the spots the light had burned in her vision. In one corner there was a slight shadow, or was it . . . ? Josie bent down and picked up a small wooden comb. Maybe it had fallen from the dead man's jacket? She shrugged and tucked it in a pocket of her overalls. Someone was calling her.

She fled down the long stairs, through the entryway, and outside.

"Where have you been?" Chris asked. "We were just getting ready to send up a search party."

"Yeah. We thought maybe you'd been murdered," the muscular man leaning against the side of the large green crane joked. His arms were crossed and the early-spring sun gleamed off well-developed muscles.

Betty had decided the day was warm enough to discard her sweatshirt, and Josie noticed that the blue-and-white batik halter underneath had attracted Jason's eye. "Why were you calling me?" she asked, trying to focus on the situation before her.

"Well, we could put in the window just any old way, but we thought maybe you'd like to have some say in it all," Jason answered in a slow drawl. "Rumor on the island is that Noel Roberts must have thought pretty highly of you to leave you his company. 'Course, Noel sure believed in getting his hands dirty. . . ."

Josie was too preoccupied to concern herself with the implied insult in the man's words, but her crew immediately sprang to her defense.

"Josie is on-site and working along with us during every minute of the day—and she sometimes works for hours and hours after everyone else has gone home," Melissa stated flatly.

"And that happens a lot," Evelyn added. "We all work hard, but she works harder than the rest of us."

"What sort of shit are you saying?" Chris asked, sounding furious. "Josie—"

"Can defend herself." Josie had gathered herself together enough to insist. "You have to understand," she added to Jason, "there are some subjects on which we're just a little sensitive."

"Sure. I understand. Women are often like that."

"It was very nice of you to bring over the crane so quickly!" Josie almost shouted the words, praying that her crew would take the hint and not insult this particular gift horse until they had finished their task. Under normal circumstances, she wouldn't have ignored the implied insult, but today was anything but normal.

"It really was," Betty said, edging closer to Jason. Josie hoped that she was flirting to help out on the job and not because she was actually attracted to men like this bulky-limbed chauvinist.

Whatever Betty's motivation, Jason was obviously inspired by the wide expanse of chest she displayed, and he leaped up onto the seat of the crane and flexed a muscle or two in response.

Chris turned to Josie and rolled her eyes skyward. Josie tried to bend her lips into a grin. She was having a difficult time coping with all this. Where had the body gone? Who had moved him? Who, for heaven's sake, had killed him? Who was he—the dead man, and his killer?

"Josie!"

Josie returned to the present. She had no choice, she reminded herself. She had to finish this job successfully if she was going to save her company. And she was going to have to find that dead man and the person who killed him at the same time—and for the same reason. Josie got to work.

The crew was inspired by her sudden enthusiasm for the task at hand, and with Jason's help, the window was installed without incident.

An hour later they were taking a well-deserved lunch break on the front porch, basking aching muscles in the warm sunlight.

"You always go to the deli to pick up lunch?" Jason asked, biting into a roll with bloody roast beef dripping from the edges of its golden crust.

"You imagined us fixing little gourmet snacks at home in the evening that we then wrapped up in gingham and carried to the job in straw baskets?" Melissa asked sarcastically.

"Actually, I was wondering if you'd tried the new fried-fish shack down at the other end of the island," he answered, grinning at her. "My uncle owns it. Good fish and good prices until the summer people arrive in a couple of months—then the prices will skyrocket. You know how it is."

"Where is it?" Evelyn asked, staring with amazement at the pile of carrots that Betty was consuming.

"Back of the row of new condos on the bay at Nineteenth Street. He makes pretty good potato salad and coleslaw too, if you're a vegetarian."

Everyone checked to see how Betty was reacting to a comment so obviously directed at her (or at Betty's chest, Josie thought, noticing where Jason was staring). But Betty was gazing off into space, apparently intrigued by the facade of the blinding white box next door.

"Ugly, isn't it?" Jason asked. "They must be fashionable, though. Rich people are putting big white geometric things up all over the island. You ladies ever build one of those?"

Josie was relieved when Melissa and Evelyn began relating horror stories about contracting houses. She was fine when they were working, but during breaks, visions of the body forced their way into her consciousness. But she had no choice other than to keep working, she reminded herself again as she stood up and stretched.

"Where are you going?" Chris asked.

"Just need to check something out," Josie muttered. "Finish eating. You deserve a long break. We've accomplished an awful lot already today." She stretched again and moved away slowly, hoping that her crew would assume she needed to use the Porta Potti behind the house.

Actually, she headed there first. It was as logical a place to begin her search as anywhere.

It was a big house, but many walls had been torn down over the past few weeks and Josie was pretty sure she knew every nook big enough to conceal a body. Fifteen minutes later, when Chris found her in the laundry-room-to-be, Josie still hadn't discovered any sign of the dead man.

"What are you doing here?"

Josie reminded herself that this was her problem and dropping it in anyone else's lap would only spread around the responsibility. All she knew about the law she had learned from cop shows on TV, but she was pretty sure it was illegal not to report a murdered man. Why spread around the guilt by telling anyone else about it?

"Just checking stuff out," was Josie's obscure answer.

"Have the john and sink arrived for the first-floor bathroom yet?"

"No. And neither have the tiles. Maybe someone should run down to the liquor store and make some calls. Would you like me to do it?"

"Sure, why not? Now that Jason has finished helping us out, I suppose there's no reason for you to hide your interest in another man."

"Wow." Chris looked at her curiously. "Running this company has sure made you cynical."

"That's not all it's made me," Josie answered obliquely. "How is everything going upstairs?"

"Fine. I thought you were crazy this morning, but it looks like we're really going to have some impressive work to show the Firbanks this weekend. The window is fabulous and we may even get that bathroom finished."

"As long as the deliveries are made on time," Josie reminded her. "So you'd better get going. I'll probably be working in the bedroom when you get back."

"Great. See you in a few minutes," Chris said, waving as she left the room.

Josie glanced around the area one last time, then followed Chris.

The afternoon was short, and everyone was tired and relieved when Josie suggested they call it quits a little after five.

"I thought plumbing supply was going to make a delivery today," Melissa said.

"They are. I'll hang around to wait for them. You all head on home—and think twice before you party. We all need a good night's sleep."

"You keep running your hands through your hair like that and you're going to be bald by the time you're forty," Melissa suggested as she stood up, a smile on her weary face.

Josie forced her hands down to her sides. Chris and Betty were looking at her curiously. She wasn't doing a very good job of hiding her nervousness.

"Maybe you should try an organic cream rinse," Betty said. "You could be allergic to the chemicals in the one you're using now."

"Maybe I will," Josie answered, knowing she wouldn't. "Have a good night's sleep," she repeated. "I think I hear a delivery truck out front."

The women split up on the porch. Josie, watching them leave before heading back into the house, noticed that Jason was waiting to give Betty a ride home, and that Chris had driven off in the direction of the liquor store even though she lived off-island and the north bridge was a more direct route to the house she shared with her mother.

"You are a single woman raising a child, running a business, and concealing a murder, Josie Pigeon. You certainly don't have time to moon around over the new man in town!" she lectured herself aloud as she circled the house, making sure all the materials stored outside were covered securely for the night. "You've been acting like an adolescent asshole," she was still muttering as she stomped up the stairs. She tripped on the top step, landing flat on the floor. It had been a long day; she was confused, frightened, and tired. She burst into tears.

"Are you all right?"

Josie's scream reverberated about the stairwell.

"Hey, it's just me. Sam Richardson. The guy at the liquor store. Remember? You were in yesterday. You used the phone."

Josie, sniffling, accepted the hand he offered and pulled herself up from the floor.

"What," she began, wondering if he could hear how loudly her heart was beating, "are you doing up here?"

"Looking for you. Well, looking for someone." He amended his statement with a slightly crooked smile.

Josie took a deep breath and ordered herself to ignore the fact that his eyes matched the faded chambray of the pressed shirt he wore. "Why?" she asked shortly, fidgeting with her hair.

"I just wanted to make sure that you—or whoever was in charge here—were aware of the light that was left on. I wouldn't have worried about it if I hadn't noticed it last night, too. The light being left on I mean," he added.

"What . . ." Josie started slowly. "What light? What are you talking about?"

"There's a small window on the side of the house. I

don't know if you noticed it. . . . But, anyway, there was a light on in there all night last night. Well, maybe not all night. But it was on around eleven when I drove by on my way to my house and it was still on this morning around five when I drove past on the way to the store."

"Don't you sleep?"

"Not much. I have insomnia. And there's a lot to do at the store these days. The inventory I was given is a mess and I don't want to duplicate vintages when I turn in my first order." He adjusted his horn-rimmed glasses on his nose. "But none of this matters to you. I'm sorry to babble on. Wouldn't your boss want you to check out that light? It's on again."

"I don't have a boss."

"Oh . . . then who runs this company?"

"I do." Despite the circumstances, despite the extraordinary events of the day, Josie made the statement proudly. "I own it, too." She suddenly realized that ancient overalls and a sweat-stained T-shirt were not exactly the garb of management. "I work, too. I mean, I'm a carpenter. I do a lot of the building . . . along with the rest of my crew."

"I think one of your workers borrowed my phone a few times today." Josie noticed that when he nodded, his graying, sandy hair fell forward into his eyes.

"They're all women."

"Excuse me?" He brushed his hair back and looked at her curiously.

"Every one of the workers of Island Contracting is a woman."

"Oh. And that's unusual, isn't it?"

"Of course it is. Do you know any female plumbers and electricians?" Josie asked a little defensively.

"No, but I could use a good refrigerator repair person—male or female. No one likes to drink warm beer in the summer, but no one seems to be able to fix my refrigeration system."

"Melissa might look at it. She can fix almost anything and she needs the extra money. She's putting her husband through graduate school."

"Good for her. Maybe you'd ask her to give me a call."

"Sure." Josie had found a knot in one of her unruly curls and she pulled a comb from her overalls to tame it.

"Aren't you going to check on that light? It's on the south side of the house. On this floor," he added, when she didn't respond.

Josie was staring at the comb. Was it possible . . . ?

"Are you all right? Are you always this nervous or is it me?"

"Not usually. Just when I find a dead body and lose it all on the same day," Josie answered, horrified as she heard the words come out of her mouth.

SIX

HE WAS LOOKING at her as though she were crazy. "Excuse me. Did you just say what I thought you said?"

He spoke softly, trying to soothe the savage beast, Josie guessed. She jutted out her chin a bit and threw her shoulders back. "You heard what I said. I found and lost a dead body today. That's why I'm so nervous," she added.

"Why don't you sit down here." He indicated the top step.

Josie sat.

"Tell me all about it."

She took a deep breath and did as he suggested.

When she was done, he stared at her for a few moments before speaking. "Sounds like you have good reason to be nervous. You're sure you got a good look at the man?"

Josie nodded. Stupid or not, she was feeling immense relief at sharing her horrible secret.

"And you don't know him?"

"Definitely not." She paused and continued. "His face wasn't smashed in at all or anything." She frowned.

"Don't worry. I understand." He took off his glasses and cleaned them on a shirttail. "How long have you lived here—on the island?"

"Almost fifteen years."

"Would you say that you know by sight most of the year-round residents?"

"Probably."

"How well do you know the women on your crew?"

"Pretty well. We're together every day and we talk a lot while we work."

"And would you have noticed if anyone was in the house besides the members of your crew?"

"Not necessarily, but I think someone on the crew would have noticed a stranger around." He was going to have the best polished glasses in the universe if he kept going, she thought.

"Interesting case."

" 'Interesting case'?" She felt a little insulted by the comment. "Who are you? A cop moonlighting in the liquor business?"

"No. A retired prosecuting attorney who has owned a liquor store for slightly more than forty-eight hours."

Josie looked down at the elegant leather loafers he wore with his pressed jeans and chambray shirt. "I guess you have to be a rich lawyer to retire so young."

"I said prosecuting attorney—I was paid a barely respectable salary by the government. It's the defense side that makes the big bucks. I retired for personal reasons."

Josie didn't know what to say about that.

"I couldn't stand being ineffective any longer," he added. "I suppose it was selfish of me, but . . ." He noticed the look on her face. "Sorry. You have more important things to worry about than my midlife angst. I moved here less than a month ago and I don't know many people. I guess I've been spending too much time alone." He finally put his glasses back on. "Let's do something about your problem."

"What?"

"I think the first thing we should do is call the police and explain—"

"No way! Not a chance!"

"Why not?"

"It would ruin my company."

"I don't see that—"

"Look, Island Contracting is in a very vulnerable position right now. We owe money, and if this job isn't a major success, we won't get another. And that will be the end of us."

"But the police are trained—"

"You haven't had much contact with the local police department, have you?"

"None. Why?"

Josie hesitated. "I have a sort of history with them," she admitted slowly.

He looked at her curiously. "Something more serious than a couple of speeding tickets?"

"The son of the chief of police hates me. . . . It's something personal." She glanced at him. "Why are you smiling?"

"Relief. You were so serious I thought you might have been in real trouble for a moment there."

"Dating Rick McCorkle was real trouble."

"What—"

"That's not true. I mean, what I said wasn't true. Dating him was okay. It was the way we broke up that caused all my problems."

"What—"

"He and his father are still mad at me. And they are one third of the police department on the island."

"You're saying that this Rick is a policeman, too?"

"Yeah."

"So what happened?"

"Nothing important." She frowned. "Except that I can't expect the police department to help me out—even if they could. They're more familiar with stopping speeders and breaking up parties for underage drinking during the season than dealing with murder." She stopped speaking and stared off into space for a moment. "Murder," she repeated slowly.

"Serious stuff," he agreed. "You can't ignore it, you know."

"It will ruin my business and the lives of everyone who works for Island Contracting," she stated flatly.

"I don't mean to insult your friends, but you should think about the fact that one of them could be the murderer. And it is more than likely that one of them moved the body," he continued before she could protest.

"I've . . . I've thought about that. I even thought I heard the closet door open at one point this afternoon and I'm pretty sure that only the crew was in the house then—although Jason was outside.

"But don't you see," she continued desperately, "that's just one more reason why it will destroy my company if anyone knows about the body now."

"And why do you think it will get better later? Think of it this way: Right now you're connected with a murder that may or may not have happened on your job site. You panicked and hid the body. It's just possible that someone on your crew did the same thing."

"You're right," Josie said slowly. "It could be that Chris or someone found him in the closet and reacted the same way I did. Just tried to get him out of the way for the time being."

"Were you here late last night?"

"No."

"Was anyone on your crew?"

"You're thinking of that light, aren't you?"

"Yes."

"I wondered about that," Josie admitted. "You said just one window?"

"It was shining out one small window. Definitely. You'll find that I'm very precise."

"There aren't any rooms with just one—"

"Couldn't there be curtains over the other windows in the room?"

"Nope. We ripped down all that junk the first day on the job. It was carted away with the first Dumpster load."

"Look. I think you should go to the police right away." He put up his arm as a sign for her not to interrupt. "But I don't think a few more hours will hurt when you've waited this long, so why don't you show me around this place? Maybe we can pinpoint the room the light was in."

"And you think it might have something to do with the murder?"

"When something unusual happens around a murder, I think it's more than likely to be significant."

Josie got up. "Then I guess I'd better show you the house. I sent everyone home so I could look around one last time."

"For the body," he said.

"Yes," she admitted, nodding. "I looked around as much as I could without attracting attention this afternoon, but I wanted to make sure."

"Why don't we start with the place where you found him and then the closet where you hid him?"

"Fine with me. The bedroom is right down this hallway," she added.

He followed her a few steps. "But a lot has changed since this morning," Josie explained, opening the door to the large bedroom and flicking the switch that turned on the lights dangling from ceiling rafters. "There was a large pile of rubbish covered with a dropcloth over there." She pointed. "That's where I found him."

"Under the window?"

"Not exactly. There wasn't a window there then."

"I mean that large window." He pointed.

"I know what you're talking about. That window was installed this morning. It replaced most of the wall and the two standard double-hung windows that were there before. That's why I had to move the man. We were scheduled to work in this room. We even had a crane coming to lift the window into position."

He walked across the room and examined the floor. "No sign of blood?"

"I didn't notice any."

"And I would imagine that a lot of people have been walking around in here all day long?"

"Definitely." Josie nodded vigorously.

He frowned.

"Did I do something wrong?"

"You could be accused of destroying the purity of the crime scene."

"Is that worse than moving the victim or not reporting finding the body?"

He chuckled. "Not really." He walked slowly around the room, glancing out the window, squatting down to check out spots on the floor a few times, and then stepped back, staring at the large new expanse of glass.

"What do you think?"

"You do very nice work. I gather there is going to be decorative woodwork added?"

"Yes. It will go in when we install the cornices and moldings."

"You're going to finish this room before the rest of the house?"

"Yes. We want to have something to show the Firbanks when they come out for a visit this weekend."

"So that's not the way you'd usually remodel a house as big as this one?"

"There isn't a usual way," Josie admitted. "Each job is different. In the first place the houses are different. You break into a wall that is supposed to be load bearing and discover a rotten two-by-four. The remodeling is different. There are architects who think it's desirable to turn an old friendly shingle-style cottage into a modern building like the one next door. And then, of course, there are deliveries and the subcontractors. Materials don't arrive on time. The wrong materials are ordered. The right materials are ordered, but the wrong ones are delivered. Subcontractors have to work Island Contracting into their schedule. But for us, for most contractors, the biggest difference is the owners."

"And the people who own this house are a problem?"

"Pains in the butt." She frowned. "Do you think the dead man was a friend of theirs?"

"Could be. Do you have any reason to think that? Was he wearing clothes that looked like he came from the city? A three-piece suit?"

"You don't have to be wearing a suit to look like you're from the city." She glanced down at his elegant loafers.

"And I thought I blended in nicely."

"You will—with the summer people."

He stared at her for a moment. "Want to show me that closet?"

"Follow me." She started to leave the room. "I had to drag him there. I'm pretty strong, but he was a big man. Luckily the closet is right out here in the hallway."

She pulled open the door.

"Well, son of a gun! So this is the light I've been seeing."

Josie leaned back against the wall, astounded. "You must be right, but it doesn't make sense."

"Why not?"

"I turned off the light. I know I did. I came in here to check on the body and I had to turn on the light to look around. But the closet was empty. I picked up the comb on the floor and then I reached up, pulled that cord, and turned off the light."

"You were in shock. You can't be sure of that."

"I don't think so. I'm usually very careful about that type of thing." She walked slowly around the small room. "I didn't realize that this tiny window was here, I have to admit. Look, it's covered with brown paper so that it looks just like the old insulation."

He peered at the spot she indicated. "Interesting. But it doesn't look like it was done recently."

"No. Probably ten or twenty years ago. The paper is old and brittle. We would have found it when we pulled the old insulation out of here."

"You said you found a comb on the floor?"

Josie nodded and started to search through her pockets for the item. "Do you want to see it? It's nice. Wooden." She handed it to him.

He held it up to the light. "Either the dead man had long red hair—gorgeous long red hair, I might add—or you've used this."

Josie felt herself beginning to blush. "Yes. I . . . my hair gets tangled when I work and the comb was handy. Did I do anything wrong?"

He sighed. "You're certainly good at polluting the evidence."

"And that's not good."

"You're a prosecuting attorney's nightmare. Any halfway

competent defense could claim that you were intentionally doing it and turn you into a major suspect."

Josie leaned back hard, banging her head against the wall. "Damn. I've made everything worse, haven't I?"

"You should have called the police immediately," he said, a serious expression on his face.

"Then I have only one alternative."

"Good idea. We can use the phone at the store."

"For what?"

"To call the police."

"I'm not going to call the police," Josie cried. "I'm going to find out who killed him myself!"

SEVEN

"YOU'RE NUTS!"

"Thanks for the compliment," Josie responded sarcastically.

"You're a carpenter. Is there anything in your background that leads you to believe that you can solve a murder?"

"I can certainly do anything that Rick and his father can," she argued. "And I was once around when a murder was being solved."

"When you were dating a policeman?"

"Actually, when I was remodeling a house. It was solved by a housewife," she added quickly.

"I'm sorry, but I don't have a lot of faith in amateurs. And what happened between you and this Rick that led you to have so little faith in his abilities? He's a trained police officer."

"He is an idiot who is always looking for a way to get

back at me. And this won't just hurt me and my son, it will hurt everyone on the crew and their families as well."

He looked at her more closely. "You're married? You don't wear a ring. . . . I didn't know you were married."

"I'm not. And I certainly do not want to talk about that right now."

"Hey! What's going on up there? Josie Pigeon? Is that you screaming like a sick seagull?"

Gasping, Josie ran over, looked out the window, and recognized the car parked before the house. "Damn!" She pulled her hair back and frowned. "Damn. Damn. Damn." She grabbed the man's arm. "Just promise me you won't say anything about this—yet," she pleaded as loud footsteps were heard coming up the stairs. "I'll explain as soon as he leav—"

"Well, if it isn't Miss Josie Pigeon." They had been joined by a man dressed entirely in denim with a red baseball cap perched on his straight brown hair and scuffed black motorcycle boots on his large feet. "I heard screams and thought they might be of distress, as they say in the movies. Anything I can do?"

"Nothing. I'm fine. I just got a bad splinter," Josie lied, sticking a filthy thumb in her mouth.

"You don't need any help?" the young man asked, looking curiously at Sam.

"I am fine," Josie insisted, turning her back on him.

"But it was very nice of you to offer to help," Sam Richardson said, wondering why Josie was being so rude.

"No problem. Josie and me go way back, don't we, Josie?"

She didn't say anything and the young man grinned at the older, shoved his hat farther down on his head, and turning on his heels, clopped back down the stairs.

"Whew!" Josie sighed and leaned back against the wall. "Thanks." She looked at him curiously. "Why did you go along with me just now?"

"About what?"

"About not telling the police . . ."

A look of dawning understanding appeared on the man's face. "You're telling me that man is a cop?"

"That was Rick," Josie answered. "I thought you knew."

"I've lied to the island's police?"

"Don't worry. Everyone lies to the island's police. Not because this is an island full of criminals, but because the police are totally incompetent."

"I assume that not everyone lies to them about something as serious as murder."

"True," Josie admitted. "Actually, I don't think there's ever been a murder on the island. I can't imagine that it's something the editor of the *Island Times* would ignore, could you?"

"I gather that's the local newspaper? I don't subscribe yet."

"No one subscribes. It will be flung against your door Wednesday afternoon—unless Arnold is fishing. Then it will arrive a little later."

"Is this Arnold fishing often enough to miss a murder?"

"No one on this island could miss a murder. No one on the island misses anything. Just wait until you start dating . . . I mean, if you're not married. I noticed that you don't wear a ring or anything either."

He seemed interested in a different subject. "Of course, if I get involved in this, I could lose my liquor license."

"Then—"

"And the bar could revoke my license to practice law."

"Then—"

"Just because I didn't speak up when a police officer was in the room. Or, in fact, a man who did not identify himself as a police officer was in the room. That's something, I guess."

"So you—"

"So I did exactly the same thing you did after lecturing you on your mistakes."

A wide smile appeared in the midst of Josie's freckles. "Sure did," she agreed happily.

"This," he said slowly, "is going to take some serious thinking. I have no idea what to do."

"You could help me find out who the killer is."

"Even supposing that isn't one of the craziest ideas in the world, it wouldn't absolve us of any legal responsibility."

"Why not?"

"Because we would have to explain how long we'd known about the murder when we turned in the culprit."

"We could worry about that later," Josie staunchly insisted.

"Well . . ."

"And, if we did find the murderer, who is going to complain? Isn't that what's called a technicality in court?"

"No, it's not."

"Oh, well, then—"

"I'm thinking," he interrupted.

Josie spun around and left the room. He could think by himself. She set about to thoroughly search the house. She tramped through the hallway and yanked open the old mahogany door to the attic. The painted stairway was chipped, the worn center of each tread testifying to decades of heavy use. The large space under the eaves had been partitioned into a half-dozen sleeping cubicles when Island Contracting had arrived. The studs and wallboard had been ripped down and the bathrooms at either end of the room were no longer enclosed. But there were two large box rooms that had been next to each of the bathrooms and the decision had been made to keep them in place. One was going to be used for storage and the other was to be converted into a steam room. Josie opened the door to the one on her left, knowing if she paused for a moment, the image she'd conjured up of the body would stop her. The room was empty. She fled across the attic and discovered the same thing on the other side. There was no way for anything as large as a body to be hiding up here. Josie ran back down the steps.

She almost collided with Sam at the bottom of the stairway.

"Seen a ghost?" he asked casually.

"No. There's nothing up there. I just wanted to look around quickly and get out in case Rick decides to come back."

"Would you mind if I looked with you?"

"Fine." Did this mean he had agreed to help her investigate? Josie decided not to ask. "This floor next, then."

"You know your way around. I'll follow you."

He did, and ten minutes later they agreed that the body

was no longer in the house. "How about buildings outside? Is there a garage?"

"Not anymore. The last big winter storm leveled it as efficiently as we could have done—and much quicker. There was a large pile of rubble." She paused, remembering that was where she had found the glasses that her landlady so admired.

"Anything wrong?"

"No, just thinking . . ."

"Haven't you been creating piles of rubbish as you clear out the house?"

"No, it's stupid to dump things on the ground and then, later, lift them into the Dumpster to be carted away—oh, shit!"

"I gather that's your way of indicating that you just thought of something significant?"

"There was a Dumpster hauled away today."

"After the body disappeared?"

Josie considered the question. "It's certainly possible."

"And could the body have been lifted into it?"

"No need to lift. We had a slide out the second-floor hallway window. All anyone would have to do is slip the body out the window—it would end up in the Dumpster. Then something else could be tossed out to cover it up."

"If that was done, how long do you think the body would have been exposed to anyone passing by?"

"Well, being carried through the hall, the time on the slide and in the Dumpster until it was covered up." She thought. "Probably less than ten minutes. Maybe a lot less."

"Who carts the Dumpster away?"

"The private contractor who owns it. . . . And if you're going to ask me where it is dumped, I have no idea. Certainly not on the island. The garbage contractor is from off-island, in fact."

"You hired him?"

Josie nodded and he walked over to the window. "Is Rick back?" she asked nervously.

"No. It looks like we have about two more hours of daylight. I think it might be a good idea to check out where that Dumpster is . . . if we can. What we need is a good story."

"For what?"

"To explain why we have to search the place where the Dumpster was dumped. Couldn't you say that one of your workers lost a valuable piece of jewelry today? Although that's a little small."

"Size isn't the question. Do you really think we would wear anything valuable on the job—even if any of us could afford to own something like that!"

"I guess not. But it doesn't matter. We can figure out a more plausible story in the car."

" 'In the car'?" Josie repeated slowly.

"On the way to the dump—unless you think it's too far away to find while we still have daylight."

"I have no idea. I'm just . . ." She made a quick decision that she would get nowhere by admitting her surprise at his involvement. "I was going to suggest that we take my truck. It's a little more suited to running around dumps than your MGB."

"Fine. So how do we find this place?"

"I'll have to call. The number of the company is always prominently displayed on their Dumpsters."

"Closest phone is at my store."

"Why don't I lock up here and meet you there," Josie suggested.

"Sure. I'll see you," Sam agreed.

But when Josie had checked the windows and replaced the heavy padlock on the front door, he was just standing by the side of his tiny car.

"Something wrong?" she called out, tossing her lunch bag into the truck and hopping up in the driver's seat.

"Thought there was a nail in my tire, but it turned out to be a piece of shiny shell," he answered, ducking down into his car and starting the engine with a roar.

Josie realized that he didn't want to leave her alone. Was he afraid she was going to murder someone? she wondered, finding her keys and starting the truck. She glanced in the rearview mirror and tried to arrange her hair. Her face, she noticed, was filthy. Sam Richardson must really be concerned about lying to Rick; he couldn't possibly be getting involved because he found her appealing. Nonetheless, she'd try to clean up, she decided as she pulled her truck into a parking spot beside the small car.

"Come on in!" Sam called out through the door he'd just opened.

"Thanks. Do you mind if I use your bathroom before I make the call?" Josie asked, stuffing her hands in her pockets and wondering what could possibly be under her fingernails.

"No problem. It's that doorway beside the champagnes."

Josie followed his directions and entered the small bathroom.

"Hey, it's neat in there," she cried out when, cleaned up, she returned to the room. "Where did you get all the labels up on the wall?"

"Like it? I just finished it yesterday," he admitted.

"You did that?"

"Yes, why are you so incredulous?"

Josie shut up before admitting that she didn't know many men who decorated—with or without wine labels in foreign languages. She didn't know whether to admit that would make her sound like a hick—or suggest that he might be gay—an idea strangely depressing for a woman who was completely uninterested in emotional entanglements, she realized. "It just looked like a very professional job," she muttered, looking around. "I didn't know there were so many different kinds of champagne," she added, wondering why he made her so nervous.

"I don't have nearly as many vintages as I'd like, but I thought I'd see how they sell before stocking up. Don't you think you'd better make that call?"

"Yes, I—damn!" Josie smacked herself on her forehead.

"What's wrong?"

"I forgot to get the phone number off the Dumpster."

"No problem," he said, pulling a small slip of paper from his shirt pocket. "I did." He handed it to her.

"Thanks."

"The phone's in the same place it was yesterday," he said, a grin on his face.

"Thanks," she said abruptly, not happy that he was making her feel like a fool. She hurried to the phone and dialed.

It was answered on the second ring. "Hank? Josie Pigeon

here. I have a question for you. Do you know where the Dumpster is that you picked up from my site today? No, nothing like that," she added with a frown. Did every man have to say something sexist about her company? Besides, it was men who were always losing things!

But beggars can't expect political correctness, she decided, after she heard the answer and hung up.

"Shouldn't you write it down? Not that I think you'd forget," Sam added quickly as she frowned.

"No. The answer is etched in my memory," she said, knowing she sounded bitter. "It's on a garbage scow headed thirty miles out to sea."

EIGHT

"THAT'S LOUSY LUCK. We may never see that body again."

"Sounds like we're going to have to go through missing-persons reports." Sam frowned. "I need to think about this. Maybe you'd like a glass of wine? Or something to eat?"

"Wine?" It didn't seem like an essential at this minute.

He looked around his store. "Well, we have a large selection. And I can't offer gourmet meals yet, but we're well stocked with chips, dips, and maraschino cherries. Or perhaps you'd prefer Scotch."

"Potato chips sound wonderful," Josie admitted, accepting the bag he offered and ripping the top with a practiced hand. Out of the corner of her eye, she noticed that he was opening a bottle of red wine with equal skill. "I've always liked those big ball glasses," she added as two large goblets appeared from beneath the cash register. "I don't have any, but I see them all the time on TV," she added, feeling like a fool. "I have some pretty glasses. I found them in a junk pile near the house we're working on. My landlady thinks they might be—" She stopped, feeling only more foolish. She knew nothing about wine or wineglasses. And what sort of hick had to defer to her landlady's knowledge of crystal?

"You really like those things, don't you?"

Josie, realizing that he wasn't discussing the crystal, looked at the half-empty bag in her hand. "I work very hard and I get hungry," she said, putting it down. Using greasy fingers, she picked up the wineglass he had offered.

"I'm sure you do," he said quickly. "Is something wrong?" he asked, noticing a definite change of expression on her face.

"No, I'm fine." She took a second sip from her glass. "This is wonderful," she said, not wanting to add that it was nothing like anything she had drunk before.

"It's a nice Amarone. Lots of depth. I thought it might go well with the chips."

"It's really wonderful," she repeated, knowing she should mention bouquet or something similar, but afraid of making a complete fool of herself with an inappropriate or gauche comment.

"You know, we could go out to dinner and discuss this whole situation."

"There's no place open this time of year."

"We could go off-island. It's a couple of miles. There must be someplace to eat."

"I'm awfully tired. And busy," she added in case her excuse sounded like an excuse. "I have a lot of paperwork to do tonight."

"You have to eat," he said gently.

"Yes, but I can eat and work at the same time at home," Josie insisted. It wasn't exactly a lie. After all, she could work and eat. She didn't actually have to watch television during dinner. She stood up. "I really have to go," she repeated.

"If I'm going to help you solve this murder—"

"Help?"

"You don't think I'm going to just sit around, knowing that I've committed a crime as serious as neglecting to report a murder, and not do anything, do you?"

"No, I . . ." Actually, she had been hoping he would do just that.

"So, if I'm going to help you, it would be nice if you told me more about the situation at your work site. And it would be easier to do that over a good meal, wouldn't it?"

"I'm not exactly dressed for a restaurant."

"There's a bar that one of my distributors told me about, and places like that aren't usually very dressy. It's just changed hands and is supposed to serve wonderful food."

"Well . . ." Josie began to try one last excuse.

"If we're going to be working together . . ."

Was there no stopping this guy? "Fine. But you'll remember that I have to drag myself out of bed very early in the morning."

He smiled. "I understand that not everybody has the advantage of chronic insomnia. Shall we go?" he asked as Josie nervously finished off her glass of wine.

It was the smile that did it. "Fine."

"Why don't we take my car?"

Josie, remembering the mess that she usually left on the floor of the truck, nodded her agreement and followed him to his small MGB. Her nervousness at being with him was momentarily overcome by the thrill of riding in a classic sports car. "This is very nice," she said, stroking the tan leather seat.

He smiled. "I had the interior reworked last year. The original color was black, of course, but I couldn't resist this. Like the burl on the dashboard?"

Discussing wood was something Josie did well and the merits of walnut versus chestnut burl got them across the bridge and to the main highway, but almost immediately, he turned his car onto a road Josie didn't recognize, and within minutes the car pulled up to a fake Tudor building with a sign identifying it as THE GULL'S NEST. It could have been confused with any of a dozen similar spots near the shore except for the number of expensive, imported sedans parked before it. Josie got out of the car and nervously glanced down at her overalls as she entered the door Sam Richardson held open for her.

The interior was as ordinary as the exterior. Dark-stained wood paneling covered the walls, tanks swarming with tropical fish and improbably colored fans of fluorescent coral separated the maroon plastic-covered booths. Shiny swordfish looking down on customers spoke of a typical shore hangout. The patrons, however, were less typical. Dressed in pressed jeans or slacks, shirts fashioned from an array of natural fibers, and shod in imported soft leather, they matched their autos, Josie decided, moving closer to the wall as if the pockmarked wood could camouflage the dirt on her clothing.

And then she heard a familiar voice. "Well, if it isn't Ms. Pigeon come to roost with the gulls. I am so thrilled that you are here to try out my new place. Would you like to introduce me to your companion?"

"Sure. This is Sam Richardson. Sam, this is Basil Tilby."

Basil was a thorn in Josie's side. A failed actor who ran numerous businesses on which the wealthier of the summer people seemed to depend, he was loud, gay, and possibly the most self-centered person she had ever met. He loved to talk—but only about himself. She found him irritating, childish, and extremely boring.

Basil, apparently not knowing her thoughts about him, was leading them to a choice table near the windows. "Not like Samuel Richardson, the writer? Are people always quoting *School for Scandal* to you?"

"I believe you're thinking of Richard Sheridan. Sam Richardson wrote *Clarissa*. And we're not related."

Josie had no idea what they were talking about. "Sam is the new owner of the liquor store on the north end of the island," she explained, on surer ground here.

"Oh, of course, I've been hearing all about you," Basil said, pulling a chair over to their table and joining them without waiting for an invitation. "And a little birdie told me you're going to be upgrading the Italian whites that you carry. I spent January in Tuscany and Umbria and I visited some very interesting little vineyards, maybe—"

"Could I have a light beer?" Josie interrupted. "And, I don't know about Sam, but I'm very hungry."

Basil leaped up gracefully. "Well, I can tell that at least one of you wants to be alone. I'll send your waitress along immediately."

"Stop in the store anytime at all. I'm there every day

now and would appreciate your advice," Sam said quickly, giving Josie an annoyed glance, which she ignored.

"I'd love to. And I've been thinking about calling you, too, Josie. I bought this hideous place a few months ago and am desperate to have some remodeling done before summer. I wondered if Island Contracting could take the job."

"We are in the middle of a major project," she said rather abruptly.

That seemed to startle him. "Oh. Well, maybe you could just recommend another contractor that Noel—and you—respect. Ah, here's Maisie. She will be waiting on you this evening and I'll leave you both in her very competent hands."

It took only a few minutes for them to place their orders. Then Sam took control of the conversation. "A friend of mine who's a freelance director told me that there are two equally important parts to his job: doing it and getting the next one. I assume that would be true for your work as well."

"Thanks," Josie said to the hand that had delivered her beer. Then she looked up at Sam and spoke slowly. "I know what you're saying and of course you're right. I've only run Island Contracting for a few months and the job we're working on was arranged by . . . by the previous owner," she said, not wanting to get involved in complicated explanations. "And it's the last one we have under contract. I'll talk with Basil later and see if I can arrange something for him. He just bugs me, for some reason."

Sam looked at her curiously, but didn't ask any other questions. "So, since you need a good night's sleep, maybe we should get right down to work." He pulled a notebook from the pocket of his jacket. "It would help me if we start right off with the women you employ."

"What do the women who work for me have to do with this?" Josie sputtered, horrified to see that she had spit beer in his direction.

"Well, if one of them isn't actually the murderer, it's still most likely that one of them moved the body, isn't it?"

She took the time to wipe her lips before replying. She knew he was right, but that didn't necessarily make it easy to talk about. "True, but isn't it possible that one of them—say Chris—saw the body and reacted the same way I did?"

"Just wanted to get it out of the way to protect Island Contracting? So whoever it was just tossed it out the window into the Dumpster?"

"It's possible."

He shrugged. "But not likely. Although the unlikely does happen, of course."

"Of course," she agreed as a bottle of wine and two glasses were delivered to their table. "Did we order . . . ?"

"With Basil's compliments," their waitress explained before leaving them alone again.

Josie sat back and examined her companion as he read the label, poured himself a glass of the wine, sniffed, and then tasted. He did these motions automatically, as familiar with them as dressing each morning. She frowned. Everything he did was making her feel more and more like an unsophisticated idiot. How was that going to help her solve this murder? Unless . . .

"You mentioned lists of people who are lost?" she began slowly.

"Missing-persons reports." He nodded. "I thought it might be a route for us to go. It probably would be easier to find the killer if we can identify the dead man."

"There's no way we can just let him remain lost?" Josie asked hopefully. It would be too easy, but she had to try.

"Now, what do you think the answer to that is?"

"You're treating me like a child," she said angrily.

"Your wishful thinking is a little childlike."

"I—"

"And this isn't getting us anywhere. I'm sorry," he apologized as a large bowl of soup was placed before him.

Josie, busy pouring catsup on her hamburger and fries, didn't say anything.

"I said I was sorry," he repeated.

Josie looked up into his remarkable blue eyes. "I am, too," she admitted, realizing that the sincerity of her statement was muffled by the fact that she was chewing french fries. "I'm not used to this type of thing. Dead bodies and all."

"You're lucky. I'm more familiar with murder than anyone should be. That's why I came to the island, in fact."

"Why?" Josie was always more comfortable listening than talking. And it was easier to do with your mouth full.

NINE

"I WAS A trial attorney for almost thirty years. And for the last nineteen of them, I prosecuted felony cases. I've put in prison men who tortured and then shot unfaithful wives, teenagers who stabbed to death a friend who wouldn't give them a ride home from school, mothers who . . ." He looked at her face and changed the subject. "These are things no one wants to hear about during dinner."

Or ever, Josie thought, trying not to stare at the catsup on her fries.

"Anyway, about two years ago, I realized that I couldn't do it anymore."

"Why not? If you were sure that they were guilty . . . ?"

"That's not it." He removed his glasses and polished them before propping them back on his nose. "At least it wasn't for me. I found that no matter what horror story I was telling as the prosecutor, I had frequently heard a similar horror story while interviewing the suspect. Some had been tortured as children, sexually molested. . . ." He noticed her pale face. "Sorry. Suffice it to say that they were victims before they were murderers. Not that anything can justify taking another person's life, but I found I had lost the stomach for the whole process." He leaned on the table and spoke earnestly. "You see, Josie, a trial lawyer, no matter on which side he's arguing, has to believe in the law. And I had begun to see the faces of people—murderers, victims, relatives of both—in my sleep. I had a hard time going to prisons to interview suspects. . . . Everything was inhuman. And the law had no answers for me. So I left."

"Which explains why you're rather overqualified for your present occupation."

"Yeah, well . . ." He had the grace to look embarrassed. "My years as an overachiever have come to an end. Of course, a lot of my colleagues think this is just a rather dramatic midlife crisis and that I will be back."

"But you don't agree."

He shrugged. "It may be a midlife crisis. But I won't go back. It was time for a change."

"Why a liquor store?" Josie asked.

He glanced down at the wineglass he had just refilled. "Wine was something of a hobby for me. Part of the yuppie eighties thing, I guess," he added. This time Josie appreciated the embarrassed look on his face. "I had no idea what to do. When I decided to leave the prosecutor's office, I had imagined that I would look for a position teaching law, but the more I thought about it, the more inappropriate it sounded for someone as disillusioned as myself.

"I was so lost that I decided to sign up for a tour of European vineyards. I had never thought of myself as the type of person to go on a tour, but a . . . a friend of mine convinced me that it would be fun." There was something about the way he said the words that convinced Josie that the friend was female.

"And, actually, it was. I learned a lot, and one afternoon while walking through a vineyard in the Chianti region, I got to talking with a fellow traveler who told me about this wonderful island where she had a summer home and a liquor store there that had been on the market since last fall. I'm not usually an impulsive person, but I signed a contract to buy that store within twenty-four hours of arriving home."

"Did she tell you about winters on this wonderful island?"

"She got the summerhouse in the divorce settlement," he added.

Didn't he know any men? "You didn't answer my question," Josie replied. "Winter on the island is very different than the summer season. Or aren't you planning on hanging around then?"

"Oh, I plan on being here full-time. I don't have an income coming in and I don't have a lot of spare cash. In fact, I won't have any spare cash until I sell my co-op in the city—and right now that's not possible." He frowned. "Anyway, in the winter, I figured I'd get caught up on my reading."

"You must like to read," Josie commented, thinking about the long blustery months between Labor Day and Memorial Day.

"But I won't even be here in the winter if I'm in jail for concealing evidence in a murder case."

"So . . ."

"So why don't you tell me a little about the women who work for you? I don't even know how many women you employ. I have met one—I don't remember her name. She came to the store to use the phone a few times today."

"That would be Chris," Josie explained, thinking that her friend would be distressed to discover how little an impression she had made on this attractive man. "She's the person I depend on the most. I really am having trouble getting a handle on the management part of this job, so she does a lot of what I would usually do."

"Like what?"

"Well . . ." Josie thought for a few minutes before answering. "Like when we started this job, she went and checked out the house while I finished filling out the paperwork and getting orders in to our suppliers." She frowned. She sometimes needed to be two people at once. "Chris is a carpenter—like I am. In fact, she's probably the best finish carpenter on the island."

"There's a difference between a finish carpenter and an ordinary carpenter?"

"Sure. Both carpenters do some of the same work, but a finish carpenter specializes in the intricate, custom touches—woodwork and the like—while all carpenters do the basics—like framing in. Island Contracting is a small company and we all pitch in to do everything. But we all have our specialties, too. And, of course, we hold different licenses."

"You're all licensed by the state?"

"The electrician and plumber are, of course."

"And the company and its employees are bonded?"

"Definitely."

"So there were extensive background checks made?"

"I have no idea," Josie said slowly. "I didn't hire them."

"That's right. You said you'd only been doing this for a few months." He frowned. "So why don't you finish telling me about Chris?"

"Kelly. Her name is Chris Kelly and she is a good friend."

"Good enough to dispose of a body that might damage Island Contracting's reputation?"

"I don't know."

"Well, we'll worry about that later. Go ahead, tell me more. I only know what she looks like."

"Well, she's younger than I am—"

"And you're about thirty-five?"

"Thirty-four." She resisted brushing her hair off her forehead. She was fairly sure it would make little difference in her appearance. "Chris is in her middle twenties."

"Married?"

"No, I . . . Oh, you mean Chris." The color of her cheeks rivaled her flaming hair. "No, Chris is single. Well, divorced. She lives with her mother."

"And her ex-husband?"

"I never met him. She was divorced before we met. She and her husband went to high school together, and were married and divorced before Chris was twenty-one. That's pretty much all I know about that. She doesn't talk about him. And it was, after all, a while ago."

"You said she lives with her mother."

"Yes, she has for as long as I've known her . . . about five years," she added before he could ask. "They live off-island. Near here, in fact, in the tract house where she grew up. Chris is an only child and her mother is an invalid . . . multiple sclerosis or something . . . and Chris takes care of her. That's one of the reasons that Island Contracting is a great place to work. Chris knows that she can come in late if there is an emergency and we all know that she will get the job done."

"Does she date?"

"Yes." Was he interested for a personal reason? "But no one seriously," she felt compelled by honesty to add.

"And her father is dead?"

"Ye—well, I always assumed so," Josie admitted.

"But she never actually told you that?"

"No, I guess not. . . . Are you thinking that the dead man could be Chris's father? I got a good look at him and I suppose he was old enough."

"I don't have any reason to think so. Just trying to get a general idea of the situation."

"Well, Chris is a hard worker and very responsible. I couldn't do my job without her."

"And there are three other workers. A plumber, electrician, and another carpenter?"

"Sort of. Evelyn is a carpenter, an electrician, and she is studying to get her plumber's license. Melissa is a qualified plumber and she is busy teaching Eve everything she knows—when she's not working on this project. The house is getting all new piping—we're even replacing the cast-iron drain to the street. It was used as a boardinghouse for a while and there was a sink in each room and two large bathrooms—nothing appropriate for family living. Besides, there were cracks, rust, and leaching lead solder everywhere. The Firbanks would have loved to just replace the stuff outside the walls, but their inspection made it quite clear that everything had to go."

"Tell me about Evelyn and Melissa. One at a time."

"Well, I told you Melissa is the person you should call about your refrigeration problem. She's good at that type of thing. She's also younger than I am," Josie added quickly. "Twenty-nine, I'm sure of that. She's always talking about how she wanted to have two children by the time she was thirty and that's less than a year off. But her husband is in graduate school—he's been there for the past five years—and there seems to be no sign that he will ever get his degree."

"What is he studying?"

"Some sort of linguistics. I just see him once in a while—at parties or when he comes to pick Melissa up after work—

and he rarely speaks about what he's studying." And when he did, she didn't understand a single word of it.

"Do they have a happy marriage?"

"I suppose so," Josie answered, not admitting that she and Chris had discussed just this question on more than one occasion. "Melissa is a hard worker and not one to complain. Even when she talks about the children she would like to have had by now, it's more a joke about her age than a complaint about the situation she finds herself in."

"Do you know anything about her family? Her parents or any siblings?"

"She was raised in California and the rest of her family still live there. She does have a brother and a sister—I think. I've never met either, but she has two nieces and two nephews who sometimes stay with her in the summer. I've met them, but they're not even teenagers yet. I don't see how they could have anything to do with this."

"Her husband is in graduate school? Do you know anything about Melissa's education?"

"Sure. That it was completely worthless. She has a degree in aerospace engineering—and has never held a paying job in her field. Luckily, she also happens to be a licensed plumber. And that's how she makes her living."

"Interesting," was all Sam said before asking his next question. "Tell me about Evelyn."

"Evelyn has been working for Island Contracting less time than anyone else on the crew. She's a licensed electrician and a good one. She could make a great living just working on her own—if she were a man—but people seem to feel more comfortable with a male than a female, so she works for us."

"Why doesn't she just put an ad in the Yellow Pages with only her first initial? An electrician isn't like a carpenter. She could work alone instead of on a crew. And why would anyone object to a woman showing up at their house when they need a ceiling light added or something similar? I know I wouldn't turn away a craftsperson that I needed just because of their sex."

Josie appreciated that he had said craftsperson instead of worker, but she didn't know the answer to his question. "Maybe she just hasn't thought of that. You'll have to ask her. As I was saying, we've only worked together for a few projects and I don't know her all that well."

"Married?"

"Yes. Her husband is some sort of salesman and travels a lot. I thought he sold aluminum siding, but recently she said something about him making a big profit in some sort of home water-purification system, so I guess I had misunderstood. Anyway, they have three kids. I get their ages confused, but I think they're all in junior high. They are all old enough to take care of themselves, I know that. Evelyn is older than the rest of us. She must be in her forties."

"Does—"

"I really don't know much else about her background. I know she loves her family from the way she talks about them. Oh, and she was a Deadhead when she met her husband."

"A Deadhead? You mean a fan of the Grateful Dead?"

"I mean one of the fans that travel with the Dead. The kids that set up in the parking lots and park wherever they're playing. You know?"

"Not really. Do you think it's significant?"

"It is if you have to listen to that music all day, every day. Evelyn's husband gave her a fabulous portable cassette player for her birthday. Everyone on the crew is going to suggest a nice piece of jewelry next year."

Sam chuckled. "So that leaves . . ."

"Betty Patrick. You haven't met her?"

"Not that I remember."

"Oh, you'll remember," Josie said, not bothering to explain Betty's figure or her clothing preferences. "Betty is very attractive and something of a flirt. If she sees a man as good-looking as you, she'll . . . Oh, wow." She leaned against the back of the booth. "I think I've had too much to drink."

Sam was grinning. "She's another carpenter, right?"

"Right. And she's the youngest of us. I think twenty-one. She's having a wonderful time being single. She's very open about her various boyfriends and all the partying that goes on on weekends. I had no idea the island was such a social place."

"So she lives on the island?"

"She has all her life. Grew up on Eleventh Street, but now she lives in an apartment over the bakery on Dune Drive. Her parents owned the original grocery shop on the island, but they sold it and made enough money to move to Florida and set up a market there. She has two brothers. One is in college on a basketball scholarship. The other goes to law school in Chicago.

"Betty is a good carpenter, but I imagine that she'll fall for some really nice hunk and get married."

"But she's not seriously involved with anyone right now?"

"Not that I know of." Josie yawned. "I'd really better be heading home."

"Why don't we meet for dinner tomorrow night? You could come over to my house. I'm not exactly ready for company, but if you don't mind the mess, I'll do the cooking. I'm a pretty good cook."

"I . . ." Josie searched her brain for a polite excuse.

"And you can tell me about yourself." He grinned, his blue eyes twinkling. "I always like to get to the primary suspects first thing."

TEN

SHE WAS STILL furious when she woke up the next morning. The alarm had gone off fifteen minutes early, to give her time for the shower she had been too tired to take last night, and she stumbled out of bed, ripped open the moldy plastic curtain, and cursed loudly as the faucet came off in her hand.

The threads were stripped and had been for a while. That's why the wrench was sitting on top of the Kleenex on the back of her toilet. She grabbed the tool and started to work. In just a few minutes she was in the shower. She had run out of shampoo a few days ago, but reasoning that detergent was detergent, was making do with dishwashing liquid. Of course, she had yet to figure out a substitute for cream rinse, she thought as she peered among the three disposable razors on her tiny tub shelf, trying to choose the sharpest. Oldest or newest, it removed a large chunk of skin on her shin along with a minimal amount of hair.

"I will go to the drugstore during lunch today, Urch," she announced to the cat that, heedless of the water dripping from Josie's hair onto her fur, wound around Josie's ankles as she stepped from the shower. Dressing as she walked, Josie headed into the kitchen, where she discovered the reason for Urchin's uncharacteristic affection. The cat's food bowl was empty.

"And to the grocery store," she added, reaching for a can of fancy white albacore tuna and a can opener.

Urchin, anticipating a treat, leaped onto Josie's shoulder and smacked her forehead into Josie's ear. Josie dumped the fish into the bowl and headed back to her bedroom to finish dressing. That accomplished, she emptied the contents of the pockets of yesterday's overalls into today's clean pair and hurried out of her apartment, down the stairs, and to her truck.

Risa motioned and opened a window to call out, but Josie wanted to stop at the office before going to the Firbanks' home and merely waved a greeting as she started up her truck and roared off down the road. She was halfway to the office when she noticed strobe lights flashing in her rearview mirror.

"Shit!" She pulled over to the side of the road and slammed on the brakes. The patrol car stopped immediately behind.

Either in keeping with the casual, vacationlike mood of the island or as a dramatic example of bad taste given free rein, all three marked police cars had been painted bright yellow with fluorescent orange stripes. Turquoise letters identified the district. But the navy uniform that Chief McCorkle wore was regulation police issue—as was the scowl on his face as he marched up to the window Josie had rolled down.

"Well, if it isn't Miss Pigeon," he said, resting an arm on her roof.

"I prefer Ms., but feel free to call me Josie," she answered, afraid to use a title while speaking with him. In the past it had seemed that every time she called him by what she thought was the proper title, he had just been promoted. Josie didn't think this was the right time to make a mistake.

"Did you know you were traveling over forty miles per hour in a twenty-five-mile-an-hour speed zone?" He peered through the open window and across her lap as though expecting to find a couple of kilos of cocaine lying on the seat beside her.

Josie frowned. Everyone on the island knew that such an idiotic speed limit was rarely observed off-season and never enforced against year-round residents. But, as the chief of police was saying, "the law was the law." It was a statement even Sam Richardson couldn't fault.

"I won't mention that broken brake light. But you better get it fixed before I see this truck on the road again." He pulled a worn black notebook from his back pocket.

Josie reminded herself that there was nothing to be gained by arguing with a police officer. Suspects in a murder investigation should be extra careful. "I didn't know it was broken," she said in a meek voice. Good thing she'd skipped breakfast; this false humility was making her nauseous. "I'll have it fixed right away." Right after I go to the grocery, the drugstore, and the office, she amended the promise to herself.

"And don't forget to sign this and pay your fine at the municipal center. Don't want to have a bench warrant out for your arrest, Miss Pigeon," he said, handing her the printed form.

"I'll be sure to do that, Officer," she answered, bending her lips into a smile and turning the key in the ignition.

"Most people address me as chief, Miss Pigeon." He did not return her smile.

"Well, most people call—"

"You must be Chief McCorkle. I have been wanting to meet you. I'm Sam Richardson. I just bought the liquor store at the other end of the island."

"Sam!" Josie squeaked. What was he doing here? Had

he rethought his decision to hide what he knew from the police? "Chief McCorkle just gave me a speeding ticket."

"He did? How interesting."

"You two know each other?"

Both men spoke simultaneously and Josie brushed her still-damp hair back over her shoulders and smiled nervously. "Ah . . . yes. I can see you two don't need me. Guess I'd better get going. Have a busy day today. And I have to buy that new brake light, don't I?" She accelerated so quickly that she was speeding in just a few minutes. She grimaced, stomped on the brakes, and glanced in the rear-view mirror. No flashing lights. She drove conservatively the rest of the way to the office.

Fortunately, the foundlings in the office had become the responsibility of the entire crew and she found plenty of packets of Tender Vittles and a box of Friskies in the bottom drawer of an extra file cabinet. She poured food into the Styrofoam take-out chicken dishes that served as crockery for the tiny animals and promised herself that the first thing she would do (after finishing all those other first things first) when she had some free time was go through Noel's files. Josie was intimidated by paperwork and it was easily put off when there were so many other things pressing.

But she had read through the headings on the file folders while visiting the office the evening of Noel's funeral. And she had gone to sleep last night wondering if the answers to some of Sam Richardson's questions were tucked between those layers of yellow cardboard. She pulled open the drawer closest to hand and began her search.

Fifteen minutes later she sat back and admitted to herself that the personnel files of Island Contracting were missing. Not misplaced but missing.

"And they could have been stolen," she said to the tiny calico that was playing with threads hanging from the seams of her overalls. And what did that mean? she asked herself as the phone on the desk rang.

Josie leaped to grab the receiver before the answering machine picked up. "Hello? Oh, I mean, this is Island Contracting," she added quickly.

"Josie? It's Chris. What are you doing at the office?

Everyone is up at the site, and without a key, we can't get in and start work."

"I just had to check something out here. I'll be right up," Josie answered, and hung up the phone. A tiger kitten stuck her pink nose on the end of the receiver and Josie frowned. "There has to be some way to keep you all off this thing," she muttered, and inspired, formed a Kohler catalog into a tepee and gently set it over the machine. "If that doesn't stop you, at least it will be more difficult." She resisted the urge to check out the crab trap and drove straight back to the Firbanks' house, glancing all the way in her rearview mirror for the police.

Betty, Evelyn, and Melissa were sitting on the front porch, sharing an early-morning snack and arguing vehemently.

"Hi, guys! Where's Chris?" Josie called out, parking her truck and hurrying up to the house.

"She went to the liquor store to call you—"

"And to scope out the hunk that works there," Evelyn interrupted Melissa.

Betty, busy stuffing gelatinous white squares into her mouth, merely nodded.

"She talked to me. I wonder why she isn't back yet," Josie said, finding the key and unlatching the padlock.

"He must be some hunk," Melissa said, giggling.

Betty swallowed loudly. "I hear he's a rich lawyer, too."

"Where did you hear that?" Josie asked. "And what is that glop you're eating?"

"At a party Saturday night. Tofu."

"Tofu to you, too," Chris said, trotting in the door with a happy expression on her face.

"Why were you at the liquor store such a long time? Was something wrong?" Josie added the second question when she realized that the first sounded rather abrupt.

"No. Where's the coffee?"

Josie realized that her first question had not been answered, but Chris accepted the coffee that Betty poured for her and was starting for the second floor. "I had a thought about the ceiling molding last night and I want to see if it will work before doing the finishing on the window. Maybe you'd like to come up and see if you approve before I get started?" she asked Josie.

"In a minute. I want to make sure we all agree on where we're placing the bathroom fixtures down here first."

"That means she wants us to work," Melissa said to Evelyn.

"The woman is a slave driver," Evelyn answered, getting up from the floor where she had been sitting.

"I just want to put the rest of these back in my cooler," Betty said.

"Are you eating the same thing for breakfast as you eat for lunch?" Melissa asked.

"And for dinner," Betty said, nodding. "I've already lost three quarters of a pound."

"Who owns a scale that weighs in quarter pounds?" Evelyn asked.

"A thin person," Melissa answered, picking up a screw from the floor and tossing it to hit Betty.

"Good arm. It's difficult to hit those skinny butts," Evelyn cheered her on.

Betty turned and stuck out her tongue.

Josie just smiled. Island Contracting's workday had begun. She checked out the bathroom downstairs, consulting with the other three women, and then hurried on up to Chris. She expected to find her busy, but instead of working on the window jams, Chris was leaning against them, staring out into space.

"Something wrong? Or is something fascinating going on out there?"

"You won't believe this, but I think he's interested in me," Chris said obliquely.

"Sam Richardson?"

"Yes, it's a wonderful name, isn't it? I must get to the library and take out some of those novels."

Josie didn't understand what Chris was talking about, but she understood what she was feeling. "Why do you think he's interested in you? Did he ask you out or something?"

"No, not yet. But he asked me all these questions about myself. You know, where I grew up and how I became a carpenter—that type of thing." Chris turned to her friend. "And he looked as though what I was saying was the most fascinating thing in the world. He has these real intense blue eyes and he stared at me like he was looking right down into my soul. Why would he do that if he wasn't interested in me?"

Perhaps because he was trying to decide if you were a murderer. But Josie kept her thought to herself.

"He's such a kind person. You should have seen the sympathy on his face when I told him about my mother's illness and how she deteriorated after my father abandoned her."

"Your father is still alive?" Josie blurted out. "I mean, I thought your mother was a widow."

But Chris didn't seem to find her response unusual. "I have no idea. I haven't seen him in almost eleven years. I used to think that he left home the very second he thought I was old enough to take care of my mother. The bastard."

Josie opened her mouth, but she had no idea how to justify asking what Chris's father looked like, so she shut it again without saying anything.

"But Sam was so kind. His mother just moved to a retirement community in Arizona. He says she's a competition bridge player. Not a sign of memory loss."

"So . . ."

"I think my mother would like him, don't you?"

"What is there not to like?" Josie asked rhetorically.

"Do you think we could forget to recharge the phone permanently?"

"I suppose. . . ." But she suspected that Sam Richardson would get further along with his investigation if Island Contracting's employees took turns going down to his store.

ELEVEN

JOSIE WAS HAVING a bad day. Not that she had expected anything else. Visions of the dead man, suspicions about her crew, worries concerning the Firbanks' reaction to Island Contracting's work were all fighting to become an overwhelming obsession. Until, that is, Melissa discovered that the wrong toilet and sink had been delivered. And since they were broken, the plumbing supplier was refusing to accept their return.

"I could go down and call." Chris paused in her work to make the offer.

"Melissa is already on her way. She knows the men there better than anyone else on the crew. And if she can't get results, I think I'd better handle it," Josie answered. "But thanks for the offer."

"You're probably right. I don't want to look like I'm running after him."

Josie watched Chris measure, remeasure, and cut a piece of cherry quarter round and then fit it into the intricate wooden mosaic that she was creating above the window. She was tempted to tell Chris why Sam Richardson was so interested in her. But then she would have to tell the whole story. And she couldn't do that.

Except, of course, that was exactly what she was dying to do. Josie sighed deeply. She desperately needed a confidant. And she had known Chris for years. If she couldn't trust Chris, whom could she trust?

Chris seemed to have read her mind. "Anything I can help with?" she asked, putting down her hammer and nail setter.

"Excuse me?"

"You seem distracted today. Not like you usually are. Is anything wrong?"

Josie would have given most anything to say yes. But she said no and used both hands to push her hair off her forehead. "Running a business is a lot more difficult than I thought it would be. I . . . I wasn't prepared for all the things that would come up," she continued. Well, it wasn't a lie. Noel never had explained what to do when you find a murdered man under a trash tarp. If only she knew whether or not Chris had anything to do with him. She wondered if a little judicious questioning would help out.

"It's amazing what you find around here, isn't it?" she started out casually enough.

"It sure is!" came the enthusiastic reply. "Mother couldn't believe those great candlesticks. I almost wished that I had waited and given them to her for Mother's Day—or even her birthday. I never manage to pick out anything she's liked so well."

"What candlesticks?"

"The beautiful ones I found in the house before we started demolition." She looked at Josie curiously. "You knew about them, didn't you? Evelyn said she had talked with you about all that stuff."

"Oh, sure," Josie said, remembering the conversation. "She found something that she wanted to take, too, didn't she?"

Chris nodded. "A couple of things: a window and some sort of vase that she was going to make into a lamp. You know Evelyn, she'll make anything into a lamp. You should see what she's done with driftwood that she's picked up for free on the shore."

"But she can't make a window into a lamp. Besides, she can get windows wholesale at the building supply store."

"Not like this one. It was stained glass. She has it hanging on the wall in her living room. I don't usually like things like that—too ornate—but this one is quite attractive. Tall and narrow and mostly clear glass. I can't imagine that it was ever in this house. At least not as a window. Maybe a room divider or part of a piece of furniture . . . We didn't do anything wrong by taking them, did we? I thought Evelyn asked you about it."

"She did. And I told her that you guys could take everything you wanted. It only saved the company the cost of hauling it off. The Firbanks were quite emphatic that they didn't want any of what they called 'the old junk' that was left around." In fact, she had double-checked after finding her wineglasses, but she didn't mention that to Chris. "Did anyone else take anything?" she asked.

"Probably. I didn't check. Do you want me to?"

"Don't bother. I was just curious." What she really wanted to know was whether or not anyone had found one recently dead body, not a few antiques.

"I was wondering—" Chris began, and then stopped abruptly.

"About what?"

"Have you spent any time with Betty lately?"

"Not more than usual. Why?"

"She's been acting strange."

"What do you mean?" Josie asked sharply.

"Hey! Don't get so excited!"

Josie took a deep breath and tried to calm down. "Is it anything other than that weird food she's eating?"

"Yeah. Yesterday I found her staring out a window and crying her eyes out. You know that's not like Betty—usually she makes Pollyanna look like a candidate for Prozac."

"Where? What room was she in?" Josie knew the moment the questions were out of her mouth that they were the wrong ones to ask.

Chris looked at her strangely. "She wasn't crying over a scratch in the woodwork."

"I was just wondering about . . . you know, if she was looking at something out the window. Something that was making her sad or something . . ."

Chris seemed to accept the awkward explanation. "It was one of the back bedrooms. The one on the right as you come up the stairs."

"When?"

"What?"

"When was she crying? What time of day? Before or after lunch?"

"Before—oh! I get it. You're trying to figure out what

she might have been looking at outside the window. Good thinking."

Actually, Josie had been trying to figure out if Betty's upset had anything to do with the dead man. "Exactly." She nodded.

Chris was silent. "Let me think for a moment. I . . . actually, I'm sure it was after lunch, because when I asked her what was wrong, she tried to deny that she had been crying. But then she realized that she couldn't because I'd seen her and she made a joke that all the carrots she had eaten for lunch had made her depressed. It was a pretty weak joke."

"That's the only explanation she gave?"

"Yes, but I didn't grill her."

"No, of course not. What did you say?"

"I asked her if I could do anything to help out and she said something dramatic like 'no one can help me now!' "

"Sounds serious. Is that all she said?"

"Well, I don't like to be nosy, but I couldn't leave it at that. I mean, I'd hate it if I could have helped Betty only she wouldn't tell me what to do." She grinned. "Besides, I was curious as hell."

Josie managed to fake a chuckle. "And did she tell you anything else?"

"It's a man." Chris had been talking while she worked, but now she took the time to glance around at Josie. "Why do you look surprised? With Betty it's always a man."

"That's true." But could it be a dead man this time? Josie asked herself. She certainly couldn't ask out loud.

"Betty has a crush on some older man. That's how she put it. I suppose he's probably thirty-five or something equally ancient."

"Now wait a second. Tell me this from the beginning."

Chris picked a small chisel from the toolbox on the floor and turned back to her work before answering. "She said that she thought she was being dumped by some man that she had been dating."

"She thought she was being dumped?" Josie was distracted by the statement. She had always known that she was being dumped—even by men who had raised dumping women to a fine art.

"That's what I said. But she explained. This man she's been dating is in business for himself. She didn't tell me more than that, and in fact, I got the impression that she didn't know all that much about his business. But apparently a while ago—days or weeks—he said that he had to go on an urgent business trip and that while he wasn't sure when he'd be back, he would call her immediately."

"And?"

"And apparently he's back and he hasn't called."

"Then how does she know he's back? Did she run into him at one of those clubs she goes to on weekends or is she so serious about this man that she's staying home on Saturday night?"

"Not a chance. We both know Betty better than that. But, in fact, she didn't actually explain. I thought it was odd at the time."

Josie had the feeling this was important. "What? What did you think was odd?" Her voice sounded strange even to her, but apparently Chris didn't notice.

"Well, I asked her where she had seen him and what he was doing—because I was wondering the same thing you were—and her answer was that she hadn't actually seen him doing anything."

Was lying dead on the floor doing something? Josie wondered. "It's a strange answer."

"It is. And it's just not like Betty to be so upset about a man. Especially when you think about how she was acting yesterday."

"What do you mean?"

"Well, first she was desolate about this man who claimed to be on a business trip and then it turned out that he wasn't—and that same morning she was flirting with Jason for all she was worth!"

"That's right," Josie said, remembering Betty's reaction to Jason's good looks. "It doesn't make much sense, does it?"

"It sure doesn't," Chris agreed. She might have said more if Betty hadn't appeared in the open doorway.

"Anyone up here want a doughnut?"

Josie didn't think Betty looked devastated. She looked

the way Josie felt: hungry. "Since when is fried dough covered with sugar on your diet?" she asked.

"Since I gave up men."

"You? You're kidding," Chris whooped. "You'll give up men about the time Mother gives up . . . Well, that doesn't matter," she added quickly. "The point is, I'll believe it when I see it! And not before." She did, however, give Josie what Josie thought would be called a significant look. Josie looked back. She didn't know how it was interpreted.

"Why have you given up men?" Josie asked Betty.

"Because I'm like that book—I always get involved with the wrong ones."

"What book?" Chris asked.

"Millions of them," Melissa said, entering the room. "Apparently you can make a million dollars if you write a book about how women always choose the wrong men and why. At least, a lot of people seem to have thought that—and given it a try. I've considered it myself, in fact. Something like how to choose a man who will spend the rest of his life in college. I'm thinking of calling it *Men Who Love to Matriculate*."

"Wahoo! Sounds dirty," Chris exclaimed.

"I'm going to call my book *Carpenters Who Care Too Much*," Betty said dourly.

"Anyone seeing that title would assume that it's about men," Josie suggested. "And they'd think it was about professional standards. You know, the old measure twice, cut once."

"Fine. I'll write the companion volume and call it *Men Who Measure*," Chris said.

"And we know what they'll be measuring," Betty said, causing both other women to scream and giggle their appreciation.

Josie leaned back against the wall and watched. These were such nice women. Who would ever think one of them could have anything at all to do with a murder?

"I would like to kill that man!" Evelyn announced, marching into the room.

On the other hand . . . "What man and why?" Josie asked, getting right to the point.

"My rotten husband. You will never believe what he did now!"

"I wouldn't believe anything that my husband did—mainly because he doesn't actually do anything. He has something. He calls it writer's block," Melissa said. "It's his excuse for not finishing his thesis."

"What about your husband?" Josie asked, realizing that Evelyn was becoming angrier and angrier as Melissa spoke. "What did he do?"

"He told the twins that they can go on some sort of expensive wilderness vacation with the science club at the high school over spring break—that's next week! How the hell does he think we're going to come up with the money on such short notice?"

"I thought your husband had made all sorts of money selling some sort of water conditioner or something," Chris started.

"It was a water-purification system and he didn't make any money. He lost money. Not that that would make any difference. If he makes money, he just invests the profit in the next harebrained scheme that comes along and loses it all again. Men!"

"You're telling me," Betty said, stuffing the last of an extra-large Milky Way bar in her mouth.

"Hey! That was going to be my midmorning snack," Josie cried out.

"Don't worry. You can have my tofu tart," Betty offered, licking her lips and smiling with contentment.

TWELVE

When Josie turned around, she discovered that Chris had vanished. "Chris?" She said the name as a question.

"She left a few minutes ago," Betty explained. "About the time I came in."

"Did she say where she was going?" Josie asked, edging toward the door.

"Does she ever?" Evelyn wondered out loud.

"Why would she?" Melissa asked. "We're all working on the same house. There's nothing else open at this end of the island. She probably ran downstairs to get something. She'll be back."

Josie just nodded. Melissa was right. It was impossible to keep track of where everyone was and what they were doing—especially in a house as large as this one. And Chris probably would be right back.

Apparently they were all taking an early midmorning break. Josie sat down with her crew and consumed her share of the doughnuts that had arrived in their familiar pink-and-orange box. "Anyone have any idea when the bakery opens for the season?" Evelyn asked casually. "It will be nice to have a larger selection of baked goods."

"I don't know." Betty, who lived over the bakery, answered. "There's a large sign in the window that says SEE YOU NEXT SUMMER in block letters, but no one has been around since early October. I don't think they usually open much before Memorial Day."

"I bought Mother a Mother's Day cake there last year," Chris said, reappearing in the doorway holding a red thermos.

"See, I told you she was around someplace," Melissa said to Josie.

"Were you looking for me?" Chris asked.

"I was just wondering where you were," Josie explained vaguely.

"I was checking to see if our phone was working. Mother wasn't feeling very well this morning."

"That phone is a real problem. I'm still trying to get those fixtures replaced and I have no idea how long the charge on those batteries is going to last," Melissa interrupted.

"You could call down at the liquor store."

"Sam wouldn't mind," Josie said. "I guess it's time Island Contracting invested in a new cellular phone." She sighed. "I don't suppose anyone knows anything about phones."

"Sure I do," Evelyn announced. "I could even get one for you, if you want. I can get it wholesale from a distributor that I know."

"Would you mind?" Josie asked, relief in her voice.

"Of course not. I would have offered before, but I didn't want to offend you."

"Offend me?" Josie repeated the words, bewildered.

"Well, sometimes you're a little sensitive about not being superwoman. I mean, you don't want to admit that something is difficult for you because you think that you should be able to do everything. Oh God, I really did offend you this time," Evelyn added quickly. "It's just that I'm a lot older than you are, and I guess I don't worry so much about being a standard-bearer for the woman's movement anymore. Will you forgive me? You're not going to fire me, are you?"

The last question was asked as a joke, but Josie thought she heard an undercurrent of real concern. "Of course not. I'd give you a raise if you could get me a good price on the cellular. If Island Contracting could afford it, that is, which it can't," she added quickly. "Maybe it's time," she continued, "to get back to work."

The women all got up immediately. Josie rarely did more than suggest a change in their work habits, so they responded quickly when she did. She, however, rose a little more slowly. Was she imagining it or was Evelyn really concerned about losing her job? And why would that be true? Sam had been right: good electricians were hard to find. And that scarcity would—for many potential employers—overcome any prejudice against Evelyn's sex. She began to wonder exactly what had been in Evelyn's personnel file. And if Evelyn had some reason to want the contents of the file kept a secret. And was that reason enough to steal the files?

She leaned against the wall, wondering about these things. Josie carried one set of keys to the office, but a spare set was hidden in the old minnow trap that hung under the dock. And anyone could have known about them, Josie realized suddenly. She had asked Chris to use them to get something from the office more than once and, she remembered with horror, she had misplaced her keys just last week and had retrieved the spare key in front of the entire crew as they waited for their paychecks.

The next question, she mused, secretly pleased with her own logical thought process, was had the files been missing before the day she introduced everyone to the spare key's hiding place?

Too bad she didn't know the answer to that one. She was back where she started, she realized, going out to the hallway to fetch a sawhorse. So she might as well continue where she'd left off: with Chris. "You know what I was wondering," she began as she toted the wooden horse through the master bedroom's doorway.

"Uh . . . not really." Chris was frowning at a design of wooden laminate veneer that was laid out on the floor. "This is a little complex and I need to concentrate . . . if you don't mind?"

"Of course not." Josie began the time-consuming and irritating job of repairing ceiling joists. As she worked she mused over the conversation with Sam Richardson last night. She had told him, briefly, what she knew of the women on her crew. And had realized how little she really did know about them.

There was a lot of easy bantering between the women as they worked. All of them kidded Betty about her active social life, but apparently the happy-go-lucky young woman's involvement with an older man was making her unhappy, and Josie, at least, had had no hint of a serious relationship. Melissa complained about her husband's career as a student, but was there more to her life than that? Her own college degree in aerospace engineering couldn't get her a job. Falling back on being a master plumber might be causing more heartache than anyone noticed. And why was Evelyn working for Island Contracting? There were more and more hints that her past wasn't as clean as it should be, that something kept her working for a small place like Island Contracting. And, Josie realized, rubbing her aching neck, it would be just like Noel to take a deserving woman under his wing. Remembering Noel brought a few tears to her eyes, but she wiped them away before Chris noticed.

Chris, however, wasn't noticing anything. Josie glanced her way and saw that the other woman was working with an air of intense concentration. Looked like her mother was worrying her again, Josie thought. There were, she reminded herself, some benefits to being estranged from her family. At least she didn't have to worry about her parents as well as about her son.

But she didn't want to think about her parents, so she concentrated on Chris's mom instead. And found that there was very little to concentrate upon. She had never actually met Mrs. Kelly. Their sole personal contact was a wave out the front window when she had—as she did occasionally—gone to pick up Chris at her home in the morning. Less frequently, she dropped Chris off in the evening, but there had been no sign of Mrs. Kelly later in the day. Maybe her condition grew worse as the day went on? She wondered if there was a tactful way she could ask about it. Chris had always been reluctant to speak of her mother's illness. And Josie had been equally reluctant to intrude.

Or had she just been selfishly uninvolved? Josie sighed and decided that she might as well do something right. "You said your mother was having a bad day. . . ." she began.

"I wish people wouldn't keep asking me about her." Chris slammed the ball peen hammer down on the wooden chisel she had been using and a piece of pale ash flew across the floor. "Now see what you made me do!"

"I . . ." Josie truly did not know what to say. "I'm sorry. I was just being polite. I didn't know you were going to get so upset." She could feel herself getting angry and bit her lip. She had the temper that went with her hair color, but she had lived with it long enough to know that any anger was short-lived. She picked up the piece of wood and carried it over to Chris. "Do you need this?" she asked, handing it to her.

"Shit! Shit! Shit!" Chris slumped down on the floor and glared at Josie.

"I said I was sorry."

"It's not you. I mean, I'm not mad at you. I'm mad at my mother."

"Parents . . ." Josie began to babble some conventional pablum.

"My mother is a drunk," Chris announced. "But you probably guessed."

"Guessed? No, I had no idea." Josie was too shocked to know what to say. "Absolutely none," she added, feeling like an idiot. And feeling like she was failing—had, all this time, been failing—her friend. "Oh, Chris, I'm so sorry!" she cried out, awkwardly resisting an urge to throw her arms around the other woman.

"Yeah; me, too. But there's not a damn thing I can do about it. I've lived with her drinking for years. Every once in a while it would stop and I would think she was done with that part of her life. But then I would discover that she had been sneaking drinks, then she was drunk again regularly. Every year it gets worse. Every time I tell myself anything different I just find out that I've been lying—to myself as well as the rest of the world," she added with a crooked attempt at a smile.

"What are you going to do?" Josie asked before she realized that it was a stupid question.

"I'm going to move out."

"That's probably a good—you're going to what?" Josie asked as soon as she realized what Chris's answer had been.

"I'm going to move out."

"But what will happen to your mother? Can she live on her own?"

"I have taken care of her since my father got disgusted with the drinking and left home when I was fourteen. And she was never much of a mother to me. When other girls came home from dates and told their mothers about the movie they had seen, I came home and mopped up my mother's vomit from the bathroom floor where she had missed the toilet. My mother never showed up at a single church or school function. I had the lead in the high-school play in my junior year. My mother was too sick to attend any of the three performances. The only contact she had with me was that she would party anytime and anywhere, with anyone. And some of her partying was with people closer to my age than hers. I used to live dreading the moment that someone I knew would see my mother disgustingly drunk." She paused. "I guess I was worrying about all the wrong things back in those days."

"But it's just drinking, not a real disease, then," Josie said, beginning to realize the pain Chris had been keeping to herself all these years.

"Oh, believe me, alcoholism is a real sickness. It's as real as any other fatal disease. Just ask anyone who has lived with it.

"But I made up the bit about multiple sclerosis in eighth grade," she continued her explanation. "We studied MS in health class and I thought it would explain my mother's symptoms—she was falling down in grocery stores at that point in her life—and I decided it was more socially acceptable to have a mother with MS than to have a mother who was a drunk." She paused. "I think, in fact, that I was probably right.

"Anyway, I became my mother's mother, and when I couldn't stand it anymore, I married the wrong man to get away from home. It didn't work, of course. We were divorced in less than a year and I was back home with Mother."

"Why?" Josie asked.

"Because I was as addicted to my mother as she was to her vodka. It's called codependence by some people. I'd heard about it for years and thought it was just one of those New Age excuses for people not taking control of their lives. And then I realized that I had no control over my life.

My mother's drinking was controlling me as much as it was controlling her."

Josie nodded. It made sense, but Chris's next words came as a complete surprise.

"That was when Noel took me to my first Al Anon meeting."

"Noel?"

"Of course, I didn't quite get it all at that meeting," Chris continued as though there had been no interruption. "In fact, it's taken me almost two years to admit that the only thing I can do is leave my mother to sink or swim on her own—and I guess I assume that what she will choose to do is swim in alcohol, but I can't live like this any longer."

"Noel?" Josie asked, repeating the part of this surprising story that had startled her the most.

"Yes, his sister was an alcoholic. He's been a member of Al Anon for years—even after she drank herself to death. He said it had become important to him."

Josie was finding all this just a bit much to comprehend. "I guess I knew that Noel had a sister. . . ." she began slowly.

"I don't know much about his family," Chris said. "I didn't want to annoy him by asking a lot of personal questions. He was so wonderful to me. I would have spent the rest of my life clerking in a store if he hadn't offered to help me become a carpenter."

"But you once told me that you and Noel met building a house together," Josie protested. She had a terrible memory, but she hadn't begun to make things up. Or had she?

Chris smiled for the first time since answering Josie's initial question. "We did. It was a Habitat for Humanity house. It was ten years ago, and may have been the first one in the area. I had volunteered along with some people at the church I attend and Noel came to the site to deliver materials that Island Contracting had and didn't intend to use. We were making a royal mess of installing the sheathing on the outside walls. Noel hung around to hand out some professional instructions and ended up working on the project every Saturday and Sunday until the last bag of grass seed had been spread. Can you imagine that? He worked building all week long and then did volunteer building on weekends."

Josie wasn't a bit surprised; it sounded just like Noel.

"Anyway, I had started out doing demolition work on the original structure and, by the end of the project, had discovered that I loved doing the small finishing details—you can imagine that I was given all the work I could handle."

Josie could. Most people liked to do work that went quickly. Human nature, she supposed.

"And Noel and I got to talking and he suggested I take some night classes at the regional technical school. I was doing odd jobs to support myself, clerking in a shoe store, waiting tables in a bar on weekend evenings, and going nowhere, so I did what he suggested. I would have been foolish to do anything else when he said I could come work for him once I had finished my training."

"But you didn't start going to Al Anon meetings then? He didn't know about your mother then?"

"I don't actually know when he found out about Mother. I thought I was keeping her problem a secret, of course. Probably Noel began to suspect pretty soon after I came to Island Contracting."

"I wish you had told me. . . ." Josie began.

"I wish I had, too. I wish I had told every single person that I know. You don't know what a difference it would have made—but I couldn't talk about it at all outside of meetings until recently. And I don't want you to feel guilty about that. It doesn't mean you were less of a friend. It means I was.

"Anyway, Noel told me about himself one evening about two years ago when we were working late—remember all the molding we put around that custom stairwell over at the house on Ninety-third Street? The fake Victorian?" She continued after Josie nodded. "Well, he just asked me if I was busy the next night. I made some excuse about Mother. And Noel said I needed to go with him to a meeting because of my mother. I didn't understand then, but I went. . . . And here I am almost two years later. Noel is dead and I am going to move out of my mother's house and start living my own life."

"And your mother?" Josie asked quietly.

"I don't know, but I can only hope that she has the courage and the strength to change her own life."

THIRTEEN

Josie and Chris worked side by side for the next couple of hours, and by lunchtime, they had completed most of the intricate woodwork around the window and were closer friends than ever. They said very little about Chris's mother. Josie did offer Chris the use of the couch in her living room if the apartment she was going to sublet for a few months didn't become available, and Chris offered a few interesting comments about Noel's background.

In fact, after Josie had become accustomed to the fact that Chris had felt obliged to keep her mother's alcoholism a secret, most of her jumbled thoughts were of Noel. As she measured and fit the tiny pieces of wood in place, she tried to remember any references Noel had made to his sister.

And failed. She had known that he was an orphan, but she couldn't remember Noel saying anything directly about that either. Her only real memory of a statement on the subject had been from a plumber on one of the first jobs she had handled for Island Contracting. That woman had made a scathing comment about how Noel could almost adopt members of his crew since it made up for the lack of family in his own life.

But that his sister had been an alcoholic who drank herself to death was a bit much for Josie to fit into her concept of Noel's life. She was still thinking about it when Chris took a break from her work and reminded Josie of Betty's uncharacteristic behavior.

"So what do you think about Betty's decision?" she asked, rubbing her back with one hand and reaching for a thermos of coffee with the other.

"Giving up men or giving up the macrobiotic diet?"

"Well, I know that if I had to give up either brown rice or men, I'd probably choose brown rice," Chris said. "Fried rice, on the other hand, would be a tough decision."

Josie laughed. "How about rice pudding?"

"Hmm. All crusty, warm, and full of raisins! Maybe if the choice were between rice pudding and Brad Pitt . . ."

"Or Tom Cruise?" Josie suggested.

"Or Sam Richardson?" was Chris's contribution.

"Sam . . . Oh, yes," Josie realized who Chris was talking about. "You know, I had dinn—" In the midst of the newfound closeness between her and Chris, she began to tell her friend who she had been with the evening before when Evelyn walked into the room.

"Well, I got everything settled with my husband, but I'm afraid that the phone is on the fritz again. I'll go out at lunchtime and see if I can make a few calls about getting us another one right away." Evelyn looked over at Chris. "And maybe I'll be able to meet this wonder man who has you looking so happy these days."

"I hardly know him," Chris protested.

"Then why are you blushing? I may be old, but I still remember that 'I just met the most wonderful man in the world' feeling."

"I don't know him well enough to know if he's all that wonderful," Chris said.

"No man is all that wonderful," Evelyn announced. "And that initial feeling doesn't last all that long. But while it lasts . . . Well, it does make life worth living, doesn't it?"

"I hardly know him," Chris repeated.

"So why don't you come with me to pick up lunch and we can stop and make a few phone calls. There's time if you eat in the car on the way back here."

"Go on!" Josie laughed at the expression of longing on Chris's face. Living with an alcoholic mother must be hell—Chris deserved all the happiness she could find. And why couldn't Sam fall in love with her? She brushed aside her own unadmitted feelings. "You deserve a long lunch break today. Just be sure to pick up a ham-and-cheese hoagie for me."

"And a large Diet Coke," Chris added, putting away her tools.

"And maybe a couple of Hostess cupcakes for dessert. We have been working hard all morning."

"We'll get them," Evelyn promised, pushing Chris out of the room before her.

"And the phone! Don't forget the phone," Josie called after the two women. She knew they would take lunch orders from Betty and Melissa and then be on their way. She nailed up the last pieces of ceiling molding and went downstairs. She planned to help out in the bathroom until lunch arrived. The rough plumbing should be finished today, and with luck, the building inspector would appear before the replacement fixtures.

Heavy brown boxes were lying in the middle of the kitchen floor approximately where an island cooktop would be located.

"What the . . . ?"

"The tiles were delivered," Melissa announced, appearing with large pieces of PVC pipe under both arms.

"Damn. I didn't even think about calling the tile layers." Josie leaned back against a sawhorse and frowned.

"Betty and I were talking about that," Melissa said. "And she has a great idea. She thinks she can do it. Look, just let me dump these outside and she'll explain. Betty is in the bathroom," she added, and vanished through the open door into the backyard.

Josie headed to the bathroom. Betty was there, peering down the DWV system in the floor.

"Problem?" Josie asked.

"Nope. Just wanted to make sure everything was okay. Evelyn promised to call and request an inspection as soon as possible."

"Great. I ran into Melissa and she said that you had some sort of idea about the tiles."

"I do. I think I could try to lay them myself."

"Well," Josie began, "I suppose you can do it, but probably not as well as the experts and definitely not as quickly.

And the time you take laying tile should be spent in other ways."

"But it would cost Island Contracting less if I did it."

"Look at the pattern that the architect drew up," Melissa added, walking into the small room, papers in her hands. "This only looks like a custom job. It will be a piece of cake. Betty could do it in her sleep."

"I—"

"And I could stay late tonight and get it done," Betty continued.

"If the inspector gets here so we can close up the floor and walls," Melissa reminded her.

"Right. Of course. I'd really like the chance to do this," Betty continued. "It will look good on my résumé. You're not the only carpenter who wants to become management, you know."

"That's not how I became management," Josie said. She had been peering down the hole in the floor, but noticed a significant look pass between Betty and Melissa in a broken slab of mirror propped up against the wall. "Okay. If you want to give it a try, feel free. But if it starts to take up too much time, let me know and I'll find out which tilers can help out.

"This is good work," Josie continued. "But you always do good work," she added to Melissa.

"Nothing like being overqualified," Melissa answered.

"Did you remember to tell Evelyn that I wanted a super hoagie?" Betty asked the plumber, dumping a box of copper fittings on the floor and picking out a T-coupler.

"Sure did."

Someone hammering on the front door interrupted them.

"Who the hell?" Josie said, startled.

"Oh, I hope it's not a social call. The kitchen is a mess," Betty simpered, giggling at her own joke.

"It's the building inspector!" Melissa cried. "I saw him coming up the walk."

"Fantastic." Josie ran to greet the man. Maybe some things were beginning to work out.

The inspection was a quick one, and the building inspector, an avid surf fisherman, made a few comments on the excellence of Melissa's work and the scarcity of flounder, then headed on his way by the time Chris returned with lunch.

"Where's Evelyn?" Melissa asked, passing out the greasy paper-covered oblongs to the crew.

"Talking with Sam Richardson. I hope he knows that she's married with children," Chris grumbled, jabbing a straw into the plastic top of a wax-covered cup.

"Hanging around to chat doesn't sound like Evelyn," Josie murmured.

"Well, she said that she had to make more calls to the phone distributor," Chris answered. "But I think it was just an excuse."

"You're telling us that Evelyn was flirting with this guy at the liquor store? That doesn't sound like her," Melissa insisted.

"Well, she sure managed to get him interested," Chris answered.

Josie knew what was happening. Sam, still investigating, was this afternoon giving Evelyn the attention that he had bestowed upon Chris earlier. She was going to have to speak to that man. She couldn't run a remodeling job if members of her crew were fighting over him among themselves. "Maybe this Sam Richardson is the flirt," she suggested aloud. "You know. Men." It was, in her experience, a comment that was universally hailed in any group of women. She was not actually sure what it meant.

But it worked. "Yeah. Men," came the reply from one or two of the women. Lunch continued.

The women worked hard, and despite their morning break, they were always starving by lunchtime. They chatted as they ate humongous sandwiches, mixing talk of the work they were doing with comments about their lives. Today Josie did more listening than talking.

She had never stopped to wonder what the other women who worked for Noel had thought of her legacy. Whether they were jealous. Whether they thought it was deserved or undeserved. Whether they thought about it at all. Well, she had known the answer to that last question when she saw the look that had passed between Melissa and Betty; they had not only thought about it, they had discussed it.

She watched her crew. She had never felt a bit of hostility from any of them. No one had ever questioned her abilities or her qualifications. And she was qualified—although barely. But the same could be said of more than one other crew member. In fact, except for Betty, probably everyone here could have done what she was doing now—if Noel had given them the chance.

She didn't know what to think about that, so she thought about Betty. The young woman was uncharacteristically quiet. Usually bubbling and happy, today even her clothing was drab. Josie thought about what Chris had told her about Betty's change of diet and abandonment of the opposite sex. Could it have anything to do with the murder? Had Betty discovered and moved the body? Had she recognized the man? Could that account for the change in her behavior?

Betty was, Josie realized, the only person on the crew who had been born on the island, whose roots were here. That made her uniquely qualified to talk about some aspects of life here. It was Betty who had grown up on stories of the year train service connected the island to New York City and how a boardwalk was built the next summer. Betty's family remembered when the only competition for their grocery store had been a huckster's cart that offered farm produce in the summertime. The fact that her family had sold out and moved away when a large chain located a store on the island was the reason why there were very few natives like Betty around anymore. The economy had changed and more money had attracted large businesses from off the island. Only the islanders who could adapt to the times, like Basil Tilby, had survived economically.

"What or who are you thinking about so seriously?" Chris asked, noticing Josie's preoccupied air.

"I was just wondering if Betty knows anything about Basil Tilby. They both grew up here and all," she added, the first thing that came into her head by way of explanation. Betty was looking at her curiously.

FOURTEEN

"HOW THE HELL do you ever get a house built?"

"What?" Josie's question was almost a shriek. "I'm telling you what I learned today and you start to criticize my professional abilities—about which, may I say, you know absolutely nothing." Why did she always sound like a character in a PBS drama when she tried to be sophisticated?

"Sorry, but it seems to me that if you built a house the way you go about collecting information, you'd end up with the basement on the roof." Sam Richardson reached across the salmon-colored Formica-topped kitchen table and refilled her wineglass.

"Look, just because I didn't go to law school . . ."

"I am not enamored of the mental abilities of all of my colleagues."

"Is that supposed to explain why you're treating me like the village idiot?" Josie glared across the table.

"I'm not. If that's what you're hearing me saying, I'm sorry. Very sorry. It's just that we need to organize our information and material."

Josie continued to glare. Dinner was excellent. As promised, Sam Richardson was a good cook—which hadn't thrilled her. Just another thing that he could do better than she could. On the other hand, the kitchen of his seaside cottage was filled with some of the most hideous fifties furniture she had ever seen. Her apartment wasn't wonderful, but that was because she couldn't afford anything better. A man who could buy beachfront property could, in her experience, afford all the goodies that went with it. She should know, she had remodeled enough of them over the years.

But he had been taking notes as well as eating while she told him about her day, and his sighs had increased in frequency as the meal went on—and they weren't sighs of ecstasy.

"I've told you everything everyone on the crew said. And I thought there were some interesting things. Like Chris—this stuff about her mother explains a lot, doesn't it?"

"Like what?"

"Well, all the mysteries about her. Why she was late for work sometimes. Why she was upset. Things like that."

"And what do you think that has to do with the murder?"

"Well . . ." Josie poked a tine of her fork into a tiny piece of green left on her salad plate and stuffed it in her mouth. It was too small to chew, but it did give her time to think.

"It also creates a lot of questions. Was the dead man the right age to be her father? Could her father have reappeared in her life, and in the anguished state, Chris smacked him over the head with the hammer she just happened to have in her hand? People who live with alcoholics get very good at keeping secrets. Maybe this man did have something to do with her life."

"I don't think—"

"But you don't know," Sam interrupted gently. "All you know is that a dead man was found, that you panicked and moved him, and then, sometime later in the day, the man disappeared."

"Taken out to sea and dumped from a garbage scow."

"It's possible, but you don't know that either, do you?"

"Well, we think so, don't we? I mean, isn't that what we were talking about last night?" She was getting confused.

"We don't have any proof. . . ."

Josie had watched enough *L.A. Law* to know the answer to that one. "But we're not in court, are we?"

Sam grinned the grin that crinkled up his eyes and Josie had to remind herself that he was irritating the hell out of her. "You're right." Then he frowned. "Although we may yet be brought up on charges of destroying the evidence in a murder case."

"Have you ever heard of living in the present?" Josie asked.

"Yes. I'm not real good at it. I have been accused of being sort of a type A personality."

"What a surprise," Josie said rather sarcastically.

"Maybe we should get back to those people working for you," he suggested.

"Great. Why don't you tell me what you learned about Evelyn and Chris while they were at your store today," she suggested. Maybe he wouldn't be so organized himself.

"Not all that much," he answered reluctantly. "In fact, my impression of Chris is not of the levelheaded young woman who has been heroically coping with an alcoholic mother. To me, she seemed somewhat giggly for a woman her age."

"How old are you?"

If he was surprised by the non sequitur, he didn't show it. "Fifty-two."

"And in all your fifty-two years you haven't noticed the effect you have on women?"

Josie was pleased to see that she had gotten to him. He opened his mouth and closed it without saying anything, reminding her of a largemouth bass. Then he blushed.

"I don't believe it! You're blushing!"

"The curse of a Northern European heritage. And, yes, I know the effect I have on some women—I just didn't realize I was having that effect on Chris."

Josie found herself wondering about the women who didn't find him instantly appealing. Were they gay? Crazy?

"And I certainly didn't have any effect at all on Evelyn. She seemed to dislike me the second I told her that I had been a prosecuting attorney. Has she had any problems with the police?"

"None that I know about. Why?"

"Well, in the eyes of some people, my career put me on the side of law and order—if you think about the world that way—and not a few criminals do."

"And weren't you? On the side of law and order, I mean?"

"I thought I was doing a little bit to make the world a

better place," he answered quietly, all signs of pink vanishing from his face. "But we're not here to talk about me."

She knew he was avoiding the issue—and let him. "So you didn't get any information from Evelyn."

"Not much," he admitted. "When I asked her something about herself—I don't remember the exact words, but I asked a casual question like how did she end up working on a building crew—"

"We hear a lot of questions that sound a lot like 'how did a nice girl like you end up doing this?' " Josie interrupted. "We do come to resent the implication that we're equal to hookers."

"I can understand that. And I don't think it sounded like that—although I know how differently a question can sound to the person asking it than to the person who is being questioned. But anyway, Evelyn reared back and answered that she had been happily married for years and was not accustomed to men coming on to her. She has some temper, doesn't she?"

"No, she doesn't." Josie was bewildered. "That doesn't sound like Evelyn at all. She's become the mom of our group—sort of the earth mother to the entire crew."

"You're kidding."

"That's not the impression she gave you?"

"Not at all. She came in, introduced herself, and asked to use the phone. I showed her where it was and she said thank you and made a few calls."

"A few?"

"At least two. Maybe more. I thought it was polite to give her some privacy. That may have been a mistake. I'm used to investigating after a crime is over, not while it—or the cover-up—is going on. Well, anyway, I thought I was making casual conversation when I asked her what led her to become a carpenter."

"Actually, she's an electrician. But she also does carpentry."

"She didn't tell me that. She just told me she wasn't looking for a come-on and stormed out of the store."

"You know, that's a little weird."

" 'Weird'?"

"It doesn't sound like her."

He frowned. "It's always interesting when people act out of character, isn't it?"

"I suppose so," Josie answered slowly. "But maybe I shouldn't have spoken so quickly about what she's like. I've only worked on a few jobs with her."

"How many?"

She had to think a few minutes before answering. "Four. But she didn't work for Island Contracting at first. She was hired as an outside contractor."

"You told me she had had trouble getting work as an independent electrician."

"Yes. That's what she told me."

"And you don't have any reason not to believe her."

"I never thought about disbelieving her until you asked about it."

"So how did she end up being Island Contracting's regular electrician?"

"I don't actually know. She was hired three jobs ago—a few months before Noel died."

"What had happened to the electrician Island Contracting worked with before her?"

"Nothing. I mean, we didn't have one. We worked with a few electricians."

"So . . ."

"But Evelyn is different," Josie added quickly.

"How?"

"She's a carpenter as well as an electrician. So she builds along with us and does all the wiring. It's efficient. She's always there when we need her. I think Noel made a good choice."

"One that you will continue?"

"Me?"

"Well, it is your company now, isn't it?"

"Yes. I haven't made any decisions like that, though. And I won't have to if this murder wrecks our reputation. Then there won't be an Island Contracting."

Sam looked concerned.

"But I have an idea!" Josie was so excited that she choked.

"Are you okay?" Sam was around to the back of her chair in only a moment.

"Fine. Just fine. Let me . . ." She took a sip of water and swallowed a few times. "Yes. I'm fine." Actually, she was embarrassed to death. "It's just that I had an incredible thought. It explains everything."

"What?"

"Well, think about the result of this becoming public—it would destroy the company. So, maybe that's why it was done. Maybe this whole thing happened so that Island Contracting would fold." She crinkled up her brow. "It doesn't sound quite so sensible when said out loud."

"It's an interesting idea, but to kill a man just to ruin a company seems like a rather unnecessary thing—unless someone killed you or an essential member of your crew." He paused and Josie got the idea that he wasn't going to tell her what he was thinking.

"What just passed through your mind?" she asked quickly.

"How did Noel die?" he asked slowly.

"Pancreatic cancer. It wasn't murder." She frowned, remembering Noel's wasted body the last few weeks of his life.

"I'm sorry to bring back unhappy memories," he said, putting his hand on hers for just a moment. "But," he continued, returning to his seat, "I had to ask.

"When you think about it," he added, "there are a lot of very easy ways to sabotage Island Contracting—without taking the risk of killing anybody."

"Such as?"

"Well, wouldn't it be possible for someone to damage the site you're all working on? Come in at night and cut wires, punch holes in the plumbing, or something?"

"I suppose so," Josie admitted. "We keep the house locked up, but there isn't an alarm system connected yet. It's certainly not impossible."

"No sign of anything like that?"

"Nothing. And, believe me, we'd know."

"Would you really? I mean, if someone punched holes in the plastic pipes in the basement or something? You can probably tell that I have no idea what I'm talking about."

Josie was thrilled that there was something she knew more about than he did. "In the first place, the Firbank house doesn't have a basement. And every system is checked and double-checked. And the building inspector does a lot of inspections throughout our work," she explained.

"How many?"

"On a job of this size, he's probably on-site a dozen times—maybe more."

"And you're sure you'd notice any sabotage?"

"That's what I said."

Josie was becoming angry again and Sam seemed to recognize it. "Do you think," he said slowly, "that we could make a quick list of questions that you would discover the answer to tomorrow? Then we can get you to bed at a reasonable hour. And maybe you could come back for dinner tomorrow night?"

"Why don't you come over to my apartment?" The words were still in her larynx and she was regretting them. She couldn't cook this well.

"No, you'll be busy all day. Why don't we just meet at Basil's place?"

"Fine." Josie breathed the word with relief.

"Seven o'clock okay with you?"

"Yeah." She was trying to decipher the words he was writing on a notepad he had grabbed from the counter near his wall phone, but he finished quickly and pushed the pad across the table toward her. Josie read the list and looked up at her companion.

"I've been sitting here wondering if this type of furniture is now chic with yuppies."

Sam Richardson seemed surprised by the non sequitur. "I suppose so . . . I didn't choose it." He looked around the room as though he hadn't noticed his surroundings before. "It was chosen for me. A friend . . ." he began, and didn't continue.

Josie looked down at the list in front of her and shrugged. It was just another mystery that she probably wouldn't be able to solve.

FIFTEEN

JOSIE WAS DETERMINED to get organized. She had gotten up an hour early, showered (again substituting dish detergent for shampoo), fed Urchin a can of imported sardines, grabbed a mug of instant coffee (stale) made with tap water (barely warm), and driven down to the office, where she hoped she could think. But once ensconced in what she would always think of as Noel's desk chair, she read and reread the list Sam had handed her the night before with absolutely no idea how to proceed.

If only she had access to the vanished personnel files, she thought, watching two kittens skidding across the wood floor after an empty Tender Vittles packet. The first two questions on the list (1) When did you come to work for Island Contracting? and (2) Did you work for a contracting company before Island Contracting, and if so, what was the name of that company? should be in those records. It seemed so embarrassing to run around and ask questions like that, although . . .

She was, after all, the boss now. Maybe she could think up some sort of reason for the questions. Maybe something related to taxes. Her crew probably had as little knowledge about such things as she did. She could claim that their accountant needed the information. She could even bring a notebook and write down the answers, she decided happily.

So what was she going to do about the third question?

Think about it later, she concluded, bending down to scoop up a black kitten. "Animals who chew on electric wires do not live to a ripe old age," she admonished the tiny creature. She set the cat back on the floor, where it resumed its suicidal habits. "Well, aren't you stupid!" Josie bent down and yanked the plug from the wall. "I guess you need to be saved from yourself."

Sunlight was beginning to stream through the windowpanes and Josie glanced at her trusty Timex. She had a few more minutes before she had to leave. Unable to resist temptation, she went out on the back deck and pulled up the crab trap hanging in the water. A half-dozen large blue crabs scurried around in the metal mesh. She grabbed the long tongs from an old set of barbecue equipment that she used for the task and flipped over the crustaceans, tossing the females back into the sea. She replenished the pile of moss bunker in the trap and gently lowered it back to the bottom of the water, barely managing to rescue a brown-and-white kitten from the briny deep.

"I'm beginning to understand why, with such large litters, the world isn't covered with cats," she announced, taking the small miscreant inside the building with her.

She had to find homes for some of the animals, she thought. It was only a matter of time before these cute little kittens were going to be beautiful big cats, and with her luck, the next potential client to walk through the door would have allergies. Besides, she thought, looking around, it just wasn't professional to run a kitten orphanage in the middle of a place of business. She noticed that the calico was asleep on top of the computer monitor. It sure was cute, though, she decided, heading off to work.

Her toolbox was on the floor of the truck. A small notebook was tucked in the pocket of her overalls. She was putting the key in the ignition when she realized what had been wrong with the picture she had just left. Kittens didn't choose to sleep on hard, lumpy rectangles of plastic—unless they were warm as well as hard and lumpy. That computer had been turned on. Someone had been in the office before her, she thought, running back up the path to the building.

And recently, she realized when she picked up the sleeping kitten and placed her hand on the monitor. She sank down in the desk chair and considered her situation. But her hand was reaching for the phone before enough time had passed for even one animal to climb into her lap. She just hoped Sam hadn't been lying about his sleeping habits.

He hadn't. The phone was answered on the first ring. "Sam. It's Josie. I need some help. What do you know about computers?"

"What sort of computer?"

"You know. Apples. IBMs. Personal computers."

"I've used them for years in my work. But mainly for word processing and some record keeping. Nothing elaborate. Why? Are you having trouble with yours?"

Swallow your pride and answer him, Josie lectured herself. "Sort of."

"Maybe you should call the company that created the program you're working with."

"I can't do that. I'm not using a program . . . I don't know how to use a program. I don't even know how to use a computer." She made the admission quickly. "I've never even turned one on. That's the problem. Someone turned on the one at Island Contracting early this morning—and it wasn't me." She took a deep breath and explained what she had discovered.

"I'll be right there. Wait for me," Sam insisted, and hung up without giving her time to protest.

Josie replaced the receiver and looked around the room, thinking vaguely of tidying up. She walked about, picking a few dead leaves off the Boston fern hanging in one window and tossing two catnip mice out of sight behind a row of old oak file cabinets. She was straightening piles of unopened mail on the desk when Sam Richardson appeared in the doorway.

"Hi . . . hey, this place is great."

Josie was pleased to see that he was admiring the row of handmade birdhouses that wound halfway around the room near the ceiling. There was one for each total remodeling job Island Contracting had completed. She wondered if there was a chance in hell that one would be built for the Firbank project. "Thanks," was all she said.

"Why all the kittens?"

"They don't have anyplace else to live."

"Good thing you live here on the island and not in New York City—you'd have a more difficult time solving the homeless problem there," Sam said, casually sitting down at the desk. "You know," he added, fingers poised above the keyboard of the computer, "I don't mind closing the store for the day to help you out. I'm not selling much right now anyway, and the only way I can find out what is in here is to look at everything. I mean, I'm going to be reading all the files of Island Contracting."

Josie shrugged. "I need your help," was all she said. I have to trust someone, was what she thought.

He switched on the computer and got to work. Josie left for the building site, with a promise to bring him some lunch around one o'clock.

Josie planned on a busy morning, working as well as asking her crew for the background information that Sam had requested. She planned to start a discussion during lunch that might elicit some answers to the third question. What she hadn't planned on was the Firbanks.

As she drove up she saw Mrs. Firbank (who had never asked to be called anything else) standing on the board that had replaced the front steps. Apparently believing that since she was at her summer home, it must be summer, she was wearing white capri pants, a blue-and-white middie blouse, and magenta straw espadrilles. She looked very cold. She also looked very angry.

Josie parked her truck behind the maroon Lexus and ran up to the house. "Mrs. Firbank, how nice to see you," she lied. "I didn't think you were coming here until the weekend. Is Mr. Firbank around?"

"My husband is inside looking at plumbing. I do not look at plumbing," she explained, tossing a massive purple scarf over her shoulders.

Josie expected that neither did Mr. Firbank under ordinary circumstances, but she assumed that Betty was his tour guide, and in the presence of youth and beauty, Mr. Firbank would look at most anything that was shown him. "Have you been up to see the window in the master bedroom? I think you're going to like what we've done," she added, hoping she was right.

"It's dirty inside."

Always be nice to the person who pays the bills. "We keep things picked up, but it does get dusty when we're working," Josie admitted, wondering if this woman thought there was any other option. "Sawing creates sawdust," she added.

Mrs. Firbank scowled.

"Would you like to come upstairs and see that window?" Josie repeated her offer. "It might be a bit warmer inside."

Apparently that did it. Mrs. Firbank turned—and waited for Josie to open the door for her.

As promised, there was lots of dust in the air. One of Island Contracting's rules was, when the owner's around, work like hell. The women were doing just that—and as noisily as possible.

"Come on upstairs," Josie urged, leading the way. Happily, Chris had hung around and swept up last night. It might not look like the Firbanks' Fifth Avenue apartment after the cleaning woman was finished, but the trash was all piled in corners and the tools were put away. Josie glanced nervously at a blue tarp and ran upstairs. She didn't want to think about what would have happened if Mr. or Mrs. Firbank had discovered the body.

Mrs. Firbank tiptoed up the steps, apparently afraid of dust attaching itself even to the soles of her shoes. "It's that big window at the front of the house, isn't it?" she asked plaintively. "Is that new?"

Josie tried not to respond. Hadn't this woman even looked at the house she'd bought? Or the plans her architect had created? "Yes," was all she said. "I think you'll find it a big improvement. Very impressive."

"Oh, yes. A neighbor of mine had a Palladian window added in the bathroom of her condo. Is this a Palladian window?"

"No, it's much . . . much fancier." Apparently she had chosen the correct word.

"Really? Is it big?"

"Very. And very elegant."

Wrong word. Mrs. Firbank frowned. "I thought this house was to be . . . I think the word was casual—as a contrast to our condo in the city. Our condo is formally elegant."

"This is casually elegant," Josie improvised. "Very nineties. After all, you wouldn't want something tacky and country or . . . or anything like that. Too seventies," she suggested.

"Retro," Mrs. Firbank murmured, nodding as though she understood. "No, we definitely don't want retro." She pulled her scarf closer as if protecting her neck from the fangs of an unpopular decorating scheme. "It has been done to death, hasn't it?"

"Uh, yes. Done to death—as you say. Well, we'll see how you like this," Josie added, flinging open the door to the master bedroom—and screaming loudly.

Apparently Mrs. Firbank thought it was the thing to do because she joined in immediately.

"What are you yelling about?" Betty cried, running over to the two women.

Josie had stopped screaming. The man on the floor was moving, getting up and coming over to them, in fact. So relieved was she that they didn't have another dead body on their hands that she didn't even ask why he had been there.

Mrs. Firbank apparently didn't feel the same way. "What in God's name were you doing there on the floor?" she shrieked at her husband. "And in your new Armani, too!" She glanced suspiciously at Betty. "Is any of this your doing, young lady?"

"Now, cherry blossom. I was just trying to get an idea of the view we'd get out the window while we were still in bed in the morning. Why else would I be lying on the floor?"

"Good question." Mrs. Firbank glared at Betty.

"Mr. Firbank was just saying that he was very glad you were here and could make some important decisions," Betty said to Mrs. Firbank. If she was trying to placate the woman, it didn't work.

"I pay someone to make the decisions."

"Now, cherry blossom, no one can decorate a room the way you can. You know that."

Josie stared at the man. He had to be at least twenty years older than she was, but he had the smoothest, shiniest skin she had ever seen. She vaguely remembered Noel saying that the Firbanks owned some sort of skin-care company. She glanced at the line-free face of Mrs. Firbank and wondered if it would be polite to inquire about the name of their products.

"I do like this window," the woman that Josie was coming to think of as "cherry blossom" admitted reluctantly. "We can do things with it. Swags come to mind."

Chris was standing in the doorway and Josie cringed, thinking what the carpenter must be feeling about having her elegant woodwork covered with miles of flowered chintz—or whatever fabric was currently chic. "Do you need me for anything?" Josie asked, hoping the answer would be affirmative.

"Yes." Her fondest wish came true. "The police are downstairs looking for you," Chris continued.

"I told you there was something wrong with an entire contracting company full of female carpenters," the cherry blossom screeched at her husband. "This house is a jinx. Now we've gotten mixed up with something illegal! You have to be very careful when you hire people, you know. Look at all those illegal aliens and . . . and everything."

Josie just took a deep breath, pushed past the yelling flower, and trotted down the stairs.

Chief McCorkle was waiting at the bottom with a hammer in his hand.

Josie was fairly sure her heart couldn't take much more. The hammer was definitely stained with blood.

SIXTEEN

"MISS PIGEON, IF you keep this up, I'm going to have to put you under arrest."

Just shut up and listen. There's a lawyer back at the office, Josie reminded herself. Perhaps she'd only get life in prison if she smiled nicely. Maybe they'd give her a pass to see her son graduate from college.

On the other hand, it might actually kill her to be nice to this idiot. "Is there anything I can do for you?" she asked breathlessly. She was afraid the pounding of her heart would drown out the question.

"Stop littering," he answered, miraculously handing her the tool. "I recognized this as Island Contracting's equipment from the initials on the handle, but I'm not going to run around town picking up after you and your crew. You'd think that a bunch of women would be neater than that, wouldn't you?" He chuckled, apparently thinking she would take this as a good joke.

"Where . . . where did you find this?" She grabbed for the hammer and, once she had it, hid it behind her back. She couldn't believe that he wasn't going to ask her about the bloodstains—he must have noticed!

Apparently not.

"Why, just think back to where you left it." He was obviously milking this for all it was worth.

"It must have been someone on my crew."

"Sure. Someone who is as fond of crab salad as my son says you are." He peered at her over his sunglasses.

Josie thought the man watched too many cop shows. "What does crab salad have to do with the hammer?" she asked.

"Everyone on the island knows that you go crabbing whenever you got free time, Miss Pigeon."

"So? What does that have to do with the hammer?"

"The hammer was found on the dock down by the Twenty-second Street public wharf. I assumed you were crabbing there. It's pretty early in the year for anyone else."

"Oh."

"You were there, weren't you?"

"How else would the hammer get there? Walk?" Josie realized she was making him mad and backed down. "It was very nice of you to bring it up here. These things are expensive." She waved it in the air and then, seeing the blood, dropped her arm to her side. "Where exactly did I leave it?"

"Just sitting on the bench that's built on to the north side of the dock. Just sitting there for anyone to see—and pick up."

"Well, thank you for bringing it over," Josie said.

"I came here to give you a ticket, Miss Pigeon." He leered.

"A ticket?" Josie was outraged. "I'm not even in my car!"

"There is a strict ordinance against littering on the public docks—punishable with a fifty-dollar fine." He handed her a carbon copy of a ticket. "You can sign it and pay the fine or show up in court on the applicable date." He did an about-face on one heel and started from the room. "Have a very nice day, Miss Pigeon."

Josie was so thrilled that he was gone that she would have paid any fine to anyone—even for something as silly as littering in a public space. She looked down at the tool in her hand and, checking first to make sure the coast was clear, ran out to her truck and tucked it under the front seat. She'd show it to Sam at lunchtime—if she ever got rid of the Firbanks.

God, the Firbanks! She wondered what they thought—and whether it was possible for them to cancel their contract this far into the project. What was she going to say to them? she asked herself as she ran up the stairs to the master bedroom—which was empty. She stood still, puzzled, until she heard footsteps over her head, then she charged up to the attic. Her entire crew was there, leaning against walls and windowsills. The Firbanks were speaking together at one end of the room.

Chris saw her first. "I guess you cleared up that little traffic problem," she cried out loudly, giving Josie some hint as to the excuse being given for her absence.

"You'll never guess what my brilliant husband has decided!" cried Mrs. Firbank.

"Yes, you'll never guess." Evelyn turned her back on the couple and rolled her eyes at Josie.

"We're going to build a deck up here!" Mrs. Firbank announced.

"We're going to what?"

"Look. It is so simple. I don't know why the architect didn't think of it. It's so obvious."

Josie followed Mrs. Firbank over to the window in the middle of the east roofline. "We will knock out these two dormers and build a deck."

"A small deck," Mr. Firbank explained, joining them. "Inset rather than jutting out into space."

"And then I'll be able to sunbathe nude. Like I did at that place down in Jamaica," Mrs. Firbank added, looking up at her husband flirtatiously.

"It faces south, so in the morning—perhaps," Josie said, looking down at the studs on the floor. "It will cost—"

"Shouldn't cost too much extra. Maybe a couple of hundred for the materials—"

"A couple of thousand. At least," Josie interrupted Mr. Firbank. "The lumber alone," she began. "And who knows what we'll find when we break through the roofline. In a house this old . . ."

"What did the police chief want?" Mr. Firbank asked abruptly.

"Just a traffic ticket."

"The police on the island make house calls to deliver speeding tickets? Sounds pretty inefficient to me. I think I'll have to stop down at the police station and introduce myself if the service is so personal around these parts," Mr. Firbank said.

Josie knew a veiled threat when she heard one. "Why don't you explain exactly what you're thinking of with regards to this deck? Then I can draw up some preliminary plans and we can go over them this weekend."

"Excellent idea." The Firbanks smiled the smile of someone who had just won. "And we'll keep the cost under . . . say fifteen hundred dollars?"

Josie took a deep breath. "I can try."

"I'm sure you'll manage to do it."

Josie pulled the notebook that she had planned to use to investigate the crime from her back pocket and prepared to listen to impractical, expensive, grandiose plans. How was she going to get out of this? She knew how to read plans, not how to draw them up. Island Contracting was probably capable of planning and carrying out this new addition to their project, but not for fifteen hundred dollars! Why had she let these awful people blackmail her with an implied threat of checking out her problems with the police? How could she run a business if she didn't like to say no to anyone?

It took over an hour for the Firbanks to finish drawing up their plans and suggestions. Then Mrs. Firbank insisted on going over the kitchen blueprints again and Mr. Firbank decided to check out the foundation of the old garage with an eye to re-creating the former carriage house that had once been there. Betty accompanied him on his quest and Josie had little concern about more impractical agreements—Betty had no trouble at all when it came to saying no to men. Practice, in her case, made perfect.

Josie glanced at her watch. Sam was going to wonder what had happened to her if she didn't appear back at the office pretty soon. But she didn't want to leave before the Firbanks. Maybe she could direct them to some out-of-the-way lunch place and they'd forget all about the police station.

For the second time that day, fate was on her side. Mrs. Firbank appeared behind her. "I'm so famished," she explained. "I suppose the only place open yet on the island is that horrible deli down by the docks?"

Josie was inspired. "Well, it's still a little early in the season, but there's a new restaurant off-island—less than a mile from the bridge—that has wonderful food." She was on a roll. "No one knows about it yet, but I'm sure it's going to be one of the hot spots this summer." She wasn't sure that was the right term, but she could see that Mrs. Firbank was intrigued.

"Wonderful. If I can just find that husband of mine . . ."

"I'll get him," Josie offered, jumping up from the place where she'd been working. "You'll want to get going. I don't think there will be much of a lunchtime rush today, but you never know—" She didn't finish: it was, after all, the literal truth.

"If you'd just find Mr. Firbank, then . . ."

Josie wasn't surprised. You didn't have to be with Mrs. Firbank long to realize that she always expected other people to do all the to-ing and fro-ing. "Right away," she called out, and ran off to find Mr. Firbank.

It took almost half an hour more to get the Firbanks on their way. Noel used to say that if people paid their contractors by the hour, they'd be less likely to waste their time. The Firbanks stood around like the last guests at a long cocktail party until everyone on the crew had made their excuses and wandered off, leaving Josie to wave her employers on their way.

Then she ran around the house, taking orders for lunch, listening to complaints about the Firbanks, and finally driving to the deli while peering out the window for an off-season speed trap.

It took her ten minutes to pick up lunch and return to the office.

"Hi! I only have a few minutes," she cried, running in the door, the bag in her hands dripping red wine vinegar on the floor. She had picked up an Italian hoagie for Sam and apparently it was leaking badly. "I didn't get a chance to ask any questions. You'll never believe who appeared at the house this morning."

Sam Richardson was sitting before the computer surrounded by kittens and long rolls of printer paper. "You didn't need to ask my first two questions. I found the personnel files of Island Contracting. They were on a computer disk," he added, seeing Josie's perplexed glance at the file cabinets.

"That's probably why I couldn't find them in the file cabinets. Anything interesting?" she asked casually, opening the bag and passing him a sandwich and a tall paper cup.

"Very interesting, in fact." He looked at the food. "What is this messy thing?"

"Italian hoagie. I hope you like peppers."

"No problem. Let me ask you some questions."

"I have to get back."

"Just one question, then."

"Okay."

"Why would Noel advertise for an electrician and then, instead of choosing one of the numerous people who replied to the ad, hire Evelyn, who just walked in off the street looking for a job?"

"Ah . . . I have no idea. How do you know that happened?"

"It's all right here. Look."

Josie leaned over Sam's shoulder as he pressed buttons

and messages flashed out on the screen. "It's very interesting," he said. "But puzzling."

"Does it have something to do with the murder?"

"I don't know. All I know is that your Noel had some very unusual hiring practices."

"Like what?" Josie asked, intrigued.

"Well, it's almost as though he wasn't only looking for a competent person—he seemed to be looking for the right person. And, sometimes . . ."

Josie heard the reluctance in his voice. "Sometimes what? Don't worry about my feelings. I need to know the truth here—even if it's about me."

"If you're sure. And, in fact, it's not you specifically. The records don't actually go back that far."

"I have to go back to work," Josie said.

"Then let me explain quickly. Taking Evelyn as an example." He tapped a few keys and words scrolled on the screen. "Look. About a year ago Island Contracting put out ads to find an electrician."

Josie nodded. "Sure, I remember. We had been using Island Electric most of the time—but Bud—he was Island Electric—retired. I didn't know that Noel was looking for a crew member then."

"No. He wasn't necessarily. The ad isn't specific. But—and here's what's interesting—he got over a dozen answers. And the next week, according to the records here, he hired Evelyn. And she didn't answer the ad—at least her answer isn't recorded here and everyone else's is."

"Then how did he find her?"

"That's one of the things that I want you to discover this afternoon."

"Oh?"

"Yes." He turned to the long scroll of paper that hung from the computer printer.

"Hey, I have a house to remodel," Josie protested.

"Don't worry. There are only a couple of things here. The rest is tax info and stuff like that." He ripped the paper into sheets at the perforations and handed a piece to her.

She frowned as she read through the list he had given her.

"You found all this stuff in there?"

"Sure did."

"Let me make sure I have this right. You want to know how Evelyn found out that Island Contracting needed an electrician and if she can say why Noel decided to hire her full-time rather than just use her as needed."

"Yes."

"And you want to find out how Melissa came to Island Contracting?"

"Yes. She is the second interesting case. She was living and working in California one week and the next week she had moved here with her husband and started to work."

"Could be that she got here and just happened to find a job right away," Josie suggested.

"It's not only possible, it's likely. Let's just make sure though. Okay?"

Josie shrugged. "Okay. And what's this? You want to know about some sort of loan that Noel made to Betty?"

"No, he didn't make her a loan—well, he might have, but his personal business isn't here—or I haven't found it. I want to know why Island Contracting made a loan to Betty and allowed her to pay it off in biweekly installments. The interesting thing is that the loan was made on the day that she started working for the company."

"So it wasn't just that she needed some cash after working here for a while."

"No. And it wasn't just some cash. It was five thousand dollars."

"Wow. That's a lot of money for a first-year carpenter."

"That's what I thought."

"No questions about Chris?"

"I haven't found anything yet. But I haven't finished going through all the files—not by a long shot."

"Guess I'm lucky that you didn't find out anything unusual about my employment history," Josie kidded, getting up.

"Guess you are," Sam agreed, taking a large bite of his sandwich and spilling sliced raw onions all over his pants.

Josie didn't smile. Just why did she have the idea that he was lying?

SEVENTEEN

IT WAS ALMOST as though Melissa were waiting for her right inside the front door.

"Hi. Is everyone starving?" Josie asked, clasping a large brown bag to her chest.

"It is a little late for lunch." Melissa looked around as though afraid of being overheard. "Could we talk privately sometime this afternoon? Maybe down at the office?"

Josie thought of Sam huddled over the computer screen. "Maybe during our break? I don't want to leave the site this afternoon unless something urgent comes up."

"Fine, but it has to be private."

"Of course. Is anything—"

"We'll talk later," Melissa interrupted her as Betty and Evelyn appeared.

"Finally, food," Evelyn said, grabbing the bag that Josie still held and digging in. "Who ordered what?"

It took a few minutes for everyone to find their order and settle down on the porch in the warm afternoon sunshine. Then little could be heard except for less than ladylike slurps and munches. Josie, never in her life having been too nervous to eat, finished off half of her hoagie before speaking.

Betty, however, unaccustomed to such rich fare, was more voluble. "I do not believe that man. How does a slimeball like that become a millionaire?"

"I assume you're talking about Mr. Firbank?" Chris said.

"He probably makes wonderful skin-care products," Josie suggested, willing to give credit where credit was due—even when it was due to idiots. "He has remarkable skin for someone his age."

"You don't think he uses the junk that he sells, do you?" Betty asked.

"I assumed. . . ." Josie began.

"So did I," Betty agreed. "He explained that what he called 'that pink crap' was mainly water and cheap mineral oil. He uses something that is specially made up for him by a masseuse on Madison Avenue. He offered to give me the address."

"Ha! It would probably cost you a week's wages to buy a jar," Melissa said.

"And why would you, of all people, need something like that?" Evelyn asked practically. "You're way too young to worry about wrinkles. Anyway, that stuff is probably less effective than a jar of Vaseline from the discount drugstore."

"It would be nice to have that type of money to spend on yourself, though," Betty said wistfully.

No one disagreed with that. And Josie saw a great opportunity. "You know, we're pretty lucky to have the jobs that we do—I mean, that Noel hired us back when he did," she added. When no one responded, she tried a more direct route. "When did he hire you?" she asked Melissa. "I mean, how soon after you arrived out here from California?"

"Actually, he hired me in California," Melissa answered, picking onions from the second half of her sandwich.

"California?" Josie repeated the word.

"Yes. I had given up looking for a job where I could use my degree—no one has hired a fledgling aerospace engineer for years—so no one was going to hire a female. And, in fact, I enjoy plumbing. But my husband's fellowship had run out and he was moving into a new graduate program out here. I was planning on finding a job after we moved, but about a week before we were to leave California, Noel walked onto the construction site where I was employed and, after watching me work for a while, offered me a job."

"Noel was in California? Why?"

Melissa shrugged. "Why not? Maybe he was on vacation or something. I never thought about it. I just packed up my stuff, and when we got out here, instead of moving close to campus, we rented a house nearer the island."

"Doesn't your husband mind?" Betty asked.

"What choice does he have? He isn't the one supporting us, is he?"

"But how did Noel find you?" Josie asked, sticking to the point. "And how did he know that you were going to move to the East Coast?"

"You know, I've never been sure," Melissa answered. "At the time I was too busy to think about it—I was even too busy to realize what a strange coincidence it was that everything worked out the way it did." She paused and Josie wondered, for the first time, if she was hearing the truth. "But I think I was pretty lucky that things worked out the way they did."

"You know, that's true for me, too," Betty piped up.

"What in heaven's name do you have in common with that story?" Chris asked. "You don't have a worthless college degree. You grew up here. You've probably known Noel your entire life."

"No. Not at all," Betty protested, her eyes wide. "I mean, I did grow up here. And I didn't go to college. I took classes at tech and apprenticed off-island before I got my credentials as a carpenter."

"And when did you meet Noel?" Josie asked, remembering Sam's questions about the loan Noel had made to Betty.

"When I was looking for a job, of course. I was living with my parents then and didn't have any money. One of my teachers at tech suggested that I call all the contracting companies in the phone book and ask if they were hiring. I don't know if it was my voice or what, but Noel was the only person who suggested that I come down to the office and fill out an application."

"And you did?"

"Right away. And he hired me on the spot."

And loaned you five thousand dollars? Josie wondered. "So you hadn't met him before?" was all she asked.

"Not officially, but he had visited one of my classes at school and I remembered him from that visit. I was the only woman in some of my classes and most of the guest lecturers either leered at me or made sexist jokes. Noel didn't do either."

All the women nodded with understanding.

"You were lucky that he needed a carpenter just when you were looking for a job," Evelyn commented, taking a loud slurp of air as she reached the bottom of her soda bottle.

"Very," Betty agreed enthusiastically.

"What about you?" Josie asked Evelyn. "How did you come to work for Island Contracting?"

"I was extraordinarily lucky," Evelyn began slowly. "I was looking for work."

"But I would think an electrician would have a pretty easy time of job hunting."

Josie was thrilled when Betty made that statement. She had been thinking the same thing. And so was Sam Richardson. It looked like she was going to be able to report back to him with some answers to his questions.

"Yeah, you would, wouldn't you? But not a female electrician with a prison record."

Josie, stunned, inhaled Diet Coke and began choking. Chris slammed Josie's back so hard that she fell on the floor. Melissa hopped up and put her arm around Evelyn's shoulder. Betty gasped and crossed her arms nervously around herself. Evelyn's eyes were filled with tears.

"I didn't . . . We didn't . . ." Josie gasped. "I didn't know anything about that."

"No one did. No one but Noel," Evelyn said. "Although I've been waiting for you to come to me about it now that you own the company and have access to the personnel records."

Josie thought about those records—the ones that were missing from the file cabinets and the ones that she hadn't had access to in Island Contracting's computer.

"I . . ." Josie had no idea how to continue.

"I'd like to tell you all about it," Evelyn announced slowly. "Now that I've told you that I have a prison record, I'd like you all to know all about it. Maybe . . . maybe you'll understand."

"Of course we will," Melissa declared stoutly.

"I . . . Oh God . . ." Evelyn sank her head into her hands and didn't continue.

"It's okay. We all have secrets," Betty insisted.

"It's not much of a secret now, is it? I was in prison," Evelyn stated the fact flatly. "For four years."

"Why?" Melissa asked plaintively. "For heaven's sake why?"

"Drug possession. Possession of illicit drugs with intent to sell. Being a drug dealer. However you want to say it, it still amounted to the same thing. Four years out of my life and my kids"—she paused and took a deep breath—"... and my kids living forever with the fact that their mother broke the law. That I did something that no good mother does—destroyed the lives of young people around me. And, I was afraid at one time, almost destroyed the lives of the people that I care about the most."

"Your children," Betty guessed.

"Yes. My children."

"And Noel knew about this?" Josie guessed.

"Yes. Well, I should say we moved here to escape my past, but of course, in a business where everyone has to be bonded, that was a ridiculous idea. There was no way that we could do that. I was, in fact, planning on getting a job in a store or something similar when I saw an ad that Noel had placed in a trade journal. He was looking for a licensed electrician. Well, to be honest, I never thought he would hire me. I had been turned down by over half a dozen companies at that point."

"Why didn't you consider working on your own?" Chris asked.

"I guess I had lost all my confidence," Evelyn admitted. "I went to prison because I was dealing drugs—at rock concerts mainly—but I was an addict then, and in prison I had begun to get my life together. I left prison an optimist, but three months later I had stopped expecting good things to happen to me.

"And then I walked into Island Contracting's office and met Noel. And my life changed."

"You told him about your past?" Josie asked.

"Of course—just like I had told a lot of other people, but instead of a negative response, Noel asked me questions."

"What sort of questions?"

"Things about my life. How I got into drugs. What life had been like in prison. Whether I was still using. How my husband and kids were coping with my mistakes. And he seemed sincerely interested—not just curious because I was some sort of freak.

"And then he offered me a job—and promised to keep my past a secret as long as I wanted."

Chris nodded. "Noel was very good at keeping secrets," she muttered.

"You know, I had thought about telling you all. I hated keeping secrets about my past. And you've all been so nice to me."

"Did Noel think we should know?" Josie asked.

"He told me that I should tell you if I felt comfortable about doing so. And I guess I just couldn't face the idea of you all rejecting me."

"Rejecting you?" Betty repeated the words. "You're kidding. We depend on you."

"That's another thing, of course. I'm older. I'm supposed to be a little wiser."

"Maybe making the mistakes is what made you wise," Josie suggested.

"That's the type of thing Noel used to say," Evelyn said with a smile.

"We all miss him," Josie said, flattered by the comparison.

"Well, I was very lucky that he hired me," Evelyn said, glancing at Josie.

"Island Contracting is very lucky that Noel hired you," Josie stated flatly. "I certainly don't know what we would do without you."

"Then you knew about her past?" Melissa asked. "From the personnel files and . . . and all?"

"No, I didn't," Josie answered, not bothering to explain why she was living in such an ignorant state. "But of course it doesn't change anything. Noel believed in you. I believe in you."

Evelyn sighed deeply. "You don't know how relieved I am to hear you say that. I've been trying to screw up the courage to come and talk with you about this ever since we found out that Noel left Island Contracting to you. I have to admit that I even panicked and tried to find the personnel files in the office. But they weren't there. I even tried looking in the computer, but I don't know anything about that."

"You were right, though. They were transferred to the computer," Josie said. "It took some help for me to find them myself."

"You know," Chris started, getting up and putting her arm around Evelyn's shoulders, "I have some problems—well, since we're telling the truth. My mother is an alcoholic and I'm planning on moving out. Maybe you could give me some perspective on all this."

"Of course. I need to get the wires run up to the ceiling fixtures in the bath down here. If you could help out with the cabinetwork, we could talk."

"I can run upstairs and help Josie in the master bedroom," Melissa suggested, getting up.

"Great idea," Josie said.

"Besides, more than two people in the bathroom is something of a squeeze," Betty agreed. "I'm going to be down in a bit. I just want to check out those flashings around the vents on the roof before we go on."

The women went off in their individual directions. It had not escaped Josie's notice that Melissa had arranged to be alone with her and she was curious about what, if anything, was going to be said. Listening to Melissa's story, she had found it difficult to accept that Noel just happened upon her in California—at a time in her life when she was looking for employment on the East Coast. But that meant that there was another connection—one that Melissa was going to confess to? she wondered as the two women walked into the master bedroom. She didn't know how to broach the subject.

And either Melissa had the same problem or she had no intention of broaching the subject. "That was some story that Evelyn told, wasn't it?" she began, walking over and examining the woodwork around the window.

"I guess we all come to Island Contracting through different paths," Josie answered noncommittally.

"Yeah. What do you think is going on with Betty?"

"Betty? You mean the fact that she's actually eating normal food—or that she claims to be giving up men for life? And I doubt that last bit, don't you?"

"I suppose. But she is acting a little strange."

"In what way?"

"Just watch her and you'll see what I mean. Especially watch her when she's outside," Melissa suggested.

"Outside? Like on the roof?"

"Exactly!"

"I—"

They were interrupted. Then the two women looked at each other, looked up, and ran for the door. They had to find out what had caused that terrible noise on the roof.

EIGHTEEN

"I WAS SURE we were going to go outside and find Betty lying on the ground. I mean it. I could literally see her lying there with her bones all broken and a trickle of blood running from her mouth."

"Perhaps you've been watching too many police shows," Sam Richardson suggested gently, leaning forward in Noel's desk chair.

"Perhaps too many strange things are happening in my life these days," Josie replied somewhat sarcastically. Terrible things had been happening recently. And what was this man doing making himself at home in Island Contracting's office?

He changed his attitude immediately. "I'm sorry. You're right. It's just that you painted such an image."

"I was thrilled when I discovered that Betty was still on the roof and it was only a wheelbarrow lying on the patio. But the image of what was possible . . ." She gulped.

"You need dinner." Sam slammed shut the desk drawer in front of him.

Josie wondered if he was beginning to realize that she

could always eat—although probably, she decided, he had realized that after a quick glance at her thighs and stomach. "I am a little hungry," she understated. "But don't you have something to show me here?" She looked down at the pile of freshly printed papers lying on the desk.

"I have a lot to show you. But we don't have to do it here. Why don't we head over to Basil's place? I have some questions to ask him."

"Basil? What does that man have to do with anything?"

"He seems to be very well connected on the island."

"Is this some sort of social event that we're talking about or a murder?"

"I didn't explain that very well. What I mean is that Basil Tilby mixes with many different groups: the summer people as well as the year-rounders—even the fishermen seem to appreciate him. At least, that's the way it appears to me."

"That's true." Josie hated to admit it.

"So shall we go get dinner there? My treat."

"We'll go dutch," Josie insisted coldly.

"Whatever you want. But, I was wondering. . . ."

"What? I'm sorry," she said immediately, seeing the startled look on his face. "I didn't mean to sound so cranky. It has been a long day."

"I was just wondering if I could have one of these kittens. They're good company and—"

"Which one?" Josie asked eagerly.

"The little gray tiger . . ."

"She's a female. And why don't you take two? It's easier in the long run because they'll keep each other company while you're working."

"Good idea. But they should both be female."

"What about the cute little black one with the white feet? Then they'll both shed the same color fur." She shut up, hoping she hadn't squashed this deal. But apparently Sam Richardson wasn't a man to be deterred from what he wanted by a few stray hairs.

"Excellent idea. Why don't you leave the truck here? I'll drive to Basil's and then, after we're done, I'll drive back here, drop you off, and pick up the little guys?"

"Fine." Although she would have preferred it if he had

taken the kittens immediately. Sometimes people reconsidered when out of the immediate presence of the little furry creatures, and the opportunity to find a good home for two at once was a rare thing.

She put out fresh food and water for the kittens while Sam gathered his papers and then they left together. Josie was tired, physically and emotionally, and was glad when the conversation on the way to the restaurant consisted of ideas for names for the kittens. Josie explained her prejudice against animals having human names and Sam Richardson reminisced about a much-loved mutt of his youth that he had named Gulliver—although he had no idea why. The short ride passed pleasantly. The kittens remained anonymous.

Two of the island's three police cars were standing before the door to the restaurant.

"Maybe we should go someplace else," was Josie's nervous suggestion.

"It might look a little strange to Chief McCorkle if we just drive off now," Sam answered, nodding at the stern-looking officer, who, arms crossed, was leaning against the door, staring out at the road.

"Damn. Well, maybe they're just here to eat dinner," Josie said, opening the door and getting out of the small car.

"Or perhaps this is the meeting place of the local Policemen's Benevolent Association," Sam suggested as Chief McCorkle walked out the door, followed by his son.

Josie clenched her teeth, straightened her shoulders, and prepared to pass by the two men.

"Good evening, Officers," Sam Richardson said pleasantly.

She said nothing.

"Mr. Richardson, nice to see you this evening," the police chief responded, his voice less pleasant than his words. "Miss Pigeon."

"Hello," Josie muttered, looking down at the ground.

"Good evening, Josie. You are looking lovely tonight. As usual."

Josie ignored the words of Rick McCorkle and, without looking up, stomped into the restaurant. Sam followed closely behind.

Basil Tilby took a breath between saying good-bye to the police and hello to Sam and Josie. "I have the table you requested," he said to Sam, showing his guests to a booth in the farthest corner of the room. "And I want to talk to you—just as soon as I make sure the police cars are gone. Needless to say, their presence does not encourage drop-ins."

"Maybe, when you come back, you could bring us a bottle of the Vernaccia we were talking about," Sam suggested.

"Ah yes. I have one chilling this very minute."

"When did you and Basil talk about wine?" Josie asked.

"He came to my store to examine my stock. He won't want to buy retail, of course, but we're thinking of starting a little co-op arrangement with a few of the more select importers."

Josie nodded. She had no idea what he was talking about. But Sam changed the subject before she could ask any questions.

"That's it!" he said. "I'll name the kittens after varietal grapes. Maybe Pinot Grigio and Pinot Noir—gray and black. What do you think?"

Pretentious is what she thought. "Very clever," is what she said.

Basil's reappearance made it unnecessary for her to continue to lie. "What do you think about the big island mystery?" he asked, handing a bottle of wine to Sam.

"What mystery?"

"The man who's disappeared," Basil said, taking the bottle back from Sam and pulling a wine opener from his gold vest pocket. "You must know about it. They said he lived in the neighborhood where Island Contracting is working."

"What?" Josie could hardly speak.

"Is this man who has disappeared the reason that the police were here?" Sam asked more succinctly.

"Yes. Although I cannot possibly guess what those boorish men imagine I have to do with it." Basil was pouring out three glasses of wine as he spoke. Josie, not bothering to wait for what she thought was the unspeakably silly tradition of sniffing and tasting, picked up her glass, drained it, and held it out for more.

"That's not Bud Lite, my dear," Basil said.

"I know. And I'm not your dear. I'm not, in fact, anyone's dear."

"About this man who is missing," Sam said, and Josie felt someone kick her underneath the table—she assumed it was Sam. "We're interested in hearing about him, aren't we, Josie?"

"Yes. And in knowing why Rick and his father think you have something to do with his disappearance," Josie insisted, putting down the second glass of wine with less than a half inch of liquid left in the bottom.

"I can recommend the bouillabaisse," Basil said.

"Two bowls and some bread . . ."

"And the story of the missing man," Josie reminded them.

"And a Diet Coke," Basil said to the waitress who had appeared behind them. "And I can't tell you why the police thought I knew anything at all about this man. Apparently he was supposed to meet someone—I think they said a woman, but whether or not she was his wife, I certainly don't know. Well, he was supposed to meet her here for breakfast. But, of course, there hasn't been any breakfast served here since I took over the place and apparently he didn't know that when he set up the meeting. Or, I suppose, it could have been she who set up the meeting. If you know what I mean . . ."

"Could you possibly start at the beginning?" Sam suggested.

"Tell us the whole thing just the way that ass—Chief McCorkle told you," Josie insisted.

Basil did what Josie would have referred to as simpering. "Well, I have to admit that I share your opinion of that hideous man and his dreadful son, so I was less than thrilled when they appeared here about an hour ago."

"And they asked for you. . . ." Sam prompted.

"Daddy McCorkle asked for whoever was in charge. As though he didn't know that I bought this place a few months ago."

"Would he know that?" Sam asked.

Josie and Basil answered yes simultaneously, apparently

agreeing on something other than their opinion of the island's police department.

"It's a small island. The police department cannot possibly keep track of all the private citizens—as well as everyone who rents a house for a week or for the entire season—but they do know pretty much who owns what business. Especially businesses that have liquor licenses," Basil explained.

"So Chief McCorkle asked to speak with you—indirectly," Sam said.

"Yes."

"And?" Josie prompted impatiently.

"And so I offered to buy him—and his son—a beer. They," Basil said, "accepted. Of course. And then they explained that they were looking for information about this man. I think his name was—or is—Michael Rodney. I, naturally, said that I had never heard of the man. And McCorkle minor explained that this Michael Rodney was supposed to meet some woman here two days ago for breakfast—are you all right?"

"Yes." Josie had to work to get the word out of her mouth. "Go on."

"There isn't all that much else." Basil shrugged his thin shoulders. "She showed up and discovered that he wasn't here—of course, no one was since the restaurant is no longer open for breakfast. Although we will be serving a weekend brunch buffet on Saturday and Sunday during the season."

"When did you stop serving breakfast?" Sam asked urgently.

Basil looked at him curiously, but answered the question. "Less than a month ago, I guess. I bought the place a little over a month ago, but it took about a week to fire the old staff and bring my people in here to start setting up for the season."

"Go on," Josie urged.

"So this woman waited for this man until one of my workers showed up and explained what had happened to the restaurant. And then she left. Apparently she looked for the man, and when she couldn't find him, she called the police department."

"And they started looking for him here?"

"They checked out his house on the island, called his home in New York City—"

"How did they find out where he lived in New York?" Sam interrupted.

"Simple. They called his security service."

"And who was home in New York? You said that it might be his wife who was supposed to meet him here." Josie was confused.

"His niece was staying at the apartment—she's on a spring break from college. She was on her way to Florida when the boy she was traveling with came down with chicken pox. They had moved into her uncle's apartment, but she hadn't contacted him personally. The police got the impression that she was happy to be living in luxury with her boyfriend. She thought that her aunt and uncle were in Arizona, but she didn't know how to contact them. She said there was a son who lived in the city, but he was out of the country on a business trip."

"So the police still don't know who the woman is," Sam said slowly. "Does that mean she called them anonymously?"

"Apparently so. I didn't push them about it. I mean, I have to get along with the police in town. I don't want them wandering through and deciding to card my middle-aged patrons—although it is possible that those of them who are supporting their local plastic surgeon would be thrilled. And then there are the people that I employ who might not have all their immigration papers in order."

"You hire illegal aliens?"

"Yes. I tried using college kids, but they tend to think that they are too good to fill dishwashers for minimum wage. The people I hire don't have parents to make sure they won't starve—they're just happy to have a paycheck. In fact, that's why I don't know much about the woman who was meeting this man. The person she talked with vanished when the police showed up asking questions."

"Can you track him down?"

"I doubt it. These people all cover up for each other."

"Could you try? It's very important that we find out more about the missing man," Sam said.

"Yes. If we could just find out what he looks like . . ." Josie began.

"The police have a picture."

"You're kidding. What does he look like?" Josie practically fell out of her chair.

"Like a lot of other middle-aged upper-middle-class white men. Short dark hair. A little overweight. It was hard to tell. I think the photographer was more interested in the fish."

"What fish?"

"He won the Memorial Day fishing championship last year. The photo came off the wall of the Fish Wish Bait Shop."

NINETEEN

"THIS FOOD IS not designed to be take-away," Josie said, watching the bouillabaisse slop around in the plastic container that Basil had found to transport it. "I keep thinking it's going to spill."

"Try dipping the bread in the sauce," Sam suggested. "And then maybe you can put a small piece in my mouth? I didn't know how hungry I was until the smell of the food hit me."

"I'm afraid to drip on your upholstery."

"It won't be the first time. And I'd rather spend a Saturday morning cleaning out the car than starve to death."

"So open your mouth," Josie suggested, and stuffed some dripping bread into it when he did so.

"I'm still not sure why we're going to the store. Do you think it will be open this late?"

"You never know. People on the island don't necessarily keep nine-to-five working hours. But even if it's closed, there are lots of photos on the walls there—and there's a yearly group photo of everyone in the contest as well as individual photos of the winners and their fish. We might be able to see through the windows."

"Could you see well enough to recognize Michael Rodney—if the man you saw is Michael Rodney?"

Josie sighed. "I don't know. It's darker than I thought it would be!"

"There's a flashlight down by your foot," Sam said. "Maybe that will help."

"I hope so. It would ease my mind considerably if I thought that I knew who the dead man is."

"Does the name Michael Rodney mean anything to you?"

"No. But I don't socialize with people on that end of the island generally. I probably wouldn't know the name unless I had worked on his house."

"But he could be the dead man—the description fits?"

"That description fits almost half the men I know. Oh, turn right here. We can park on the side street."

Josie was out of the car, flashlight in hand, almost before Sam had switched off the engine. The Fish Wish was the only bait store on the island, a little cedar-shake cottage on pilings to keep it above water level during winter storms. "The photos are on the side wall," she explained. "We can see them through those windows."

"Maybe if you stand on my shoulders, you'll be able to see in," Sam suggested.

"Maybe if I stand on your shoulders, you'll develop a permanent back problem."

"I may be a lot older than you are, but I'm in fairly good shape for my age." No one could mistake the offense in his voice.

"I didn't mean that." Josie was appalled. "I . . . I meant that I'm not a nubile young thing anymore." She hadn't ever been nubile, but there was no way he was going to find that out. "Why don't we move the dinghy that's leaning against the back wall under the window and I'll climb up on the end and see what I can see."

"Fine."

They worked quickly and Josie was spying through the window in just a few minutes.

"Can you see?" Sam asked.

"I'll be able to see better if you would hold the flashlight steady." Josie leaned against the glass. "The photograph should be on the far right. They're in order of year. I can see where the missing photo went, so the next one—damn!" Josie felt the windowsill give way and the tinkle of breaking glass announced her entrance into the Fish Wish.

"Oh shit! Are you okay? Should I call an ambulance? Can I—"

"I don't believe it. The entire frame came off. Most of the broken glass is underneath me. I think I'm okay," came her reply. "Hand me the flashlight, will you? Don't cut your arm—there must be nails sticking out somewhere."

Sam gingerly passed the flashlight through the gaping hole in the wall. "How badly are you hurt? Shall I call an ambulance?" he repeated.

"I'm fine. I really am. Look." She turned the flashlight on herself so Sam could see her.

"Breaking and entering," he muttered, looking over his shoulder.

"Damn." Another series of breaking sounds could be heard through the hole in the wall.

"What happened now?"

"I seem to have smashed some sort of fish tank—or old bait tank," she added as an extraordinarily pungent smell filled the air.

"Did you cut yourself?"

"No."

"Why don't you go open the door and I'll come in and help you out," he suggested.

Josie didn't answer, but not comfortable in such an exposed position, Sam hurried around the side of the building. He was relieved that Josie was standing in the doorway.

"Let's get out of here," she urged.

"What?"

"Look, the place stinks. I did a lot of damage. And I sure don't want to be discovered here if the McCorkle clan drives by." She edged out on the porch, closing the door behind her.

"Don't you think we should just find the owner and confess to what happened and offer to pay for the damage?"

"We can't do that."

"Why not?"

"Get into the car. I'll explain when we get away from here," Josie insisted, shaking glass out of her hair as she ran back to the MGB.

"What?"

"Hurry," Josie insisted. "I've got the photograph. Let's go back to the restaurant. If we're lucky, we can pretend that we've been there all evening."

"What about the damage? What about the owner?"

"Just get going!" she insisted angrily.

"Josie!" Sam stopped the car he had just started and put his hand on her shoulder. "I think we should own up to our responsibilities. I don't feel right about running away from here."

"Would you feel better about it if I told you that Chief McCorkle's brother owns the bait shop?"

"Oh, fine." Sam started the car so quickly that the wheels spun on the pavement. "Small world," he commented.

"Small island," she answered. "Don't speed! We don't want to attract attention."

"Look, why don't we go to my house and regroup? If we pretend to have been at the restaurant all evening, someone is bound to tell that we weren't. We can just say that we left the restaurant early and went to my house."

"What excuse can we give for being alone at your house?"

"A man and a woman . . . Do I have to draw you a picture?"

Josie giggled a little hysterically. "It might be interesting," she admitted.

"My artwork is limited to stick figures." He seemed to have caught her mood.

Josie saw a flashing light out of the corner of her eye. "Is that the police?"

"No. It looks like the first-aid van."

"Good. If there's a problem, the police will go there, too. What direction are they traveling?"

"South."

"Thank heavens you live on the north end of the island. Let's get going!"

It was, as Josie had said, a small island, and it only took them a few minutes to get to Sam's house. She followed him through the back door and into his kitchen. "Don't you want to turn on some lights?"

"No. Follow me."

She did and he led the way to his bedroom. "Have a seat. I'll just light some candles."

Josie plopped down on the edge of the bed (crisply made with a batik cover pulled up and tucked in) and waited while he lit three votive candles lined up on a mantelpiece across the room. (What sort of man had candles ready and waiting in his bedroom? A sexually active man, Josie answered her own question.) She tried to look around without appearing too interested.

"It will look more like we've been . . . well, doing what we want everyone to think we're doing, if the house is dark," Sam said.

"Bring one of the candles here," Josie requested. She was trying not to think about how he looked in the candlelight—or how it might be improving her own bodily contours. "I want to see this photo." She squinted at the black-and-white photo. "Why the hell didn't they ask everyone to take off their hats? It's almost impossible to tell anything about any of—oh, wow." She took a deep breath. "It's him!"

"You're sure?" Sam leaned over the photo. "It's difficult to see in this photo and he probably wasn't looking his best."

"He's right here. Standing on the end of the row next to the fish . . . What are you doing?"

"The candle got too close to your hair. I was just making sure you weren't on fire."

Josie sniffed the odor of scorched hair. "I still smell a little like bait, don't I?"

"Uh, yes. Actually, I was just going to suggest a bubble bath."

"You have bubble bath?" She didn't even have shampoo!

"There's a bottle somewhere around here."

"It can wait until I get home." Apparently he hadn't been

admiring her appearance in the dark, but had been only aware of how she stank.

"I wasn't saying that it couldn't, it's just that it might provide us with a convincing alibi if you came to the door in a towel when the police are here."

"Why do you think the police are going to come here?"

"Because one of those hideous patrol cars just pulled up out front," he answered as flashing strobe lights shone in through the windows. "It's the dark blue bottle in the medicine cabinet!"

Josie ran for the bathroom.

She was aware of frantic activity in the bedroom behind her, but it wasn't until she walked out of the bathroom about ten minutes later that she realized Sam had mussed up the bed before answering his door.

"Sam!" She tried to trill the name the way the heroines of romance novels did, but to her ears, she just sounded shaky. "Where are you?" She paused, unable to force herself to call him honey or another endearment.

"In the living room, Josie."

Fine. Unfortunately, she had never come into Sam's house through the front door, and she had no idea where the living room was located.

"Right in here," she heard Sam add, but Josie had no intention of leaving the bedroom until she had found the photograph again. She tucked the largest towel she had been able to find in Sam's well-stocked linen closet more tightly around her and peered down under the bed.

"Did you lose something, Miss Pigeon?"

She leaped to her feet, praying that the towel had been big enough to do its job.

"Yes. An earring," Josie lied to Chief McCorkle.

"Why don't you join us in the living room, Miss Pigeon? Unless you would like to get dressed first?"

"There's a robe hanging behind the door in the bathroom," Josie said, dashing back to the room. She was hoping to be quick enough to follow the chief of police back to the living room. But it turned out that he was waiting to escort her back to Sam. Josie had no choice but to go along with him. She glanced at the rumpled bed, but there was no sign of the photograph.

There was no sign of the photograph in the living room either. But that wasn't Josie's first thought. What attracted her attention was the huge nude lying on the wall above a bilious green couch.

"Miss Pigeon seems surprised by your interior decoration, Mr. Richardson. Certainly someone with such an intimate relationship with you would have been in your living room before, wouldn't they?" Chief McCorkle leered.

"I was so anxious to get to the bedroom that I'm afraid I wasn't paying very much attention to what the rest of the house looked like," Josie said. She knew that she was about as sultry as your average mollusk, but she gave it her best shot. "Sam and I had other things on our minds."

"You two weren't acting like lovebirds at the restaurant a short while ago," Chief McCorkle insisted. "And two different neighbors of the Fish Wish said that they saw a small sports car parked outside around the time that someone removed the window from its frame and broke in."

"Are you suggesting that I own the only small sports coupe on the island? I find that highly unlikely," Sam Richardson insisted.

"And we had bouillabaisse for dinner. A well-known aphrodisiac," Josie said, pushing her damp hair out of her face.

"Oysters are an aphrodisiac. Bouillabaisse just gives me diarrhea."

Josie tried to smile. She felt that the woman in the painting over the couch was leering down at her thighs. The model had obviously never worried about the shape of her thighs—or any other part of her body.

"Perhaps you would tell us exactly what you think we were looking for at this place. What did you call it?" Sam feigned ignorance.

"The Fish Wish," Chief McCorkle said. "It is the island's bait shop."

"We were not interested in going fishing when we left Basil's place. I can assure you of that," Sam said stoutly.

"I have no idea why you and Miss Pigeon would break into the Fish Wish. But I am going to find out, I can assure you of that, Mr. Richardson. And when I find out, I will be back to see you and Miss Pigeon."

"I was not planning on spending the night," Josie spoke up.

"Well, that won't surprise some people, will it, Miss Pigeon?"

Josie, furious, glanced back over her shoulder. It seemed to her that the woman on the wall had just joined her in sisterly solidarity.

TWENTY

"YOU PACK UP the kittens and I'll see if I can find Mike Rodney in the phone book."

"It's under the bag of kitten food—over there." Josie pointed out the location of the phone book. She was so embarrassed after the police chief left them alone that she had dressed and traveled back to the office without speaking. Now she was glad that there was something for her to do. She collected cat food and a bag of kitty litter and stuffed them together in a large paper bag. Then she started her search for something appropriate for kitten transport. She was poking small holes in a box that had held computer paper when Sam Richardson spoke.

"Well, I'll be damned."

"What?"

"Guess who is the Firbanks' next-door neighbor?"

"Wh—not Mike Rodney!"

"Exactly."

"Wow," Josie said, dropping the box on the floor, where it was instantly filled with curious kittens. "So he lived in that large house, did he?"

"Looks like it. I gather you haven't met any of the people next door during your project?"

Josie laughed. "We're workers, not neighbors. People

don't wander over with plates of cookies or suggestions that we all get together for drinks in the evening. And in fact, that house is closed up for the winter. I don't think anyone's been around at all."

"Aren't most of the houses up in the dunes closed for the entire winter?"

"Most of them. A couple are open all year long. People retire and think that they would like to spend winters on the island that they love in the summer. But then they're shocked by the cold and how little there is to do—so that experiment usually lasts only one year." She wondered if this was going to apply to Sam Richardson before continuing. "And sometimes people open their houses for Christmas or New Year's Eve. And as it gets warmer, families come down and check to make sure the winter storms didn't do any damage—and spend a day at the beach. Every weekend there are more and more off-islanders around—it just depends on the weather."

"And have you noticed any activity next door?"

"None. Although that house has storm shutters that roll down over all the windows. Someone could probably be inside and no one would know about it."

"But you would see cars."

"Probably." She thought about her answer. "To be honest, I'm not sure that we would. There are delivery trucks coming and going all the time. And we're busy. It would be easy to miss someone next door—and if anybody wanted to sneak in, it would be easy as pie. They could park down the street and just walk in. The doorway is turned away from the Firbank house. No one could see who is coming and going."

"Do you have any idea if there is a Mrs. Rodney?"

"None."

"Then—"

"But it is a family house," she mused. "There is a shed—a very fancy one that matches the house, but still a shed—out in the backyard. It's filled with sports equipment—banana boards, bicycles, and fishing stuff. So there must be a family there during the summer. And that would imply a Mrs. Rodney, wouldn't it?"

"Or an ex–Mrs. Rodney."

"Or two—or three," Josie added with a grin that changed into a yawn. "I'm sorry. I'm so exhausted that I'm getting punchy."

"Why don't you head on home? There are still things in the personnel records that we should go over, and I suppose we'd better start checking out what, if any, connection there is between your crew and Mike Rodney."

Josie yawned again.

"And we'll worry about it all tomorrow."

"Good." Josie stood and picked up the box.

"What's this?"

"Your kittens. Cat food. Cat litter. Now, if they panic in a new environment, just put some butter on their paws—that will help calm them down. And make sure the room that they're in is kitten-proof."

" 'Kitten-proof'?"

"Yes. No long exposed wires that they could get tangled in. No holes in walls that they might fall down and become trapped. And they need water all the time. Feed them at least twice a day—although I just leave food out all the time. They've had their first shots, but they should go back to the vet at the end of the month."

"I don't need to set up college funds for them, do I?"

"Having pets is a responsibility," Josie lectured, and handed him the box. "But they sure are cute, aren't they?"

"They'd better be. How else would they have found a sucker like me?"

But he was scratching the little tiger on the head and she felt confident that these animals would have a good home. "I really have to go," she announced. "It's been a big day."

"You mean you don't always run around in a bath towel in front of the town's chief of police?"

Josie knew he was kidding, but she couldn't quite bring herself to kid back. "I'll check in at your store sometime during the day and let you know if I find out anything more."

"I'll be there," he promised. If he was surprised by the abrupt change of tone in their conversation, he didn't show it, but just followed her to the door. "Maybe we can actually get some dinner tomorrow night."

"Yeah, maybe." She was ready to fall asleep on her feet,

but she wanted to think before she made any commitments. "I'll see you at the store," she repeated, locking the door behind them.

"Great. Good night. And thanks for Pinot Grigio and Pinot Noir."

Josie heard the scratching of the kittens left behind in the office. "Anytime," she said sincerely, and got in the truck.

She was halfway home before she remembered the photograph that they had stolen from the wall of the Fish Wish and wondered what had become of it. The first thing she did after arriving home was call Sam, but no one was home and she had to leave a message on his answering machine. "Call me in the morning, please," she said. It wasn't romantic, but neither was it incriminating.

The second thing she did was eat an entire jar of chunky peanut butter. Then she went to bed.

Maybe it was the peanut butter, maybe it was lingering embarrassment over her appearance that evening, maybe she was just overly tired. But she couldn't sleep. She rolled over, flipped her pillow, threw it on the floor, picked it up, and generally twitched and wiggled until Urchin stalked from the room, screeching her distress to the world at large.

Josie finally fell asleep only to have dreams in which Sam Richardson and various nubile young (and thin) things cavorted in oil-scented baths and candlelit bedrooms while two tiny kittens were left in their cardboard box to starve.

She woke up with a headache.

Which wasn't helped by the loud knocking on her door. She grabbed the ragged synthetic Japanese kimono that hung on her closet door and ran to see who was there.

Risa's bright smile was only slightly less welcome than the steaming cinnamon buns she held in her hands. "You have been working too hard and not taking care of yourself. I made these for you and those other young women that you work with. They are full of calories, but sometimes what you Americans call comfort food is more important than a few extra pounds." She handed Josie the basket of food and took her face in her hand. "Let me come in and fix your coffee while you shower."

Josie was too tired and grateful to argue. "There are beans in the refrigerator," she said, and headed in the direction of the bathroom. Last Christmas, Risa had given her a coffee grinder and a miraculous drip pot, and Josie, who couldn't cook, had come to think of good coffee as one of the great luxuries of her life—when she had time to make it.

"They should be kept at room temperature," she heard Risa muttering as she leaned over and turned on the water. For once, all the plumbing worked and she was feeling much better as well as much cleaner when she returned to the kitchen.

"I was going to start washing up these dishes, but apparently you have run out of dish detergent," Risa said, passing Josie a mug of coffee and a plate with a cinnamon roll in the middle of it.

"It's in the bathroom. I have dish detergent, I was just using it for shampoo," Josie admitted, and waited for the explosion.

"Your beautiful hair! How could you do that to your beautiful hair?"

"I—"

"I despair of you! Your beautiful hair!"

"I—"

Risa narrowed her dark eyes and peered at Josie. "But who is this man I hear about you being with? This man who has the sports car?" She grew calmer. "This very good-looking man who probably does not use Ivory liquid with which to wash his hair?"

Josie had spent enough time in Sam's bathroom last night to have told her landlady exactly which brand of expensive shampoo he used, but she didn't want to have to explain everything. She wasn't actually sure that she could explain anything these days.

"He's . . . a friend. Just a friend." So what could she say? That he was a coconspirator in covering up a crime? In breaking into and robbing the local bait shop? That the two of them were working hard to protect Island Contracting from ruin? That, in fact, she hardly knew him? And that she was depending on him to save her from financial and personal ruin?

"He is much older than you are. . . . And I think that is very good. Americans do not realize that it is natural for an older man to be involved with a young woman. You invite him over to dinner and I cook you a romantic meal."

"I am not interested in him romantically."

"You say that," Risa said, "but I have—what do you call it—proof that you lie."

"What proof?"

"Only a great love can make you forget your children—even if only for a minute." Risa searched in the deep pocket of her suede skirt and pulled out a postcard. "From Tyler," she added, passing it over to his mother. "He is just fine. And he is getting an A in math."

Josie read the few words on the card; they did little beyond confirming Risa's words. "I'm so glad to hear from him!" She took a large bite of a cinnamon roll, slightly weak with relief. Then suspicious. "When did this arrive? I didn't see any mail when I got in last night."

"I guess you were thinking of other things. You did not check your mail when you were here yesterday afternoon. I found this on the floor after you had left. It is not like you to forget to check the mail these days—not since little Tyler went off to school—that is how I know that you had very powerful thoughts about this good-looking older man."

Josie had lost her appetite. "When did you think that I was here yesterday afternoon? I mean, did you just find my mail unpicked up on the floor or—"

"No. I heard you." Risa paused and her eyes became even narrower. "Something is terribly wrong, no? It was not you that I heard. I thought . . ."

"What did you think, Risa?"

"I heard footsteps over my head—up here. And I thought that you had lost weight. Or perhaps just taken off those horrible heavy boots that you wear to work."

"They're work boots. I have to wear them," Josie said absently. "When did you hear these footsteps?"

"A little after five."

"You're sure?"

"Yes. Sure. I had just sat down to watch the evening news and have a glass of Chianti. The world is so horrible; I cannot see without something beautiful in my hand and mouth."

"You're sure you didn't just hear Urchin banging around

and knocking something over? You know how loud she can be for such a little thing."

"Positive. In fact, that's how I know that someone was there. I got up to fix myself some gnocchi with Gorgonzola sauce, and when I went outside to see if any thyme had come up in the garden, I found the poor thing walking around in the hallway. Someone had left your front door open. Of course, I thought it was you. You can be very absentminded, you know."

"Yes, I know. What time was this?"

"A little before six. I do not watch sports. Not even soccer. So I start dinner then."

"And was this person you heard still in my apartment?"

"No, of course not. I went up and put back poor little Urchin—who pulled a thread in my favorite shawl on the way—and when I looked around, you weren't there and the mail was on the floor where it had been tossed through the slot. Someone—I thought you—had walked right over it. That is why I assumed you were in love. But . . ." She looked around the messy apartment. "Has anything been taken? Would you know?"

"I would know," Josie insisted. "And nothing was taken."

"What are you going to do? You cannot depend on the police for help on the island."

Josie glanced at her watch and started putting sweet rolls in a large paper bag. "I'm going to go to work."

TWENTY-ONE

JOSIE PARKED HER truck in front of the Firbanks', but she went directly to Mike Rodney's home. It was early, almost an hour before she expected her crew to arrive, and she could walk around outside, fairly sure she wouldn't be noticed.

Up until now, she had paid very little attention to the house, only concerned that her crew not infringe on the rights of the property owners next door, but now she wandered about the yard, not sure what she might or might not find.

The Firbanks and the Rodneys shared a property line along a high point on some of the last natural sand dunes on the eastern seaboard. On one side of each house was Dune Drive. On the other, the dunes themselves dropped down to a wide white beach by the sea. The Rodney property, Josie decided, had probably once belonged to the Firbanks' home. It was a large rectangular lot on which a chic architect had erected a large rectangular white shoebox of a building. From the outside, its lines were clean, if not terribly interesting.

Dune grass grew right up to the foundation of the house and Josie circled the building, unable to see in because of the metal storm shutters that were rolled down over the large panes of glass that made up the walls that faced the ocean. The building was immaculate: freshly painted and well kept. As she had told Sam, she had looked in the small shed at the side of the property. This time she tried the door and was surprised when it opened easily.

The sporting-goods store that the Rodney family patronized must be thriving. Sleek surfboards lay across ceiling beams and a family of dirt bikes (red papa, blue mama with basket, and three black male teenagers) were hung on a complicated series of hooks sprouting from the walls. She had to walk around a trio of fluorescent children's bikes in the middle of the floor. An old Hot Wheels was lying across a pile of dismantled crab traps in one corner, and a tangle of abused fishing poles had been tossed in another. Badminton, croquet, and lawn darts were scattered about. A couple of folded-up lounges leaned against a wall and one was open underneath the shed's only window. Josie sighed. There was nothing here to provide a clue about Mike Rodney's life—or his death. Maybe, she decided, it was time to check out the house.

Like the shed, the house was unlocked. Josie opened the

door slowly, teeth gritted in anticipation of the howl of an alarm. Nothing happened. She closed the door behind her and reached out for the light switch.

Years spent building houses had convinced her of the perversity of architects when it came to electric wiring. But she had never before scraped her knuckles trying to turn on a light. When she finally managed to illuminate the entryway, she discovered that the switches had been set in slabs of mica. It was unusual and attractive. Josie, concerned about light shining through cracks in the shutters, set the dimmer low and started to look around.

It was a wonderful house. The theme set by the unusual switch plate was continued throughout. Large stones had been sliced and laid as flooring. An open stairway, leading to the second floor, was composed of natural slabs of pink granite connected by shiny metal posts. A fireplace was the most distinguishing feature of the room, built of boulders piled as though they had just tumbled down from a hole in the ceiling. Josie longed to see the room in bright daylight. She wandered through the house, admiring stone countertops in the European kitchen, doubting the comfort of bathtubs created from gray and white granite, and thrilled, in the bedrooms, by headboards of polished stone that soared up walls behind mounds of pillows.

Then she went back to the living room and sat down. One thing was bothering her. Were the Firbanks, those competitive urbanites, ever going to be satisfied with the house she was remodeling after they saw their next-door neighbor's digs?

No way, she answered her own question as she glanced at her watch. Time to get back to work. She didn't want to be discovered here. She was heading to the fireplace to get one last look at the mortar holding the rocks together when she heard a jingling at the front door. Someone was there! Cursing herself for turning on the light, she ducked behind one of the massive canvas-covered couches that stood in the middle of the room and held her breath.

"Damn!" The lights flickered off and a flashlight's beam was directed up the stairway. Josie heard the footsteps follow the light. When she thought she was alone on the first floor, she tiptoed across the room, cursing the rock floor, which did little to mute the thud of her work boots. It wasn't until she was outside that she realized she had been holding her breath.

Knowing that the efficient shutters would prevent the intruder from looking out, she ran the short path between the two houses and was sitting on the front porch of the Firbanks' when Chris came whistling up the walk.

"You're in a good mood," Josie commented, amazed that her pounding heart couldn't be heard by everyone within a mile radius.

"Sure am. Have a doughnut—fresh this morning. The bakery is open for the season."

"Good news, but is it just the doughnuts that are making you so happy?"

Chris beamed. "No. Mother agreed to let me drive her to a rehab center for alcoholics last night. I don't know if it will make a permanent difference in her life, but I can't tell you how relieved I am right now." She paused and looked down at the ground. "I only wish Noel were around to see this. I'd like to thank him. Mother and I would never have gotten to this point without him.

"So . . . do you want a cruller or a jelly?"

"I was hoping for a piece of crumb cake," Josie answered, examining the bags of pastry.

"Just doughnuts today. They still don't have their summer staff. But they promised cheese Danish tomorrow. And macaroons!"

"Don't tell me you brought doughnuts, too!" Josie exclaimed as Melissa and Evelyn appeared on the walkway, full bags in their hands.

"It was my turn!" Chris protested. "And I was going by the bakery and saw that it was open—"

"Smelled! You must have smelled that it was open!" Evelyn argued.

"We were driving over here and the scent just sucked us in," Melissa said. "We bought two dozen. How many did you buy?"

"Two dozen, too."

"Who brought the coffee?" Josie asked, beginning to relax after her experience next door.

"Betty is supposed to . . ." Chris began as Betty entered the front door.

"Betty is supposed to what?" she asked. Josie was surprised that her youngest worker wasn't looking her best.

"Bring the coffee," Evelyn said.

"Don't tell us that you forgot the coffee," Melissa said. "I didn't get much sleep last night and I really need the caffeine."

"Maybe you should tell your husband that you're tired after working all day," Evelyn kidded.

"I did, but he needed me to proofread one of his term papers," Melissa answered.

"So much for romance," Betty said, passing out cups of steaming brew.

"Is there romance after marriage?" Melissa asked.

The conversation took on a life of its own and Josie sat back and let the fried pastry soothe her ruffled nerves. She was upset enough to let the socializing go on longer than usual.

"Aren't we supposed to be remodeling this house?" Evelyn finally asked rather pointedly.

"Yes. I . . . I'm a little distracted this morning," Josie admitted.

"I'm done up on the roof," Betty announced, screwing the top on the thermos. "Who needs me where?"

"We all need you," Evelyn began.

"But I don't think we can fit anyone else in that bathroom," Melissa put in, still munching on a doughnut.

"Why don't you work with Chris and me in the bedroom until they're ready for the tile," Josie suggested as the women split up to begin their workday.

Chris chatted happily about the things she was going to do now that she didn't have responsibility for her mother's day-to-day care, and Betty and Josie got to work converting a small room into two large walk-in closets. For a couple of hours the house was filled with the noise of their work. During the midmorning break, Josie added Risa's cinnamon rolls to the leftover doughnuts, and well fueled, they worked hard until early afternoon.

"I'll go pick up lunch!" Betty offered enthusiastically as the women realized that it was almost one o'clock.

"No, you keep framing in those shelves and I'll get lunch," Josie insisted. "I have to run back to the office for a few minutes and I can do it on the way," she explained. "But I'd appreciate it if you would go downstairs and find out what Melissa and Eve want."

"Fine." Betty stretched and did as Josie asked.

Josie turned to Chris almost immediately. "Do you remember those questions you were asking me about Betty the other day?"

Chris paused in her work. She was laying the last corner of the parquet top on the window seat that was being created to match the floor and wrote down some measurements on a piece of scrap lumber before answering. "Not really. She's been acting rather strangely, but she's young."

"But what do you mean by strangely? Just that she was giving up men and tofu?"

"You have to admit that, for Betty, that's pretty strange."

"True, but . . ."

"But that's not all I meant," Chris admitted. "Listen, hold this for me and I'll try to explain. But only because you know how often Noel made excuses for me."

"You're saying that I should be as kind to Betty as Noel was to you? Does that mean that Betty has an alcoholic relative too?"

"God, not that I know of. Didn't her family move somewhere down south?"

"As far as I know, they did. I was just trying to understand what you meant."

"What I meant was that I haven't always given one hundred percent to the job because of things that were happening in my personal life. And I think that's what's happening with Betty."

"I hadn't noticed that she was distracted."

"No, neither had I, but she has been spending a lot of time up on the roof."

That had nothing to do with what Josie had been thinking about all morning long. "What are you talking about? What does the roof have to do with anything?"

"How long does it take to fix flashings around chimneys and the venting pipes on most roofs?"

"Are you saying that she's been doing something else on

the roof? Beside showing off that wonderful figure of hers?"

"I suppose that's one explanation," Chris said slowly. "I suppose she could just have been working on her suntan and that would explain her taking so long up there."

"What other explanation could there be?" Josie asked, thinking that she probably knew the answer better than Chris did.

"I think she's a spy for another contractor." Chris surprised her with the answer.

"You're kidding."

"She's been having secret meetings with this man."

"A man connected with another contracting company on the island?" Josie was astounded by the turn this conversation had taken.

"I don't know about being a contractor on the island. I mean, he wasn't someone that I recognized. It's just that he was pretty old for her to be romantically involved with him."

"Look, I think I know what's going on here," Josie interrupted. "And you don't have to worry about Betty being disloyal to Island Contracting. It's something different. Something personal, not professional."

Betty walked into the room, ending the conversation.

"It occurred to me that you might want to take a break and pick up lunch with me," Josie suggested.

"Sure. I . . ." Betty seemed to be speechless with surprise.

"I'll meet you out in the truck in a few minutes," Josie insisted, and didn't turn to Chris until they were alone again. "Do me a favor," she asked the other woman. "I want to ask Betty some questions and then I have to talk with Sam Richardson. Would you give him a call and tell him that I'll be at his store in less than half an hour?"

Chris looked puzzled. "I didn't know that you had any sort of relationship with Sam," she began, obviously unhappy with the thought.

"I don't even think that I like him very much," Josie said, not knowing if it was a true statement or not. After all, being attracted to someone was different from liking them. "But he's a lawyer and right now Island Contracting needs a lawyer, so just do what I ask. Okay?"

"Sure. And—"

"And don't mention it to anyone," Josie added, hurrying out the door, confident that Chris would do as she asked.

Betty was waiting in the truck and Josie leaped in and started the engine before speaking. They were about a mile down the road before she turned to the young carpenter and asked a question.

"Just who gave you a key to the Rodney house?"

"You saw me go in?" Betty asked.

Josie noticed that Betty kept her eyes on the road ahead. "Yes," she answered, not admitting that she had been inside the Rodneys' house at the time.

Betty was silent for a few minutes. "I could say that I found the key or that someone from the security company loaned it to me, but I guess I have to trust you with the truth, don't I?"

"I'd sure appreciate it if you did."

"I'm in love," Betty announced, as though, finally freed to talk about it, she couldn't resist sharing her joy.

"And the man you're in love with lives next door?"

"Yes. He's wonderful. The most wonderful man I've ever met."

"That's nice." Well, what could she say? Too bad he's feeding fish at the bottom of the Atlantic? "Where did you meet?" Josie added, when she realized that Betty wasn't going to say anything else on her own.

"On the beach."

"When?"

"A few months ago. But it's been so difficult. . . ."

"Why don't we go back to the office and you can tell me all about it?" Josie suggested.

"I'd like that. I could use your advice."

If Betty thought that Josie was a fount of wisdom, the only thing anyone could be sure of was that her own judgment was more than a little flawed. No wonder she had fallen in love with a married man, Josie thought. A married man with a family, she reminded herself. A rich married man. Josie wondered about that all the way to the office.

Betty, with her youthful enthusiasm for almost everything, just didn't strike her as a gold digger.

"What about lunch for the crew?" Betty asked, waiting for Josie to unlock the door.

"I'll call Chris and tell her something came up. She can pick up lunch, and you and I can go out later."

Betty sighed. "I hate to be the reason that we get behind on this project. I know how important it is to Island Contracting. I could stay late tonight," she offered.

"Great. I'll take you up on your offer," Josie agreed. She didn't know how to get back to the topic.

But Betty solved the problem by bringing it up herself. "We met on the beach," she repeated. "I was jogging. He was walking his dog. He has a beautiful black Lab." She smiled dreamily.

"And?"

"Well, I was jogging along and I had this bandanna hanging out of my pocket and the dog grabbed it and . . . and we met. He asked me if I jogged there often and I told him every day, and the next morning, at the same time, there he was again. Well, he asked me if I knew a restaurant around here that served breakfast. He said he was staying alone at his house. And I told him about that place over on the mainland—and he asked if I would eat with him."

"And you did," Josie said.

"I was hungry. And curious," Betty admitted. "I mean, I could tell right away that he was older than I am. And we come from very different worlds. . . . I guess that's one of the problems with having been brought up on the island."

"What do you mean?"

"Well, my parents worked hard and we kids always had the necessities, but nothing like the money that the summer people at this end of the island have. Know what I mean?"

Josie, who had been raised in the upper middle class and now found herself in the working class, knew the differences between the two worlds, and also knew how much easier having money made everything. She also understood the longing of the outsider to be part of something richer, even if money didn't preclude a certain impoverishment of spirit. She just nodded to Betty.

"And over the years I've watched the big houses go up

on the dunes and I've . . . well, I've wondered what it would be like to live in one of them." She looked at Josie a little defensively.

"That's natural," Josie assured her. "I've thought about it myself." Maybe she was better at this giving-advice stuff than she thought!

"So we started dating," Betty said. "Only on weekends when he was down here, of course."

"Where does he live during the week?"

"New York City. He's a stockbroker with a huge firm on Wall Street."

"How nice for him." And for his wife and family, she would have liked to add, getting mad at this unknown man for taking advantage of a trusting girl like Betty. Only Betty's next words made her reassess the situation.

"If only he weren't married." She sighed.

"You know?"

"Yes!" Betty opened her eyes wide. "He was very upfront with me from the first. He told me about his wife and his children."

"And just how many children does he have?"

"Actually, I don't know. I thought just a little boy, but then he referred to his daughter. I guess I was confused. I was so disappointed that he was married that when he was talking about his life at home, I had a hard time making myself listen to the details." A tear crept down a smooth pink cheek.

"Betty, where is this going to go?" Josie asked, putting a hand on her employee's arm.

"Nowhere. I know that it can't go anywhere. I tell myself that every Monday morning, but then Mikey comes down on Saturday and I start acting like a silly schoolgirl again."

Josie tried not to smile. Betty was so close to being a schoolgirl that acting any other way would be inappropriate, but of course, that didn't answer the question of how much she was damaging her life by her involvement with a married man. "I gather he doesn't say that he's going to get a divorce and marry you?"

"No. He's much too honest for that."

TWENTY-TWO

"I GATHER THAT in this case at least, you don't think honesty is all that it's cracked up to be."

"I think in this case—as in many others—this man is using honesty as a club. He's saying I love you and you love me, but I'm married, so I can't marry you—but let's have an affair and you can feel guilty about it, and when I get tired of you, I'll just go back to my wife and kids. And . . ." Josie raised her voice. "And then you'll have no one to blame for your misery but yourself, because, after all, he was honest with you."

"So . . ."

"Not that he was honest with his wife and children. Not that he had the self-discipline and respect for either woman to not have the affair . . . not this man. But he's honest—and we're all supposed to admire that!"

"Hey! Don't yell at me!" Sam Richardson insisted, flipping off the computer in Island Contracting's office, where he and Josie had been going through the personnel files again. "Just because I'm the only man in sight, doesn't necessarily make me guilty of anything like that."

Josie frowned. She wondered why he had qualified his statement with *necessarily*. Had he, in fact, done something similar to what Mike Rodney was doing to Betty? Had he been married? Had he moved to the island to get away from hordes of angry women? Was she going crazy? "I didn't mean to accuse you of anything," she said slowly. "It's just that I hate to see anyone take advantage of Betty."

"I'm not going to defend this Mike Rodney's behavior. I don't approve of it. But I have a hard time envisioning

Betty as a young innocent. She is the woman who runs around on the roof in a bikini."

"A woman can wear—"

"Whatever she wants and it is no justification for a man's bad behavior," Sam interrupted her. "I am not unfamiliar with what you're saying. I prosecuted a number of rape cases—and I didn't let the defense get away with the suggestion that a woman had 'asked for it' because of the way she looked. We're on the same side in this one, Josie."

Josie took a deep breath. "I know. I'm just so upset. I didn't know what to tell her. She knew that I disapproved, but that doesn't make a lot of difference when you're young and in love. You make stupid decisions." She was horrified to realize that she was about to start crying. She stood abruptly. "I . . . I have to go to the bathroom." She used the only excuse she could think of and hurried off.

She was washing her hands when she heard the phone ring over the sound of the running water. She smiled at Sam's professional "Hello, Island Contracting." She frowned when she heard him agree that they would "be right there." Be right where? she wondered, wiping her hands on a fluffy hand towel.

"Did I hear the phone?" she asked, returning to the main room.

"Yes. It was someone named Risa. She said to tell you that it was very important that you come home right away. Why don't I drive you?"

"What's happened?" Josie asked, following Sam out to his car. She had a mother's vision of her son lying on the ground bleeding. She should never have allowed him to play baseball at school. She should never have allowed him to go away to school. She should never have allowed him to leave the house. Plenty of children grew up without seeing the light of day. . . . This was crazy thinking. Why was this man driving so slowly?

"Is this Risa your roommate? She said that she had heated up the dinner that you cooked last night, and if we didn't hurry, everything would get cold."

Josie gasped. "Are you telling me that she called to tell us that it was dinnertime?"

"Yes. I thought you were acting a little strangely—even for a women who is always hungry. What did you think?"

Josie decided to ignore the comment about her appetite. "I thought there had been a real emergency. I thought Tyler had been hurt. Or that someone had broken into my apartment again."

"Tyler—that's your son's name? He's fine," Sam continued at Josie's nod. "And what is all this about someone breaking into your apartment?"

Josie leaned back against the MGB's new soft leather and felt her heartbeat begin to slow down. "I guess I should have told you before," she started as they drove up to her apartment house. "Someone broke into my apartment yesterday afternoon."

"Were you at home?"

"No, I was at work. Risa was there—she's my landlady and she lives downstairs." They had arrived at her home.

"Risa is the woman who called the office?" he asked, starting up the sidewalk to the house.

"Risa is the woman you can see there in the doorway," Josie said, following Sam.

Risa was indeed standing in the doorway, although Josie thought that draped across the doorway might be a more accurate description. For a woman who must have spent the entire day cooking (for Josie expected an Italian gourmet treat), she looked wonderful. In fact, she looked more like she had spent the day relaxing at a spa. Her skin and hair glowed and she wore layers of raw silk wrapped in a manner that accentuated the youthfulness of her figure. A figure that was more youthful than Josie's despite the more than thirty-year difference in their ages. Josie resolved to stop eating completely.

The resolution lasted until she walked in the front door.

"Something smells wonderful," Sam said. He might have known how to whistle "Dixie," but he wasn't doing it now.

"You're eating out here," Risa insisted, waving toward the tiny glassed-in sunroom at the front of her apartment. "Your apartment is being worked on, remember, *bellissima*?"

Josie's foot was already on the bottom step of the stairway leading up to her apartment. " 'Worked on'?" she began to argue—and then glanced at Risa's sunroom through the door she was holding open. "Oh, Risa! How beautiful!"

Risa, however, was busy introducing herself to Sam, assuring him that Josie kept the complete novels of his namesake by her bed—and explaining that she had only heated up the dinner that Josie herself had cooked. Josie, overhearing this, wondered exactly how Risa had managed to make peanut butter and jelly smell so heavenly.

She edged toward the small table, laid with heavy ivory linen, silver, bone china, and the wine goblets she had found behind the Firbanks' house. White wine was already poured into two glasses. Two salads made from greens barely large enough to be teenagers, shimmering with dressing and slivers of pale parchment-colored cheese. A covered casserole was exuding scents of garlic and shrimp. On a tiny side table a cut-glass bowl of pears and white cherries was soaking in a mixture of red wine, sugar, and citrus zest. Josie started to protest that she couldn't possibly have imagined this meal, much less cooked it, when she began to wonder what the number of place settings meant. She started to ask about this, but Risa was urging Sam to take a seat.

"The dinner has been warmed once—I think it will not improve the food if that happens again. Sit, sit. I poured the wine, but the bottle is on the table for you to pour again."

"Risa . . ." Josie began.

"I go. I go. I have important things to do inside." She swirled through the French doors (Josie had salvaged them from an earlier project and installed them on Risa's last birthday), which she latched behind her. Within moments opera music escaped through the glass panels.

"Music to discuss murder by," Josie said grimly.

"*La Forza del Destino,*" Sam remarked. "I wonder if her choice is significant."

Josie didn't know what he was talking about. "You should know that I didn't cook this."

Sam sipped his wine. "That doesn't surprise me. I know how busy you've been recently."

Josie opened her mouth and then decided there was no point in confessing that she couldn't cook a meal this good. The way things were going, she'd be spending the next few years in prison. He'd probably never find out that she rarely made anything more difficult than a two- or three-step brownie mix. She picked up her wineglass and sipped.

"This is good, isn't it?" she asked, surprised by the taste.

"I gather you didn't buy the wine either?"

"I buy jugs of most anything that is on sale—from California," she admitted.

"California makes some great wines."

"Not the ones that I can afford."

"Honesty is important to you, isn't it?"

"Definitely. And that's why I was so upset by what Betty was telling me at lunch." She leaned forward and started eating her salad as she spoke. "Here she is—seriously in love for the first time in her life—and he's pretending to be an honest man while lying to his wife."

"Do you know that?"

"Well, I don't think that his wife thinks it's just fine if he has a weekend fling with another woman at the beach."

"But you don't know, do you?" Sam said gently. "Maybe his wife doesn't care. People do live unusual lives, you know."

"That's a little sophisticated for me, but I suppose so," Josie said slowly. "On the other hand, he could have lied to his wife about the reasons he came down here and she followed him down one weekend, discovered that he was spending his time with Betty, and hauled off and killed the man."

"Which is what you would have done," Sam suggested, smiling at her enthusiasm for her own interpretation of imaginary events.

"I would have wanted to, that's for sure."

"And then, I gather, you think she dragged the body over to the Firbank house, for some reason."

"Yeah." Josie agreed with what he hadn't said. "It makes more sense that he was at the Firbanks' house to see Betty and . . . But that doesn't make sense. Betty doesn't have a key to that house. And why would they be meeting in a filthy torn-apart building when they had that wonderful home next door with the plushest of everything available to them?"

"Good question. I gather you didn't ask Betty about it."

"I couldn't. I would have had to tell her that he was dead."

"You didn't tell her?"

"No. Do you think that I should have?"

"Not yet." He looked down at his half-finished salad. "This is excellent. Do you think she used vintage olive oil?"

Vintage olive oil? Was there such a thing? "I don't know."

"You're sure she didn't have a key to the Firbank house?"

Josie thought about it. "Pretty sure. As far as I know, I'm the only person with a key to that padlock. But it's possible that someone could have broken into the house some other way."

"The padlock is on the front door?"

"Yes, and the back door has been boarded over until recently."

"And there aren't any other doors?"

"No, but there are lots of windows—some of them at ground level. And I suppose someone could get a ladder and go into a window on the second floor—they're not locked."

"And you wouldn't know if someone had been there, would you?"

"No way. I mean, unless they left a body behind."

"And we do know that someone has been in there at night."

"How do we know that?" Josie asked.

"The light that I saw."

"Oh, yes, I'd forgotten all about that." Sam had served Josie a plate of seafood risotto and Josie looked down at her food without tasting it. "What a mess."

"This looks wonderful!" Sam protested.

"I wasn't talking about the meal. I meant the murder. We know the name of the murdered man—"

"And we know that he lived next door to the place where he was found. And we know that he had a connection with the Firbank house—he was their next-door neighbor as well as having an affair with one of the women remodeling the building. That's a lot more than we knew yesterday."

"I know. It's just that what we're learning involves Island Contracting more, not less." She frowned and picked up her fork.

"We didn't think it was likely to be an accident that the body was found where it was," Sam reminded her.

"I know, but I was hoping," she admitted. "And still I may be right. Mike Rodney and Betty certainly weren't meeting at the Firbank place for a romantic tryst—not with those big stone beds available next door."

" 'Stone beds'?"

Josie explained the unusual decorating theme at the Rodney home.

"Sounds weird."

This from a man who thought the taste of the fifties was something to preserve? "It's wonderful."

"We don't know anything about Mike Rodney. Except that he's a family man who fishes."

"And has affairs."

"And has affairs." Sam chewed a scallop thoughtfully. "Is there anyone who might know him? Maybe Basil Tilby?"

"Possibly. I do know that Basil usually enters the island fishing tournaments."

"I hate to interrupt this wonderful meal, but do you think we could give him a call right away?"

"Why not? Risa will let us use her phone. What's the name of that restaurant?"

"The Gull's Nest. I'll call," Sam offered, leaping up.

Josie served herself a second helping of risotto while Sam was out of the room. Starving wouldn't help Island Contracting stay in business.

"He's on his way over. I called the restaurant and someone there gave me the number of his car phone and it turned out that he was only a few minutes away."

"Leave it to Basil to have a car phone on an island where a good jogger can run from one end to the other in a little over an hour."

"He's running a few businesses on that island, remember.

You might find a car phone useful if Island Contracting starts to grow."

"Maybe," was all she said. "I sure hope Basil is good with names. I've spent all day on a dock fishing and crabbing and talking and not gotten to know the names of anyone around me."

"We have this picture," Sam reminded her, taking a folded photo from his pocket.

"I wondered where that was!"

"I dropped it on the floor behind the dresser in the bedroom. I knew the police couldn't claim to look there casually. And there was no reason for them to have been given a search warrant. That must be Basil," he added as the lights from a car flashed through the windowpane.

It was. He flew in the doorway wearing, of all things, a cape flung over his shoulders. And stopped abruptly when he saw the table and its contents. "Where did all this come from?" He glanced toward the French doors. "Ah. Risa. If only I could bribe her to cook for me. I could open a small place and make a fortune." He picked a shrimp from the casserole and popped it in his mouth. "Heaven. Sheer heaven."

Josie shoved the photograph in front of Basil's face. "Do you know the man who is third from the left in the back row?" she asked abruptly.

"Sure. Mike. Great fisherman. Won the tournament a few years ago." Basil squinted at the photo. "Maybe the year this was taken, in fact." He pulled a spare chair up to the table and picked another shrimp from the risotto.

"Would you like a glass of wine?" Josie offered a little sarcastically.

"Love one."

"Tell us everything you know about Mike Rodney," Sam said, pouring out the wine. "We're not just being nosy. It's important to us . . . and to Island Contracting."

Josie winced. Asking Basil to tell everything about anything could keep them here all evening.

Basil smiled at Josie as if he knew what she was thinking. "I'd do anything I could to help out Noel's company. He did me a major favor once. Changed my life." He sipped the wine. "So let me think. Mike Rodney.

"Well, he came to the island about five years ago. And he started fishing right away. The man seems to have a very healthy cash flow. Built a big house up on the dunes and his fishing tackle is the best, the very best, that money can buy."

"Do you know where the money came from?"

"My impression is that his family made it. He may dabble around in the stock market, but I couldn't be sure of it. He's a good guy. When he fishes, he fishes. And he probably is the same way at work."

"Do you know anything about his family?" Sam asked.

"That I do know about. He has two. The first produced three grown-up children. All boys. He's brought them along on fishing trips. They're in their late twenties or early thirties. All single. I know that because he brought two kids from his second marriage on an all-day charter a few years ago. I thought the young ones were Mike's grandchildren until he made a disparaging comment about the older kids not liking to fish with him."

"Have you met either of his wives?"

"No. One was waiting on the shore at the end of that cruise. Young. Blond. Thin. Typical trophy wife." Basil shrugged his elegant shoulders. "We fish together. We don't talk much about our personal lives. Or our professional lives. We talk about the fish." Another shrug.

"Have you ever noticed any changes in him?" Josie asked.

"No."

"Do you fish this time of the year?" Sam asked.

"I fish all the time. Fishing is an addiction. Ask Josie."

"I prefer crabbing," she admitted. "But I do it year-round, too."

"And when was the last time you saw Mike Rodney?" Sam asked.

"Last fall," Basil said. "He never comes down in the winter. The man is rich. When he wants to drop his pole in the water off-season, he flies someplace warm like the Florida Keys. I've never seen him down here between Labor Day and Memorial Day. He stays out of the water when it's cold."

"I wouldn't bet on that," Josie muttered.

TWENTY-THREE

RISA WAS WAITING for Josie in her apartment, Urchin curled up in her lap and a glass of wine in her hand. "Did you enjoy your meal?" she asked casually.

"Of course we did, but you shouldn't have said that I cooked it."

"Some men think food is very important, *cara mia.* And I think your Sam Richardson is one of those men, no?"

"Maybe. But I can't start a serious relationship with him now, can I?"

"*Cara mia!* Why not?"

"Because he would expect me to invite him to dinner and what would I cook?"

Risa narrowed her eyes and stared at Josie. "You kid me, yes?"

"Yes. And what I should be doing is thanking you for the wonderful meal. But how did you know that Sam and I were at the office?"

"You drive that hideous truck. He drives that divine British sports car. It is very easy to keep track of where each of you is on the island."

Josie frowned and thought about that comment. "That's true, isn't it?" she murmured. And then she realized that her truck was still back at the office. "Could I please impose on you for a few minutes more?"

"Anything. Anything. You know you can count on me."

"I need a ride to the office to pick up my truck. Sam drove here and . . . and . . ."

"And what, *cara*? What is wrong?"

Josie put her hand over her mouth. "Sam drove me

here," she whispered. "And he didn't have to ask the way. He . . . he knew where I lived."

"Ah, that proves it! He loves you. When I was a girl, all the men in my town knew where I lived. They found out. He found out. You see."

She did. She saw that maybe she had been trusting the wrong person. She began to tug on a lock of hair. "I'd really appreciate it if you'd drive me down to the office."

"Of course." Risa stood up and tucked various pieces of fabric closer around her.

It was only a few minutes to the office, but it was ample time for Risa to embroider on the theme of Josie and Sam. When Josie hopped out of the car, her landlady was discussing her supposed need for new pastel sheets. "Think of pale pink, *cara.* With your white skin and flaming hair . . . sensational."

Josie smiled, waved, and searched in her pockets for the keys to the truck. She knew that when she didn't arrive home immediately, Risa would assume she had gone to spend a smoldering night with Sam Richardson. Instead she got in the truck and drove to the small cottage on the bay where Basil lived.

She had never been inside Basil's home, although it was fewer than ten blocks from Island Contracting's office. Now, uninvited, she knocked on the door, ignoring the hour. Light seeping through white Levolor blinds indicated that Basil was still awake.

As did the fact that he answered the door immediately. "Josie! What are you doing here? Did you and Sam think of something else you wanted to ask me?" He peered over her shoulder.

"I'm alone. But I need to talk with you. Right now," she insisted.

"Come in." He stepped back out of the way.

Josie walked in—and then walked around. From the outside, Basil's cottage resembled Island Contracting's office: a small shingle-style cottage with lots of double-hung windows, a gable roof with a tiny centered dormer, and presumably, a deck out back over the water. Inside it was special—in a style that Josie quickly recognized. "Noel designed this."

"Yes," he said, although she had not asked a question.

The walls were painted white. The ceiling, trim, woodwork natural pine. Terra-cotta tiles in various natural shades of clay covered the floor. The back of the room, which looked out over the water, was glass, but a fireplace was set in the middle with a white plaster flue leading to the sky. Behind them was a small black-and-white Pullman kitchen. It was tucked beneath a balcony that Josie could see was lined with overflowing bookshelves. She looked at the puffy linen-covered couches and coffee tables that made up the decor of the room. "Where do you sleep?"

"Follow me." A bookshelf along the right side of the room hid a stairway that Basil now descended with Josie on his heels. At the bottom a small bedroom looked out under the back deck of the main floor.

"You're farther above the water than I thought from the outside."

"And I'm very waterproof in case of a storm," Basil said, perching on the edge of a bed covered in Indian cotton. Two dressers and low bookshelves completed the room's decoration. Two doors, one on either side of the bed, led to closets and a gleaming white bathroom.

"Noel used to talk about the perfect house for one person," Josie commented, following her host back to the main floor. "I guess he built it for you."

"Well, it's perfect for me. Would you like a drink or maybe a cup of hot tea? I have lots of herb teas."

"I can't stay long." She sat down on one of the couches. "I know it's late, but I just have to ask you some questions." She looked at him curiously. "Two questions actually."

He sat down opposite her. "So ask."

"I don't understand why you've been acting so different, not talking about yourself all the time in that irritating way that you used to do—" She stopped, knowing that she had been rude and surprised that Basil was smiling at her.

"This is a beautiful island," he began slowly. "And it is nice to live here, but it is very hard to keep anything private."

Josie nodded. She knew exactly what he was talking about.

"So I talk about myself all the time. I don't say anything important and some people actually stop listening and that gives me some privacy and other people think that I'm baring my soul and never seem to realize that it's all just babble. And, most importantly, I manage to have more privacy than most people on the island."

Josie narrowed her eyes at him. "Just how did you figure this out?"

"I worked my way through hotel management school at Cornell as a bartender. Most drunks talk and talk. And one day I realized that after a while no one listened." He shrugged his thin shoulders. "It's worked for me. And you would be amazed how infrequently anyone asks me any questions. But you did just now. What else did you want to know?"

"How well do you know Sam Richardson?"

Basil examined the expression on her face before answering. "I gather you're not checking out his background because there's a budding romance here."

Josie remembered the scene in the bedroom and hoped that she wasn't blushing. "No. Not really," she answered. "And although I know this sounds rotten, I really can't explain what is going on between us."

"Don't worry, my dear. I rarely can explain my personal life." He reached out and patted her knee. "And I will tell you what I know about Sam Richardson, although it's not much.

"You know, of course, that he left his job recently."

"Why don't you just assume that I don't know anything?" Josie remembered Noel suggesting this method for getting information. "When did you meet him?"

"Actually, I heard about him before we met. One of my distributors told me that there was a new owner of the liquor store—a man who knew a lot about Italian wines."

"So you went to visit him?"

"Yes, I went to his store to say hello when I saw his car parked on the street." Josie was surprised to see the rueful expression on his face. "I've had a lot of extra time since Noel died. I guess that's why I bought that awful place out on the highway—which I do hope you'll work on for me as soon as you finish that mansion up on the dunes."

"Of course." Josie was subdued. Until looking around here, she had forgotten how close Noel and Basil had been. She couldn't refuse to work for this man.

"Sam, I think, was feeling as lonely as I was that day. Of course, when you've just broken up after a three-year relationship . . ." He looked at her carefully. "I gather he didn't mention that part of his past to you."

"Only in passing," Josie lied. Well, what had she been expecting? The man hadn't been in a monastery. And those candles and the bubble bath . . . "What did he tell you about the woman?"

"Not much. She was a decorator."

And not a very good one, Josie thought, remembering the turquoise Formica table and the painting over the hideous green sofa.

"Of course, Sam claims that he came here because he was unhappy with his job, but it is possible that he couldn't deal with this woman deciding that she wanted more freedom after years and years together—such a surprise, don't you think?"

"It would be to me," Josie admitted. "You two seem to have gotten along pretty well after knowing each other such a short time."

"He's a very friendly guy."

Josie wasn't in a position to argue with that. "So he told you that he decided to abandon his career, buy a liquor store, and move to the island because this woman left him."

"No. That's my interpretation of events. Sorry. He told me that he had lost faith in the legal system—he didn't go into details. At about the same time a romantic relationship had broken up. And then this opportunity to buy the store came up and he leaped at it."

"That's not much of an explanation."

"I wasn't investigating his past, we were chatting over a bottle of Gravi. He is a very interesting man. I think he's going to be a real asset to our little community. You've been spending a lot of time with him, so you've probably noticed how well-read and well traveled he is."

Josie had driven her son to school in Massachusetts. That was pretty much the last time she had left the island—except to work. Her reading . . . well, she always meant to get around to doing some serious reading. When she wasn't exhausted. Or busy trying to make a living. She merely smiled. "How did he tell you that he found out that the store here was for sale?"

Basil frowned. "He met a relative of the previous owner on some sort of tour, I believe. I suppose there's a reason that you're not asking him these questions?"

"Yes." She was relieved that Basil's answer had confirmed what Sam had told her.

"Of course," Basil continued, "he had been here before and knew what a good place this is to live."

"He had?"

"Yes. He spent a few weeks here one summer. I don't think he rented. I got the impression that he was someone's guest, probably the interior decorator."

"Probably." Josie racked her brain, trying to remember whether or not Sam had ever indicated that he had been on the island before buying the store. Perhaps he thought that she would assume that he wouldn't move unless he knew at least something about the place he was moving to—or perhaps he had intentionally not told her. Certainly, he had never indicated any familiarity with anything on the island—like the Fish Wish. On the other hand, most vacationers were content to lie on the beach during the day and drink their gin and tonics at night. If they went fishing, they did it from charter boats that provided equipment, bait, and beer. They had no need to know the location of places like the Fish Wish.

"He bought his house and the store—"

"He told me that prosecuting attorneys don't make a lot of money."

"You're right—they are paid by the government, aren't they?"

"So how did he afford a store and a house on the beach?"

"How do the people who buy houses on the water afford those outrageous prices? Not many of them from just a salary. Maybe he inherited money. Maybe he had another business that he sold. Maybe . . . well, there are all sorts of ways that people get large amounts of money."

Josie didn't respond.

"He doesn't seem like a man who would do anything illegal," Basil continued, seeming to know what she was thinking. "He left a career that had meant a lot to him because he wanted the law to be just, but I don't think he lacked respect for the law. He just wanted the reality to be more like what he had imagined when he was in law school."

Josie, who was very aware of Sam's inherently law-abiding personality, bit her lip and wondered if she was missing something here. "Has he said anything about me?" she asked seriously.

Perhaps because he sensed her reluctance to ask the question, Basil's response was equally serious. "Yes. He's talked about you a lot, in fact. Let me think.

"He liked you as soon as he met you. He even mentioned that he thought you were cute the first time you came into his store to use the phone. I think it may have been the first time he ever saw you. And you made quite an impression."

"Of dirt." Josie nodded.

"He didn't mention the dirt. Just your red hair. Apparently he likes red hair."

Josie wondered what color hair the interior decorator had. "He just said that there was a woman who came in the store and she had red hair and that he likes red hair?"

"No. He said that there had been a young woman—I think he said a cute young woman in overalls—who came into his store and asked to use the phone. And he asked if I knew your name. But I needed more of a description, because he could have meant almost anyone on your crew. But he said that the young woman had wonderful red hair."

"So you told him my name?" Josie was working very hard to keep from grinning with glee at Sam's description of her.

"Sure did. He didn't even have to tell me about how you kept misplacing your keys. You have the best red hair on the island. Everyone knows that."

Josie blinked at the unexpected compliment. "Thank you."

"Of course, a lot of people don't like red hair."

She grimaced. "Thanks again. What else did he say about me?"

"Not much that day. I told him who you were and that you were single. I thought he might be interested. That's all. But we met for lunch the next day and he mentioned you again. He asked if you were part of the crew working on the house on the dunes. I knew he was talking about the Firbank house and told him yes. And then I explained about Island Contracting and Noel's inheritance to you."

Josie wondered if Sam had come to envision her as a single woman of substance instead of a red-haired carpenter, but she remained silent. And slightly amused. "And he hasn't mentioned me to you since then?"

"Oh yes, he has. He came in to the restaurant yesterday."

"With me?"

"Without you. It was earlier in the day—before the two of you came in together."

"And he talked about me?" Josie asked, hoping for some more flattering revelations.

Basil grimaced. "He asked me if I knew if you had any serious psychological problems."

TWENTY-FOUR

A SPRING STORM toward dawn caused Josie's ancient clock radio to abandon timekeeping and a phone call awakened her—over an hour late. Chris was on the other end of the line. She didn't bother to say hello.

"Josie. It's me. You better get to the Firbank house right away. Someone broke in during the night."

Josie was pulling her flannel nightshirt over her head as she hung up. She grabbed yesterday's overalls from the floor and the top T-shirt in her drawer; socks and work boots completed her outfit. Her morning's ablutions consisted of brushing her teeth and running a cold (and clammy) washcloth across her face. She ran to her truck and was at the work site less than five minutes later, owing to the fact that none of the island's policemen saw her zoom by. She found out why when she arrived at the Firbanks'. Every police car the island owned was parked out front, strobe lights flashing. Josie parked behind the last one in line and ran to the house and up the steps.

"I called the police right after we hung up," Chris announced, opening the front door for Josie.

Josie took the time to look around before answering. Nothing seemed out of the ordinary. "How did you know that someone broke in?"

"You'll know when you see the third floor," Chris said, leading the way.

The noise of the police department's two-way radios greeted their arrival in the attic. The first thing Josie saw was the scowling face of Rick McCorkle. But she lost interest in him as soon as she noticed the walls. Every piece of wallboard was covered with fluorescent graffiti. Even the ceiling had been decorated with the balloon lettering familiar to those frequenting highways that lead in and out of urban areas. Josie stood in the middle of the room and spun slowly, trying to interpret any messages.

"You can't read them," Evelyn announced. "Unless they're in a foreign language. We've all been trying ever since we got here."

"Don't think anyone on the island would be stupid enough to sign this particular artwork, do you?" Rick asked, chuckling at his own joke.

Josie walked up to the wall and touched the paint. Of course it was dry. The propellants in these spray cans caused that to happen almost immediately, but for some reason, she couldn't help herself. She frowned and then turned to Chris. "If we put on three coats of a fairly dark color, we can get this covered before nightfall. The Firbanks will never know."

"Can't do that, Josie."

"Why on earth not?" she asked Rick.

"Evidence. We need to keep this for evidence."

"No, we don't. We can just paint it over and forget that it ever happened. . . . Nothing was taken, was it?" she asked the members of her crew who were standing around looking concerned.

"Not that we can find," Melissa answered.

"We checked out all our tools and materials and we sure couldn't find anything gone," Evelyn explained further. "And there's nothing else here that's worth anything."

"Doesn't matter," Rick insisted in a deadpan tone. "We have to keep the evidence until Dad—until the chief gets back to investigate."

"That is stupid!" Josie was getting mad. "Look around you. What happened here is . . . is malicious mischief. Some dumb kids broke into the house overnight and thought this would be fun. They didn't do any permanent damage and they didn't hurt anybody. There's no need for the police to be involved."

"You should have thought of that before you called us. Once we're here, we have no choice but to file a report and investigate. And the investigation is going to have to wait until my father gets back."

"Oh, Josie. I'm sorry. I didn't know that or I wouldn't have called," Chris said.

"It's not your fault," Josie assured her before returning her attention to Rick. "Returning from where?" she asked, barely controlling her anger.

"He's in Philadelphia attending a conference in forensics. We have to keep up with modern science, you know." Rick smiled and the policemen around him put similar expressions on their faces. The officer closest to the stairway began to unroll the familiar yellow police line tape.

"What is he doing with that?" Josie asked.

"We're going to have to close off this space. You women will just have to work elsewhere in the house. It looks like there's enough to keep you busy."

"I'm going to go call my lawyer," Josie announced, and stomped down the stairs.

"The cellular is in the kitchen," someone called down after her.

Josie was furious, but unwilling to show it to the policemen. She dialed the liquor store and felt the first moment of relief of the morning when Sam Richardson answered. "Sam, someone broke into the Firbank house last night."

"I'll be right there." And he hung up.

Josie spent the minutes before he arrived checking out Melissa's statement. She had come to agree that nothing had been stolen when she heard Sam enter the house. "I'm back here," she called out from the tiny bathroom (which she had taken a few seconds to admire).

"Where is everyone? Don't you ever let your crew take a day off?" he asked, not bothering to greet her.

"Everyone is on the third floor. And we all agreed to work seven days a week until this project was finished," Josie answered Sam as he started toward the stairs. "Don't leave! I have to talk to you before you go up there. Sam, if I hire you as my lawyer, that means anything I tell you is a secret, doesn't it?"

"No."

"What about confidentiality between a lawyer and his client?" Josie asked, thinking of all the television shows she had watched that insisted on this particular aspect of the relationship.

"It is illegal for a lawyer and his client to enter into any conspiracy. Otherwise a lawyer could do anything he wanted to with impunity as long as a client was involved—and vice versa, if you see what I mean."

She didn't, but she knew they didn't have a lot of time before Rick found them. "What if we lied about the stuff upstairs. What if I said I did it?"

"Why would you do that?"

"Because they're putting up a yellow ribbon to keep my crew from going up there. And we have work to do," she said, starting upstairs.

"Josie." Sam grabbed her arm. "Don't lie about this. Just let it be. You're potentially in enough trouble already. Okay?"

"Okay," she agreed reluctantly.

"I gather Chief McCorkle is here?" Sam asked.

"My father is attending a professional conference in Philadelphia." Rick McCorkle stood at the top of the stairs.

"Really? How interesting," Sam commented noncommittally. "Why don't we go check out the crime scene?" he continued. "I am Samuel Richardson. Ms. Pigeon's lawyer."

"I thought you bought that liquor store," Rick said in his usually articulate manner.

"He is also a lawyer," Josie explained. She noticed that Rick opened and closed his mouth a few times, but made no comment. She and Sam continued up the stairs.

Everyone was still in the attic, presenting a strange scene. They seemed to be cordoned in by the yellow tape, rather than cordoned out. Josie thought that Sam had been momentarily stunned by the sight until she realized that he was staring at the painted walls. "Well, it wasn't done by Keith Haring," was all he said. Josie wondered if she would ever understand everything he was talking about. He lifted the tape and stooped to enter the room, and Josie followed.

Chris started toward them and then stopped. Sam saw her movement and took the time to smile at her before he examined the walls. "No tags here," he muttered.

"Good point," one of the policemen said, joining him. "I worked in New York City for two years before coming here and I've never seen anything like this. Usually the perpetrator wants his identity known. This is more . . . arbitrary is the word, I guess."

Sam just nodded and knelt down to examine a few letters that had run over onto the floor.

"Those kids back in the city can write their name and get the hell out of the area in just minutes."

Sam looked up at the speaker. "So how long do you think it would take someone to do this? Someone who knew what they were doing—you know, who had practiced."

The officer took a few moments to consider the question. "An hour. Maybe less."

"What are you thinking?" Josie came up to Sam's side. "You paint walls?"

"We usually leave the walls in condition to be painted. Sometimes we apply an undercoat, but I know how to paint walls if that is what you want to know." She started to say that she had painted her own apartment, but she didn't want him to suggest a visit.

"How long do you think it would take you to do this?"

Josie heard someone behind her gasp. She glanced around and saw that Betty was staring out one of the dormer windows. "Maybe two or three hours. Not much more. There are only three colors of paint."

He looked at the walls again. "That's true."

Josie thought that he was pleased with her observation. "And it's all the same handwriting, isn't it?"

"Good point."

"So how did he—or she—get in?" Rick had joined the conversation.

"Back door was open when I got here," Chris said.

"You and your crew don't lock up at night?" Josie knew that Rick was loving every minute of this. "I thought women were so good at all the small details."

"We usually lock up," Chris insisted.

"And Josie always checks out everything." Betty had left the window and returned to the group. "It's really sexist to say something like that," she informed Rick.

Josie would have cheered Betty on, but she had other things to consider. She couldn't remember locking up last night. She looked at the floor and frowned. When she looked up, she saw Betty staring at her.

"We will be filing a report about this," Rick said. "And we will require you to preserve the crime scene."

"What—" Sam began.

"Until my father returns," Rick continued as though he hadn't been interrupted. "My father is the department's forensic investigator."

"Hence the convention," Sam said, nodding. "But as long as you are only talking about this floor, I don't believe my client will be unduly inconvenienced."

Josie was impressed. He really sounded like a lawyer. It seemed to impress Rick as well; he stopped pontificating and agreed that there was no reason to limit activity on the floors below.

"Then we'd better be getting to work," Josie suggested. "It's late and the Firbanks may still plan on appearing the day after tomorrow."

"Tomorrow night, I think," Evelyn said. "I'm pretty sure I heard Mrs. Firbank say that they were coming down Friday night."

Josie sighed. "Why doesn't that surprise me?" she muttered. "Maybe someone should go out for coffee?"

"I picked up some at the deli on the way here this morning," Betty said. "It's downstairs."

"Did you bring doughnuts?" Melissa asked.

"Damn, I was going to get crumb cake this morning," Chris said. "I don't suppose you thought to buy some?"

"Me? Why me?" Betty asked as the women walked down the stairs together, leaving Sam and the police officers to do whatever it was that they did.

"You live above the bakery. You're the closest," Chris explained.

Josie didn't catch the rest of the conversation; she heard Sam calling for her.

"We need to talk," he insisted, meeting her halfway down the stairs.

"Fine. Tonight—"

"This can't wait until tonight."

"Then how about lunch?"

"No. Now."

"I absolutely have to get everyone working," Josie insisted.

"I'll meet you down at the store if you promise to come there right away."

"Half an hour?"

"Make it less if you can. I'll be waiting for you."

Josie found that Betty was also waiting for her, surrounded by the rest of her crew, when she got to the first floor.

"Betty needs to talk with you," Evelyn announced.

"She needs to confess something," Chris said.

"Hey, guys, it's not as though I killed someone," Betty cried. "It never occurred to me that spending the last couple of nights next door would be such a big deal."

TWENTY-FIVE

BETTY HAD INSISTED on talking to Josie alone. Josie got the impression that the rest of her crew, smelling a messy personal situation, was thrilled to give them some privacy.

"Did I hear you correctly?" Josie asked as the two women hiked across the dunes toward the sea. "You've been sleeping in the shed behind the house next door?"

Betty nodded, her tight curls bouncing in the breeze from the sea. "Yes. Chris realized that I didn't know the bakery was open and I had to tell the truth. I was closer to him in there." She sighed. "I know it's irrational, but that's how I felt."

Josie bent down to pick up a tiny black scallop shell. "Did you two ever meet in the Firbanks' house?"

Betty looked astonished. "Of course not. Why would we meet there when his house is right next door? And his house is really fabulous. I know it looks pretty ordinary from the outside, but inside—"

"I know," Josie said. "I've been inside."

"Oh." That seemed to surprise the young woman. "I didn't know that you knew the Rodneys."

"I don't," Josie admitted, not bothering to explain.

Betty didn't seem curious about that. "It's just that I thought if he came back to his house, I would see him . . . if . . . That's not true. None of this is true. I was lying to myself as well as everyone else. I was staying there to spy on him—or on his wife, if he brought her down for the weekend. That's why I didn't dare sleep in his house. I have the key, but I couldn't risk being caught."

"You—"

"I was desperate. He promised to meet me and then he didn't. I . . . to be honest, recently he has been acting less and less interested in me. I suppose I shouldn't have been surprised when he didn't show up."

"He was supposed to meet you at the Gull's Nest for breakfast?" Josie asked as the two women walked up the beach together.

"Well." Betty picked up a rock and tossed it into the sea. "I thought . . . Actually, I guess the truth is that I hoped he would be there. You see, that's where we used to meet."

"Used to?"

"He's been out of the country for almost a month. But I had called his business office in the city and his secretary told me that he was back in the country. She just thought that he might be coming down here for the weekend. I thought . . . well, he told me that he would come here to see me as soon as he was back from his trip. And I knew that he had been at the house."

"How?"

"There were garbage cans left in the side yard for weeks—then when I came to work one morning, they had been put away. He doesn't have a caretaker and his family stays away until summer. I knew that no one else would have done it. So I called his office and they said he had returned. I thought he might call, but he didn't, so the next morning I just naturally went to the restaurant."

"But he didn't arrive?"

"No." She kicked a plastic soda bottle in front of her. "I panicked when he wasn't there. After speaking with a kitchen worker, I called the police. We used to meet there when he came into town."

"Are you telling me that you weren't sleeping with him?"

Betty looked slightly offended. "What does that have to do with anything?"

"Why would you meet him someplace for breakfast if you were spending the night together?"

"Oh, that's not the way things were. You see, Mike couldn't get away from the city on Friday nights. He used to drive to the island early Saturday morning. I just assumed that he had been in town the night before and he expected me to meet him there." She gave the bottle a kick out into the ocean. "I guess it was just wishful thinking. I kept imagining that I had seen him at the house. That's why I've been acting like such an idiot freezing to death in my bikini on the roof and flirting with that stupid Jason outside when I imagined that Mike might be hanging around and watching."

"I don't want to hurt your feelings, but I really need to know more about all of this," Josie began.

"Don't worry about it. I'm pretty resilient. You have to be if you're going to get involved with married men."

"There have been others?"

"God, you make it sound like I collect them. And I never will again. I thought . . . I thought it was different for Mike and me. I thought he really loved me."

"And maybe he did," Josie suggested gently. She knew the same old story when she heard it, but she knew that everyone had to learn their own lessons.

"Yeah, and maybe he was just using me. Maybe his wife is old and chubby and knows him just a little too well to be fascinated by every word that comes out of his mouth. Maybe I was there in my running clothes wanting to believe that a wealthy man would sweep me off my feet and take me away from the island and a life as a carpenter. Maybe I'm just as stupid as he thought I was."

"Everyone makes mistakes. I have. That's for sure."

"But I have so many opportunities to do stupid things!" Betty cried. "Do you know how many men come on to me? Hundreds!"

"Of course most women aren't as attractive as you are, but—"

"But I screw up. I know that. I'm not naturally the most beautiful woman in the world. I jog and work out to keep my figure. And I guess the clothing I wear is somewhat revealing." She glanced over at Josie and grimaced. "Okay, very revealing. I know it. I'm just a stupid jerk! And after Noel gave me a second chance, you would think that I'd have taken it."

"What do you mean?"

"I was pretty stupid when I was young."

"We all were." Josie glanced at Betty. "Does this have

anything to do with the five thousand dollars that Noel loaned you when you came to work for Island Contracting?"

"He didn't loan it to me. He gave it to me. I didn't have to pay him back, I did because I wanted to. It took two years and I had to keep living with my parents when I had planned on leaving home the very second that I got a job, but I paid back every cent—with interest." Betty's pride in the accomplishment was obvious. "But how did you know about the money? I didn't think Noel ever told anyone."

"He didn't. I have the personnel records of the company and it's in there." Someplace. And right now, only Sam could find it. But she didn't tell Betty.

"Oh, I guess I should have thought of that." Betty frowned. "Then I guess you know all about the car."

"Why don't you tell me about it?" What car?

"The Mercedes that I crashed and had to have repaired. It was so stupid. I was barely eighteen and hadn't had my license very long and I should never have been driving that car. But I'd always been so jealous of the summer people in their big houses with their imported cars, and when I had the chance to car-sit, I just leaped at it. And so I was driving down the street and admiring myself in the plate-glass window of the drugstore when I ran smack into a stoplight. Who would have thought that it cost so much to have those cars fixed!"

"If you have to ask how much it costs . . ." Josie muttered.

". . . you can't afford it. I know. I know. And I couldn't."

"Whose car was it?"

"A man. Just one of the summer people who was trying to impress a poor little island girl with how rich and powerful and sexy he was—which he wasn't once he heard about the car. Turns out he didn't even carry collision insurance and he expected me to have the damage repaired immediately. And I didn't have that type of money. The guy who did the best bodywork on the island was a guy that I had dated in tenth grade—and dumped in eleventh. He wasn't real interested in giving me credit."

"But Noel gave you the money the day that he hired you, didn't he?"

"Says a lot about the type of man Noel was, doesn't it?"

"Yes. But I don't understand. The personnel records are a little brief. They don't explain every detail of everything Noel did."

Betty sighed. "What happened was that I was lucky. You see, I was on my way to apply for a job at Island Contracting when I had the accident. I was such an idiot. I had this whole image of applying for the job and being hired because whoever ran the company would think that I could bring in business—obviously I knew all these wealthy people intimately since they loaned me their cars. It sounds stupid because it was stupid. And there I was in the middle of Main Street with this damn expensive German sedan wrapped around the light pole. I was horrified.

"And suddenly there was Noel Roberts. He was on his way to the office and he recognized me and stopped his truck. I must have looked so stupid. I was in tears, of course. And I was so embarrassed that everyone was seeing me like that. I had thought I was such a big shot and I was afraid the people who knew me on the island would just think that it served me right to be acting like something I wasn't—and I was afraid that the summer people would realize that I wasn't what I had been pretending to be." She stopped. "If you know what I mean."

Josie just nodded. "So Noel stopped his truck," she said, trying to get back to the story.

"Yes. He said something about having an appointment to see me to the policeman who had appeared on the scene and he hung around while I filled out accident forms. In fact, he did everything. He even arranged to have the car towed away and he took me back to the office and called the owner for me. Because I didn't want to call and get his . . . uh, his wife."

Josie appreciated that Betty had the grace to be embarrassed by the admission. "And he offered you the money?" she prompted.

"First he offered me a job. Just like that! I couldn't believe it. Half the carpenters in my graduating class were unemployed and he just gave me a job. And Island Contracting was known to work almost exclusively for summer people. I became a carpenter because I wanted to work in the homes of the summer people, so it was the chance I had been waiting for. He said that he was sure I would do just fine."

Josie smiled. "Sounds like Noel." She couldn't remember him ever saying anything negative to anybody.

"Yes, it does, doesn't it? I miss him."

"So do I," Josie agreed sincerely.

"And then the garage called me at the office and said that the Mercedes could be fixed, but that they had called the owner and his insurance company and that they would not even begin to work on it without at least twenty-five hundred dollars. And then they explained that they wouldn't release the car without all the work paid for—and that it could be as much as five thousand dollars. I started to cry—like an idiot. Noel took the receiver from my hand and talked to the mechanic. Then he asked me if I would accept the money from him. And I hate to think what expression I had on my face, because he grinned that grin he had and added that there were no strings attached."

"And of course you believed him."

"There was something essentially honest about Noel, wasn't there?"

"Sure was. So you took the money."

"And paid it back in two years. I didn't move out of my parents' house. I didn't buy anything that wasn't absolutely essential. I lived on tuna sandwiches and water brought from home for lunch and snacks. When anyone asked any questions, I just said that I was on a diet. Of course, I was working my butt off—literally. I simply could not keep on weight that year. But I did it. And became a pretty good carpenter at the same time."

"Just like Noel knew you would."

"Yeah, I guess he did." Betty took a deep breath of the fresh sea air. "And now I'm screwing up again. Noel would think I'm a failure."

"I don't think so," Josie disagreed. "I think Noel always knew how human we were and he accepted the weaknesses along with the strengths. He would just expect you to pick yourself up and get on the right track again."

"You know, you're right." Betty bit her bottom lip. "And that's what I'm going to do. I'm going to stop acting like an idiot over Mike Rodney. I'm going to get my life back in order—and that includes getting him out of it. And I'm going to do it right now."

"No! Wait!" Josie cried. "I think there's something I should tell you first."

"What?" Betty had already turned and started back to the house.

"There is something you should know."

"What? Just tell me so I can call Mike at his office—like I promised him I wouldn't do—and tell him to go to hell. And to stop picking on vulnerable young women."

"But—"

"I think Noel would be proud of me for this, don't you?" Betty asked.

"I think—"

"I think I'm getting my life back in order."

"I think you should know that Mike Rodney is dead. He was killed with a hammer that belongs to Island Contracting and then dropped into the sea."

Betty seemed stunned. "The hammer?" she whispered.

"No. No, the body was dropped in the sea," Josie explained. She put her arm around the tearful young woman and suddenly found herself wondering exactly why the same fate hadn't befallen the hammer.

TWENTY-SIX

BETTY, FOR ALL her weaknesses, had sincerely cared about Mike Rodney, and Josie sat by her side in the sunny bowl between sand dunes as she cried at the horrible news.

"You're sure?"

"I'm afraid so. I saw the body myself."

"Where?"

"He was found in the Firbanks' house." She didn't add that she had been the person who found him.

"When?"

"Four days ago."

"That explains it! That's why I felt so close to him in the house."

Josie cringed. The last thing she wanted to do was encourage any strange attachment to the work site—although, on the other hand, maybe she could get Betty to work longer hours. . . .

"But how did he end up in the ocean?"

"Well, we're not exactly sure." It was almost true and she hoped that the plural would add strength to the statement.

For some reason, Betty accepted her answer. "So there's no way to retrieve the . . . the body?"

Josie decided not to raise false hopes. "No."

"And what are the police saying? Do they have any idea who killed him? I didn't see any signs that anyone else was staying at his house. It must have been someone here who killed—" Betty stopped, a look of dawning horror replacing the sadness on her face.

"Wait," Josie urged.

She didn't. "The police are going to think I killed him, aren't they? I'm the only person around that he was involved with. He was acting less and less interested in me. They'll think that I killed him because, if I couldn't have him, I didn't want anyone else to have him. And I can't prove anything. I'll end up in prison for a crime I didn't commit. And prison food is probably disgusting." She stopped and stared at Josie. "I'm acting like an idiot again, aren't I? I can't believe I just said that."

Josie took a deep breath. "The police don't know about this," she began.

"But you said he was murdered."

"I know. I can't explain now, but Sam Richardson has a lot of experience with murder. He was a prosecuting attorney and . . . and we're trying to find out who murdered Mike Rodney by ourselves."

"And you know that I'd never kill anyone." Betty

breathed a sigh that Josie assumed was of relief. "I can't tell you how much better that makes me feel. And you probably don't want me to tell anyone else either, do you?"

"I think he would find that helpful," Josie answered slowly.

"Fine. I won't." Betty stood up.

"Look, this has been a horrible thing to learn. Why don't you take the rest of the day off?"

"No. I'm fine."

"But, Betty . . ."

"I owe it to Island Contracting. And I owe it to Noel," she insisted, stomping off over the dunes.

Josie decided this was no time to argue. Not if they were going to get the Firbanks' house finished on time. She followed Betty toward the house, only to be greeted by Chris carrying a large bakery box.

"Crumb cake," Chris announced.

"Hello to you, too," Josie commented, reaching out for the box. "And I'm starving."

"Have some. Where is she going?" Chris asked as Betty continued back to the house. "Something wrong?"

"Just a personal problem—you know Betty," Josie said obscurely.

"Men." Chris nodded.

"Yeah. Men."

They followed their colleague up to the house.

"You're not listening to me," Chris complained.

Josie had had no idea that she was being spoken to, so she couldn't argue with Chris's complaint. "I'm sorry. What were you saying?"

"I was just talking about the lumber order. I think we might have miscounted sheets of two-four-one plywood. We're seven short. What were you thinking about so intently?"

"I have a question for you."

"Shoot."

"If you wanted to get rid of something, something fairly small—"

"Smaller than a bread box?"

Josie chuckled at the overly precise reference. "Okay. Smaller than a bread box. What would you do with it?"

"It's easy if you live on an island like we do. Just throw it in the water. In the ocean . . . but probably on the bay side."

"Sure. Less likely to get washed up by the tide," Josie agreed. She couldn't imagine anyone doing anything different around here. Something as heavy as a well-balanced hammer was unlikely to be seen again except by the crabs and other bottom eaters. Unless it was snagged by a fisherman using extra-heavy line and a very large hook, she thought.

"Of course, if it was something that floated, it would be another story. I suppose then I'd go bury it in the dunes. It would be safe there until a storm came that was big enough to wash away the dune. Then it just might reappear."

"That's a thought." But it didn't explain why someone had left the hammer on the public dock. Unless that someone had wanted the hammer found. And fairly quickly at this time of year, when Josie wasn't the only person on the island anxious to start fishing.

On the other hand, she thought, stopping abruptly. If that hammer had been found by someone other than Chief McCorkle, wouldn't the person who found it just take it home? Or, if they didn't want a tool, possibly toss it in the bay—or a convenient trash container. Was it just an accident that it had been found by the police chief? she wondered.

"Are you coming?" Chris asked, slowing down. "We're going to get further and further behind if—"

"Chris. I've got to go. I have a real problem and—"

"So go!"

"The future of Island Contracting may depend on it or I wouldn't leave," Josie added.

"Listen, I know you wouldn't leave now unless there was a real emergency. You go. We'll keep working. We won't get behind."

"Tell Betty that everything is going to be fine," Josie continued.

"Okay. If the company's future depends on you, you'd better get. We'll take care of everything. Promise."

Josie ran around the side of the house and down the front lawn to the street, searching in the pockets of her overalls as she went. She found her key chain as she reached the truck, and moments later she was speeding down the road.

She almost ran into the MGB parked in front of the liquor store. Sam was looking out the glass double doors and opened one for her as she ran toward the building. "What is going on? Are you okay?" he asked, throwing his arms around her.

"I . . . I'm fine," Josie answered, startled by his hug. "But you won't believe what I've discovered." And she told him about Betty's involvement with Mike Rodney.

"And she's been spending her nights in that shed between the houses?"

"Ever since the murder, apparently."

"I don't think I've ever seen this shed. What does it look like? What's it used for?"

"A lot of these beach houses don't have garages, and people need places to store bicycles and other sports equipment, so they put up sheds. Some people in houses worth a couple of million dollars put up a hideous plywood wonder from Sears. Other people have custom sheds that match their home. The Rodneys have a compromise. Their shed is a standard modular thing, but it was faced with the same facing as their house. It's nothing special, but it's consistent."

"And it's big enough for a person to spend the night in comfortably?"

"A person could live in it if a bathroom was added. You know, there was outdoor furniture stored there. One of those expensive lounges would be a comfortable bed. Where are you going?"

"I thought we should check out the Rodneys' property."

"But my crew will see me! How am I going to explain?"

"Don't worry about it. The ones that are innocent will think you've gone crazy and the murderer will know without asking."

"You still suspect someone on my crew!"

"Who else is there to suspect?"

"What about Mike Rodney's friends in New York City? Maybe he had professional enemies? Maybe one of his relatives?"

"Did Betty say anything about them? Do you think that's a possibility?"

Josie shook her head. "Probably not," she admitted. "In fact, from what Betty was saying, it's not at all likely."

"And she doesn't have any reason to lie about it, does she?"

"Not that I know of."

"And does Mike Rodney have friends among the year-round residents? Maybe other fishermen?"

"None that I know about, but it's possible. We could ask Basil."

Sam reached out for the wall phone. "Good idea."

"I'm going to use your bathroom. Tell him I said hi." She scurried off. Basil, she hoped, wouldn't mention her late visit last night, but right now she had more pressing problems. The tiny bathroom intrigued her even more since learning the profession of Sam's ex-girlfriend. (Was he too old to have a girlfriend? Was she too old to be one? she wondered, dealing with a bent button on her overalls.) Had he always been interested in interior decoration? Or had this woman changed him so much that papering the bathroom was the first thing he thought of when he bought a new store? Josie stood up suddenly. What was under all these wine labels? Something that it was important to cover up immediately?

She noticed that a label was puckering up near the switch plate. A few seconds with her handy Swiss army knife and she had the plate removed and was peeking under the labels closest to the door. The wall was covered with numbers, phone numbers mainly written by different people using a variety of pens and pencils. She was frowning as she slicked the labels down and replaced the hardware. Now she had another problem: should she ask Sam why he had been so anxious to hide the numbers or just go on about her business?

"Hey! Are you all right?" She heard Sam calling.

"Yes. I'm right here," she announced, returning to the room. "Did you get Basil on the phone?"

"Yes, he—"

"And why did you cover up all those phone numbers on

the bathroom walls?" she asked, her words coming in a rush.

Sam seemed startled, then his expression changed to one of amusement. "Someone who worked here was running a little business on the side—taking bets. When I realized what I had been looking at each time I went in there, I got to work and covered it all up. I don't want anyone thinking that I was involved in that sort of thing.

"So you don't trust me either. That's smart," he added before she could protest. "You're in no position to trust anyone at this point."

Josie thought for a moment before speaking. "I don't feel very comfortable with that," she admitted. "I'm a pretty trusting person. Of course, sometimes that's gotten me in a lot of trouble. And almost permanently screwed up my life on at least one occasion."

"Well, then?"

She saw that he was smiling. "Actually, I checked you out with Basil last night."

"I asked him about you, too," Sam admitted.

"Why?" Josie asked. "I'm the person with the most to lose if the murderer isn't found! If the murder goes unsolved, it will destroy the company and my life." She noticed that Sam was staring at her intently. "What are you thinking?" she demanded.

"I was thinking that you just made a very interesting comment. You said that Island Contracting was your life."

"No. That's not true. Island Contracting gave me a chance at life. I came to the island because the man who got me pregnant dumped me—which is certainly not an unusual story. And when my parents found out about my condition, their response was to refuse to support me anymore and to write me out of their wills. I was so hurt—and so angry—that I decided to keep my baby and raise him myself. And I have no idea how I would have managed if Noel hadn't found me and . . ."

"And taken you in?" Sam offered when she seemed to run out of words.

"No. He didn't take me in. I had all the skills you would expect from a freshman in college—none. I suppose if I had chosen to live in the city, I might have found a job as a receptionist or filing clerk, but here on the island, I was a waitress. And it was August. My job was going to end after Labor Day, and it was becoming difficult for me to stay on my feet all day anyway."

"You became a carpenter because being a waitress was too difficult physically?"

"I became a carpenter because Noel reached out a hand when I needed it the most. He came into the place I was working pretty regularly all summer. One day we started talking and I ended up telling him my life story. The next day he came back for dinner, and instead of a tip, he made me an offer that I couldn't refuse—because it was the only option I had. He said I could come to work for Island Contracting immediately. That he would train me and that I would get as much practical experience as I could. He said I would have health insurance and that I could bring the baby along with me when I came back to work. All I had to do was promise to work for Island Contracting for two years."

"And you agreed?"

"Are you kidding? I was thrilled. I was completely untrained and this man was guaranteeing me employment and insurance for myself and my baby. I would have been out of my mind to say no. He was taking all the risk, as far as I could see." She stopped talking and tears welled up in her eyes. "I'm sorry. I still miss him."

"Basil said that you and Noel weren't romantically involved," Sam said gently.

"You thought I had to sleep with a man to get something from him?" Josie could feel herself getting angry—and realized it wasn't helpful or particularly appropriate. (Not that that always stopped her.) "Okay. I shouldn't be mad. After all, I asked some pretty personal questions about you. And no, we weren't romantically involved. I didn't ever think of him like that. He was more of a protector and a friend than a potential lover."

Sam frowned. "There was a big difference in your ages," he muttered.

"Maybe fifteen years. It wasn't that. It was just that our relationship wasn't that way. Wasn't sexual." She used the word she had been trying to avoid. "I think it was intentional on his part. Sometimes people used to kid around and call the women who worked for Island Contracting 'Noel's harem,' but everyone knew it was a joke. And it wouldn't have been much of a joke if it had been true in any way."

"What you're saying is that Noel wasn't romantically involved with any of the women he hired."

"Or he was extraordinarily discreet about it."

"As was the woman," Sam suggested.

"That's true, isn't it?" Josie said slowly.

Sam stood up. "Let's go check out the Rodney house. We can talk while we look around."

Josie, thinking intently, just nodded.

TWENTY-SEVEN

"I DON'T QUITE know what we're doing here," Josie said, jumping down from the truck cab.

"Checking out Betty's story. If she's telling the truth, there should be some sign that she's been staying here."

Josie doubted that. "Maybe she picked up after herself."

But Betty hadn't been lying, they decided about fifteen minutes later. They had found a bag of makeup, toiletries, and clothing underneath the lounge that was set up under the window.

"Interesting," was Sam's comment as he picked up a pair of black lace panties from the floor. "Let's go see if we can get into the house."

"Betty probably locked up."

"You can break a window."

"That was an accident!" Josie protested, beginning to turn red. "Besides, there are shutters pulled down over all the windows—"

"I think we have company," Sam interrupted her. "That's the electrician, Melinda."

"Melissa," Josie corrected him, waving at the woman jogging across the yard toward them. "And she is a plumber. Didn't you want to talk to her about your refrigerator?"

"Seems to be working now."

"Then you're in trouble. An intermittent problem is the most difficult kind to track down."

"It's—"

"Of course, that's sort of the type of problem we have here, isn't it?" Josie interrupted him. "It's intermittent. Things are going along normally and then something strange happens."

Melissa joined them, so there wasn't time for her to explain further. "We have a crisis. It looks like someone threw away all the hardware for the windows. Chris said not to bother you, but—"

"Damn. I thought we were taking care of things better than that. I've got to check this out," Josie explained to Sam, starting toward the job site. "I'll be right back."

"And there is some sort of mix-up with the tile order," Melissa called after her.

Josie stopped dead. There were days when she felt like Noel was sitting on her shoulder whispering advice in her ear. And sometimes she imagined him leaning down from above and threatening to smack her on the head with a heavenly hammer if she didn't listen to him. This was one of the latter.

When problems are overwhelming, most people start running when it's really the time to stop and do a little thinking. She could hear the words; she could see him sitting in the office, feet on his desk. She spun around on the worn heels of her work boots and headed straight for the sea. "I'll be back in a bit," she called over her shoulder. "I need some time alone." She needed to take a walk on the beach.

There were always people walking or jogging on the sand, looking for health or their lost youth. What Josie hoped to find among the crumbled shells, garbage, and threads of green seaweed was the truth. Or maybe, she thought, picking up a fabric-covered elastic and stuffing it in her pocket, just a tiny piece of it.

The island was seven miles long. The Firbank house was north of the island's center. Josie frowned, squared her shoulders, and started to walk.

She marched along on the damp sand at the edge of the retreating tide, lines of sandpipers fleeing from her path.

There were people, she knew, who approached life in an orderly manner. They got up each morning and had the same meal. They went to the movies on Friday night, did their laundry on Saturday, and went to church on Sunday. These same people must have a method of putting facts in order, of separating facts from feelings, of doing what her grandmother used to call "getting to the heart of the matter." But Josie was about as capable of that type of organization as she was of thinking through this situation in a foreign language.

Her thoughts leaped from Chris's problems with her mother to Mike Rodney to the refrigeration system down at the liquor store. She wondered for a moment about the age of the woman she had come to think of as Sam's ex–interior decorator and considered whether or not Sam was taking adequate care of the kittens that he had given such silly names.

She took a deep breath and remembered Mike Rodney's wound and the way he had looked under the blue tarp. She decided it was pointless to wonder about his condition at the present time.

She found a piece of beach glass, its edges worn soft by the sand, its turquoise muted to the color of Sam's eyes . . . damn.

She wondered whether or not the window hardware had been located, and if not, how long it would take to find replacements. She wondered how Evelyn's children had dealt with the fact that their mother had been in jail. She wondered if Melissa's husband would ever get his degree and if she would continue to work after she had children.

She thought about Noel and how he had given his employees a chance at a good life when he offered them a job. She wondered about his relationship with Basil Tilby and the house he had remodeled for him.

She smiled, thinking of what Noel, who hated pretense, would say about the furniture at Sam's seaside cottage. She thought it was interesting that Sam had shown up on the island only a few weeks before the murder.

And then she realized that she had to find out more about Sam. Because she couldn't ignore the possibility that his arrival on the island and the timing of the murder had been something other than a coincidence. Her mind finally focused, she turned and walked back to the Firbank house.

One of the nicest things about the island was that the year-round community was small and, if not closely knit, at least you knew who you could depend on and who you couldn't. Josie didn't even go into the Firbank house, but headed straight to her truck, and after removing the hair elastic and the beach glass that had reminded her of Sam's eyes, she found her keys and drove straight off to Ocean Drive, the closest thing the island had to a main drag.

There was one real-estate office for every mile of the island's length and they were all located on three short blocks, squeezed in between an ice-cream parlor, a candy store, six boutiques that carried chic beachwear, eleven gift shops, and a newsstand that, during the season, carried *The New York Times*, *The Wall Street Journal*, *Barron's*, and *Business Week* for people who couldn't leave their work at home. In the winter, it was, like many of its neighbors, closed.

But selling and renting beach property was a year-round business and Josie knew she'd be able to find the information she wanted without waiting for Memorial Day. She parked in front of two adjacent realtors and, spying a familiar face, entered the door of the business to her left.

There were almost a dozen desks in the long room, but only the one immediately by the front door was occupied. The middle-aged man who sat there replaced his politely curious expression with a smile when he recognized her. "Josie Pigeon. I was thinking about you while I was showering last night."

"I hope that doesn't mean you're having trouble with the plumbing again."

"Nope. Just thinking about what good work you girls—I mean women—do. The room looks nice and neat and substantial. The way bathrooms looked when I was growing up. And I sure appreciate you talking me into having that wood around the walls."

Josie chuckled. "It's called beaded wainscoting. And it wasn't an original idea. It's probably what was there in the first place. Just think of Island Contracting when your wife talks you into remodeling the kitchen."

"Just as soon as I sell a million-dollar house. Maybe you're in the market for something larger than your apartment?"

"You wouldn't get much of a commission on anything I can afford. There are months when I have to scrimp and save to pay Risa the rent—and she doesn't charge me nearly what my place is worth."

"So if I can't sell you a house, what can I do for you? Have a seat. Maybe you'd like a cup of coffee?"

"Thanks, but I don't have time. I need some information. About Sam Richardson. He bought a house and the liquor store—"

"I know who he is. And I heard a rumor that you and he were seen together around town. You know you can't keep a secret on the island during the off-season."

Josie just smiled. She was learning, in fact, that it wasn't true. "I can't tell you why I need to know about him."

"You don't have to explain to me and I'd love to help you, but Arthur and Betsy handled the liquor-store deal and then found his house for him. I saw Betsy drive by just a few minutes ago. She could have been on her way to their office. You could try her there."

"Great. Thanks for the info. And let me know about the kitchen," Josie said as she left the office. She walked a few feet and found herself at the doorway to Harmon Realty. Betsy Harmon was at the rear of the room, talking into the phone, but she waved for Josie to enter before continuing with her conversation.

"Hi, Josie. What can I do for you?" she said, after hanging up. "I know you're busy with the Firbank house, so you're probably not interested in idle chat these days," she added before Josie could explain the reason for her visit. "And I hear the new owner of the liquor store is keeping you busy in the evenings."

Josie just smiled. She wondered what Betsy would think if she realized that one of the ways she and Sam had been kept busy was investigating a murder—and breaking into the Fish Wish. "Actually, Sam is the reason I wanted to talk to you," was all she admitted. "I understand you and your husband sold him the liquor store—and his house."

"Sure did. We're not as young as we used to be and the commission on the store is going to let us hire extra help this summer. And the house is my trip to Venice in the fall—at least that's what I'm trying to convince Arthur to do with the money. He wants to buy a new Boston Whaler—but you're not interested in that. So what do you want to know?"

Josie suspected that "everything" would elicit only vague generalities. "Do people usually buy two properties at one time?" was, she thought, a subtle way to start.

Apparently, she was wrong. Betsy leaned back and hooted. "Well, if that doesn't take the cake. I never would have thought of you as a gold digger, Josie Pigeon."

"Oh, I'm not. I'm not even interested in him romantically," Josie protested. "I want to know for . . . for some other reason." So much for spur-of-the-moment thinking.

"Listen, you don't have to lie to me. If you're interested in the man, I hope you get him. Just let me see what's in our files about those sales. Arthur handled them, so I don't know anything personally, but the least I can do is look. There's fresh coffee in back."

"Thanks." Josie accepted the offer this time. "Can I get a cup for you?"

"Sure. Here's my mug. I'll go look through the files. It will only take me a moment."

Josie found the coffee and an extra mug. As she returned to the desk, two steaming mugs in her hands, she heard Betsy cheer. "Eureka! You better snag this one and keep him on the hook, Josie. He's good-looking and rich."

"You're kidding! How rich? How do you know?"

"Well, he paid in cash for the store. And then had no trouble getting a very large mortgage on the house that he bought. The papers were filed, and five banking days later the mortgage was approved—it's one sign of an exceptional credit rating. Arthur doesn't keep the most complete records in the world, but as far as I can tell, he didn't show Mr. Richardson anything that cost less than six hundred thousand."

"Wow." All that and an MGB, too. Too bad she was so young and chunky. "You don't happen to have the address of where he lived in New York City, do you?"

Betsy looked over her wire-rim glasses. "Sure do. And I wouldn't give this to just anyone, but I'm a real sucker for young love. One fourteen East Seventy-second Street. Apartment 1007. I don't know much about the city, but it sounds like a pretty nice area to me. Between Park and Lexington probably. Where are you going?"

"To see for myself just how nice an area it actually is—and maybe meet a former neighbor or two who can give me some information," Josie answered, halfway out the door. "Don't tell anyone I was here or where I'm going. Okay?"

She didn't hang around to wait for an answer.

TWENTY-EIGHT

JOSIE DIDN'T WORRY about speeding on her way to the city; the truck didn't have enough power to go over the speed limit. And thanks to the person who used a nice neat grid to lay out the center of Manhattan, she easily found the apartment house. But if she hadn't managed to squeeze into the spot that a disintegrating Pontiac roared out of, she didn't know what she would have done with her truck. She waved her gratitude to the driver, but the deeply tinted windshield didn't allow her to see if the gesture was appreciated. Ignoring her stomach's wails that it was long past lunchtime, she locked her truck and headed into the sleek apartment lobby.

She would have liked to walk about for a few minutes and examine the mosaics formed from thousands of dollars' worth of Carrara marble, but the glare of the man sitting behind the large desk in the center of the room demanded her attention.

"I'm here to see someone in apartment one-oh-oh-seven," Josie explained.

Apparently she didn't explain enough. "Name?" he asked, showing no interest in whether or not she answered his question.

"Josie Pigeon." She smiled politely, thinking he could use an example of good manners.

"No one named Pigeon lives here."

"That's my name."

"And what is the name of the party you want to see?"

Josie realized she had been mistaken. He did know how to smile; it was just that he did it rather nastily. "I don't know the name. I only know the apartment number. You see, Sam Richardson lived—"

"Mr. Richardson. Yes. Is he expecting you?"

Josie blinked twice. Well, what the hell. "Yes."

"I gather you're here to do something about his leaky pipe while he's out of town?"

Josie suddenly realized how differently she was dressed than the rest of the people who had been traversing the lobby during this conversation. She would obviously never pass for a friend of a resident here. "Yes," she lied again. "My tools are in my truck. I wasn't sure what I would need."

"Apartment is on the tenth floor. Service entrance is to your left."

"Excuse me?"

Josie might never have gotten to 1007 if the leash connected to a large white poodle hadn't become entangled in a revolving door, requiring immediate attention. As the dog's owner's screams threatened to drown out the animal's outraged howls, Josie headed directly for the elevator and, ignoring the curious glances of the other passengers, proceeded to the correct floor. The apartment was across the hallway from the elevators. Josie found and pressed the tiny doorbell.

The door was answered immediately.

Josie was so stunned by the appearance of the woman on the other side that she could only stare. Besides, the confusion of the last hour had completely driven the explanation she was going to give for her presence out of her mind. "You . . . You're . . . Haven't I seen you before?" she asked, feeling like an idiot.

But the young—almost childlike, in fact—girl didn't seem at all surprised by the question. "Everyone says that. I'm all over the city."

"I . . . I don't live here." Josie explained, wondering if Sam could really be the law-abiding person he claimed to be; certainly a relationship between him and this child would be illegal.

"But you are here now. And Benetton has me plastered on every other bus shelter on the East Side." She surprised Josie by flinging her arms up in the air, bending her knees slightly, lowering her eyelids, and pouting. "Of course, my hair isn't braided now and—"

"You're a model!" Josie cried, recognizing this waif as the young thing that was displayed at twice life size to convince city dwellers to buy white cotton T-shirts, baggy jeans, and canvas boots. Josie wore a variation on that theme most every day. And she never looked at all like that photograph.

The girl grimaced. "Not really. I'm modeling for six months to get together enough money to travel. See, I was accepted at Sarah Lawrence, but I want to travel around the world for a year first. Wicked idea, yeah? And you'd think, like, if the admissions office understands, that my mother would, wouldn't you? But no. She said no way unless I could pay for it myself. And I did! Ha!" Suddenly she seemed to realize that she didn't know the woman she was talking to. "Do you know my mother? Or maybe Sam?"

"Sam Richardson?" Josie asked hesitantly.

"Sure. Sam. He and my mom used to date. This was his apartment."

Josie seemed to blank out after the phrase *used to date*. But she did realize that the young woman had used the past tense twice. "Who lives here now?" was her next question.

"Oh, well, my mom and I are using it for a while." For

the first time the teenager's extraordinary self-confidence seemed to diminish slightly. "It's a little difficult to explain. Did you come here to see my mother?"

"Actually yes," Josie answered. She didn't feel comfortable questioning this child.

"She's at Pizzocheri."

"I'm sorry?" Josie knew *pizzocheri* as a pasta-and-greens dish that Risa sometimes made.

"It's the new hot restaurant. About three blocks from here. They have good *grissini*. My mom is there with some friends."

Josie decided to be blunt. "I don't actually know her. How will I recognize her?"

"Oh, easy! She's wearing this really wicked shirt. Taupe silk with French cuffs. And black silk slacks. And black high-heeled sandals. I'll give you directions to the restaurant—in fact, they're on the back of this." She dug in her jeans pocket and pulled out a book of matches.

"Thanks," Josie said gratefully. She took them and left, after saying thanks again. Pizzocheri was a short walk away. But while the waif's mother was probably dressed exactly as described, so were half the women seated on the raw silk banquettes that ringed the tiny room, dimly lit even in the middle of the day. Josie would have loved to take notes. If Island Contracting survived the present crisis, Basil would adore this look.

She had attracted the attention of a young, thin man wearing his hair long and his tux pants slightly short. His socks were peachy (or maybe they were his ankles?) and, surprise, he was smiling.

"May I help you?"

"I'm Josie Pigeon—"

"Ms. Pigeon. How may I help you?"

"I'm . . . I'm looking for . . ." Why hadn't she asked for the name of the woman she was looking for? "Sam Richardson." It had worked once today, but it drew a blank here.

"I don't believe I am acquainted with Mr. Richardson."

"Well . . ."

"But I am." A lovely woman turned from the conversation she was having at a nearby table and trotted to the front of the room; she was wearing taupe and black, and it was easy to see where her daughter's looks had come from. "Sam has left the city, but we were friends once. I'm Jinx. Jinx Jones," she said, offering her hand.

"I . . . I know him now," Josie said, offering her own. "My name is Josie Pigeon."

"Nice meeting you." But her smile vanished as another thought struck her. "Is anything wrong? Has something happened to Sam?"

Josie was appalled. "Oh no. He's just fine. I just wanted to . . . to meet you and . . . and talk."

Jinx Jones smiled. "I'm with friends, but they're young parents and have been making noises about getting home to their baby for the past fifteen minutes. Why don't you join us for dessert and we can talk once they leave?"

"I'd like that," Josie admitted.

"I'll get you another chair," the helpful host offered.

"Thanks."

Josie suddenly realized why everyone in the room was so thin. No other body shape could easily slink through the narrow spaces left between the chairs and tables. She followed Jinx Jones as well as she could, feeling fat, foolish—and surprised by the warm reception she was receiving from strangers. Unlike the doorman over on Seventy-second Street, the people here didn't assume she was looking for the service entrance.

"I gather Shelby told you where I was?" Jinx asked, after she had introduced everyone and ordered fresh cappuccinos and pastry for all.

"If Shelby is your daughter, yes. I went to your . . . I was looking for Sam Richardson. Sort of."

Her last few words were drowned out by the general consternation that his name engendered. "How could he?" seemed to be the general feeling. Phrases like "a wonderful career," "fabulous lifestyle," and "paid-off co-op," were exchanged as a list of what Sam had given up. Josie was tempted to reply with a list of her own, beginning with fresh air and ending with jeans and T-shirts that cost a fifth of those Shelby was wearing all over town. But she listened.

Everything she learned verified what Sam had told her.

Apparently he had been a popular single man, working as a prosecuting attorney by day, eating and drinking with friends at night. She leaned forward when the woman in green mentioned a recent inheritance, but the topic moved from Sam to their baby's teething, and conscience-stricken at discovering themselves having fun while their infant was miserable, the parents departed, leaving Josie and Jinx alone together.

Josie toyed with the handle of her small cappuccino cup and waited for Jinx to continue the conversation.

But Jinx suddenly changed from outgoing to quiet and shy. "You're hungry, aren't you?" she asked, flipping silky brown hair off her forehead.

"No," Josie lied. Well, it wasn't really a lie; actually she was starving.

"You ate rather a lot of biscotti."

"Oh, I'm sorry!" Josie knew she was flushing.

"It doesn't matter. We're all on diets—always are. That was one of the things Sam used to complain about."

He didn't like thin women? Josie felt her heart start to beat a little faster.

"Of course, he could eat a pound of butter a day and not gain an ounce," Jinx continued.

Damn.

"Are you from his island?" Jinx asked, looking at Josie intently.

"Yes. I've lived there for almost fifteen years."

Apparently Jinx was having trouble knowing what to say, too. She picked up crumbs of biscotti with the tips of her long apricot-stained fingernails. "What did Sam tell you about me?" she finally asked.

"Oh." Josie was stunned by the question. "He said that you were an interior decorator." She stopped, realizing that she knew nothing else about Jinx Jones. "And that you had dated for . . . "—she improvised—"for a while."

"Three years. Off and on. Mostly on."

"I didn't actually come here to find out about you," Josie admitted. "I was interested in learning more about Sam. It's important," she added. "We're not dating or anything. It's more a business thing." She knew she sounded stupid. But apparently Jinx didn't mind.

"Sam is Sam," Jinx said. "He's one of the most honest men I've ever known. Well, that's no big compliment. But Sam is really absolutely honest and up-front. With him, what you see is what you get."

"Your friends seem to think that he made a major mistake by moving to the island."

"What did he tell you about that?" Jinx asked, leaning across the table.

"He said that he had become disillusioned with the legal system. Something about the criminals being victims first. And that he just couldn't be a part of it anymore. But your friends seemed to think that he left because he came into a lot of money."

"My friends don't exactly understand why a lawyer would become a liquor-store owner. They would have understood exactly if he had become a defense lawyer and started making more money, but conscience is slightly beyond some of them. I don't bother to explain much. And there was an inheritance. But it was years and years ago. Sam probably did use it to buy the liquor store—or his house. He must need money. He hasn't sold his apartment. In fact, my daughter and I are staying there."

"Why?"

"I'm a decorator, but a fair amount of my living comes from buying old apartments, remodeling them, and then selling at a profit. I sold my last loft right out from underneath my daughter and myself. And Sam came to the rescue. He did that even though we're not dating anymore." She looked at Josie. "You were curious about that, weren't you?"

"Sort of. We're not . . . you know, dating or anything, like I said. But there aren't many single men on the island and one of my coworkers is . . . you know, interested in him. Sort of. But you've pretty much verified everything that Sam told me . . . and her." Josie made a move to push herself away from the table.

"What do you do?" Jinx asked, following Josie's example.

"I own my own contracting business," Josie said proudly.

"Really? Then we have something in common, don't we?"

"Sort of." Josie waited while Jinx paid the bill and then they left the restaurant together.

"You must have a lot of pull there," Josie commented when they were out on the street.

"Why do you say that?"

"Because they let me in and treated me well even though I was dressed for work."

"Oh, they just assumed that you were an eccentric artist. No one else would have the nerve to try to get a seat in Pizzocheri dressed like that." Jinx took a step back and examined Josie from head to foot. "You know, you may be just what Sam was looking for."

TWENTY-NINE

"YOU CHECKED ME out?"

"I thought I should tell you about it," Josie said, after explaining the meeting she had had with Jinx. In truth, she hadn't been able to bring herself to ask Jinx not to talk about her visit to New York, so she had little choice but to admit how she had spent most of the day. Which reminded her . . . "I have to get back to the Firbank house."

"I'll go with you. I'd like to talk with you some more."

"My crew is going to think it's a little strange if you come along. I'm pretty sure at least a couple of them are still there."

"I wouldn't worry about that. They already think it's pretty strange that you just drove off and abandoned me this morning."

Josie gasped. "Oh, Sam, I'm sorry. I forgot about you."

"Please. I'd hate to get an inflated ego."

"Actually, I want to talk to you, too. I've been thinking

all the way back here and I have an idea," she said proudly. She thought it was a good idea.

"So do I. Why don't I give you a few minutes to get together with your crew and then come up to the house?"

"Sure." She was anxious to see what the crew had accomplished during the day, so she didn't hang around to chat.

She had taken the new bridge to the island and had recognized the cars in front of the Firbank house as belonging to Chris and Evelyn. They were still there when she returned and she parked the truck, hopped out, and trotted up the path to the house. Chris opened the door for her.

"I'm sorry. It was really important," Josie immediately started apologizing for her absence.

"Hey, don't worry about it. Wait until you see everything we've done!"

"What?"

"In the first place, we're going to be finished with the downstairs bathroom by tomorrow morning."

"Really? You're kidding!" Josie followed Chris to the room.

"Yeah. Betty has gone out to get some dinner and then she's going to come back and start laying the tile. She says she owes it to you to work all night. With the Firbanks coming so soon, I figured you wouldn't argue with her."

"Then the tiles were delivered?"

"Yeah. They're in those boxes over there. Betty arranged that, too," Chris added as Josie went over to peek in the top box. "Apparently she once dated the son of the man who owns the tile store out on the highway."

Josie chuckled.

"So what do you think?" Chris reached around the doorless doorway and flipped a switch. "Evelyn just finished with the ceiling fixtures. She pulled wires for the lights around the sink. They're back-ordered out at supply."

"Fantastic! Really fantastic. Where did this come from?" Josie asked, pointing to the beveled-glass window that had been placed in the wall.

"Evelyn found it upstairs when we were looking for the hinges."

"I don't suppose they've been located?"

"Since when did you become the local pessimist? We found them right where Betty left them. Of course, she didn't remember leaving them until Evelyn found them. Betty's been a little distracted recently."

"She's had good reason to be," Josie said, walking over for a closer look at the window. "This is very attractive. It must have come from the house in another remodeling. Where did you say it came from?"

"In the closet at the top of the stairs."

Josie took a deep breath. "You're kidding." She was absolutely sure it hadn't been inside when she had put Mike Rodney there. "Who found it?"

Chris frowned. "I think Evelyn. She's still working upstairs. You can ask her. If it's important."

"In the bedroom?"

"Yeah. She's working on the ceiling fixtures in there—so she might be up on the third floor. She pulled up some of the boards in the floor and wants to get them back down before tomorrow morning. In case the McCorkle family returns to do some more investigating."

"Oh no! I forgot all about that. Is Evelyn allowed to work up there? Didn't they tell everyone to stay on this side of the tape?"

"I told her that, but she said that if no one finds out . . ."

"Okay. Just make sure someone is down here to warn her if we get unexpected company."

"Fine. God, those guys are assholes. Someday I'd appreciate it if you would explain to me how you ever ended up dating Rick McCorkle," Chris said.

"I think lawyers call it temporary insanity."

"Speaking of lawyers," Chris said, "what's going on between you and Sam Richardson? He was a little distressed to discover that you had deserted him today, you know."

"I didn't mean to. I just forgot that I had driven him here," Josie confessed. "And there isn't anything going on between us. We're friends. Sort of."

"What does 'sort of' mean?"

"We have something in common." Well, what could she say? That they were both amateur detectives investigating a murder? It didn't sound likely to her—and she knew that it was true.

"Yeah. He told me that you two had talked a lot about crabbing. He was very interested in whether I went crabbing or not and which docks I thought were the best ones."

"You hate crab. And crabbing."

"I know, but I didn't tell him that. I figure I could learn to like most anything for an attractive single man like that. So I made up some answers and told him about the public dock down on Twenty-second Street."

And made yourself into a primary suspect in a murder investigation by lying, Josie thought. That would impress Sam. "Let's go upstairs."

They went, and a few minutes later Josie stood in the middle of the master bedroom, completely stunned. "This is wonderful! What a day's work!"

"Well . . . You've been awfully upset for the past few days," Chris began. "And we all know how hard you've been working and worrying about the company. We just got together after Sam left and decided that we'd give a hundred and ten percent to the job. I told you that we wouldn't let you down."

Josie felt tears begin to well up in her eyes. "You guys—"

"We know," Chris cut her off. "But I'm waiting for a compliment on how well I finished off the closet doors."

"They're fantastic," Josie said, not exaggerating one bit. She smiled at Chris. "You know, you look exhausted."

"To tell you the truth, I am. I thought I'd head home, go to bed, and then get an early start tomorrow morning. Tonight I have the entire house to myself and I'm looking forward to it. Unless there's anything else you want me to do today?"

"No, go. I'm going to go up and talk to Evelyn."

"I'll stop at the bakery on the way in tomorrow," Chris offered.

"My hips will love you. Get a good night's sleep," Josie called out, starting up the stairs to the attic. She heard the telltale rhythmic hammering of an experienced carpenter as she carefully lifted the yellow plastic tape that was strung across the banisters at the top of the stairs. Evelyn was in the far right corner, nailing floorboards back into place. She looked up when Josie started across the wide, empty room.

"Thank goodness. For a moment there I thought you were the police. Give me a minute, I'm almost finished here."

Josie saw that Evelyn had been working so hard that she was sweating and Josie knelt down to give her a hand. "I can't tell you how much I appreciate this," Josie said. "You guys have really come through for Island Contracting."

"Hey, a good job with a good company is something to protect," Evelyn said, sitting back on her heels. "What did you think about the ceiling fixtures above the windows downstairs?"

"I guess I didn't notice," Josie admitted, wondering what was underneath the spot where they were standing. "But I have a question for you," she added.

"What?" Evelyn got up awkwardly and stretched.

"Chris said that you found the great window that she put up in the bathroom on the first floor."

"Sure did. I was looking for the hardware that Betty had misplaced and came across that window leaning against the wall."

"Where? Chris said you found it in the closet under the stairs here." They were walking down from the attic as she spoke.

"Yes. I did. I thought Betty might have stashed the hardware in there. You know how crazy things have been around here recently."

"Yeah. Would you show me exactly where you found it?" She had to be sure that she hadn't missed that window the last time she had looked in the closet.

"Sure. Follow me." She put her tools down by the side of the hallway and they headed toward the closet. "I've got to get home to the kids, but it would help me if someone would mark out the location of the outlets in the master bedroom. I don't want to cut into the wrong place in Chris's moldings."

"Good thought. We'll let Chris do it. Then, if there's a mistake, she won't have anyone else to blame." Josie reached around Evelyn and opened the closet door. "Now, where . . . ?"

Josie dimly realized that she had just discovered the truth

of the expression *having your heart leap into your mouth.* She jumped back onto Evelyn's feet and gasped for breath.

Evelyn seemed to be more in control of herself. "Exactly what are you doing here?" she asked Sam Richardson.

"Looking for Josie," he answered blandly.

"In the closet?"

"Seemed as good a place to look as any. The light was on. Josie and I had a date," he continued. "She was expecting me."

"In the closet?" Evelyn repeated her question.

Josie was calming down enough to recognize a gleam of amusement in Evelyn's eyes. "I was up on the third floor with Evelyn," she explained, taking control of the situation.

"And I'm on my way home. So you two can be alone together in your closet," Evelyn said, now grinning broadly.

Sam had the grace to look embarrassed. Josie moved to help Evelyn pick up her tools.

"I'm fine. See you tomorrow," Evelyn said. "Talk to Chris about those outlets if she gets here before I do."

Josie promised to do just that and she and Sam stood together awkwardly until they heard Evelyn slam the front door and her boots clunk across the porch outside. Then she grabbed Sam's arm.

"I am so glad to see you. Let's get out of here. I want to talk. Something else has come up."

"What?"

"Evelyn found a window in here today when she was searching for some hinges that were lost—that doesn't really matter. The point is that someone must have put the window in here. Because I know it wasn't here when I was looking for the body!"

"So what do you think that means?"

"It means that I'm right about what I've been thinking."

"Well, I've been thinking, too," Sam said as they walked back out into the hallway. "In fact, I haven't been able to do anything but think about this all day. We've been checking out everyone, going in circles. Why don't we check out where the circles overlap?"

"That's what I've been thinking!" Josie cried, excited. Too excited to admit that she wouldn't have been able to put it so well. "We have to look at what all the suspects have in common . . . at the Firbank house." She sat back, a smug smile on her face.

Sam appeared astonished. "No. Not at the house. The house just happens to be where everything happened. It's located next door to the victim's home. Noel Roberts is where everyone overlaps. He personally chose everyone on your crew—you told me that yourself."

"Yes, but Noel's dead. What could he have to do with the murder?"

"Now listen. Just try to follow my thinking," Sam urged her.

"Try to follow your thinking? Are you saying that it's going to be difficult for me to follow your train of thought? That you are so sophisticated, so articulate, so brilliant and well educated that it just isn't possible for a poor little carpenter like me to make head or tails of your deductions?"

"It's not really deductive thinking."

"Now you think I don't know what deductive thinking is?" Josie knew she was overreacting. She knew that the strain of the last week had finally gotten to her. She knew she was looking and acting as unappealing as possible. She just didn't seem to know how to stop. And she wasn't actually sure that she did know what deductive thinking was.

"I think that this is the time to use logic and you seem to be more than a little emotional."

"That's one of the most sexist—"

"I didn't say anything about sex."

"What the hell were you talking about th—"

"Is this a lovers' quarrel or should I call out the National Guard?"

For some reason the quiet question seemed to stop the argument. Sam and Josie looked at Betty, standing in the doorway with a puzzled expression on her face, and then turned to look at each other.

"Would you like to come over to my apartment?" Josie heard herself ask.

"I'd love to," he answered.

And without another word, they walked out the door together.

Betty shrugged and returned to the tile job awaiting her in the bathroom.

THIRTY

"I'M A CARPENTER, not a housekeeper," Josie stated flatly.

"You didn't hear me say anything," Sam reminded her, folding up a cat-fur-covered afghan and placing it neatly across a pile of dirty laundry before sitting down on the couch. "Ouch!" He leaped up immediately.

Josie slid her hand under the flowered cushion. "Hey, look! You found my remote! Thanks." She added it to the pile covering her coffee table.

"It would be easier to find if you'd keep it on top of the set—but I'm sure your way suits you best," he added quickly, having no trouble interpreting the expression on her face.

Josie sighed. "Do you want a glass of wine?"

"Sure."

"I'm afraid it won't be what you're used to drinking."

"That's okay. Listen, do you have any notepaper or anything like that?" He glanced around the messy room as though uncertain where to look first.

"Under the phone book," Josie answered, heading for the refrigerator. "It's on the stereo," she added, when he started for the telephone. "The phone book is, I mean. And there's a notebook underneath." She knew she was confusing him, but her nerves seemed to have gotten the best of her. She hurried to get the wine.

"Pen?"

Josie opened her mouth. Did he think she was the local lost and found? Where had she seen a pen recently?

"Don't worry. I found one on the floor by the TV," he

called as she started opening and closing drawers in her kitchen.

Josie watched a lot of television and she knew that Jinx and women like her did not pour out two glasses of wine and carry them into the living room. They set the glasses on a tray and served them accompanied by tiny napkins and little tidbits to nibble on. But she didn't own a tray. She used paper towels when she wanted to wipe her hands and the last tidbits she had had in her kitchen were the sardines that she'd fed to Urchin yesterday.

"You're going to find out that I'm not much of a housekeeper—or a cook," she said, walking back to the couch.

"But you have lovely crystal."

Josie looked down at the glasses in her hands. "They are, aren't they? I found them out at the Firbank house."

"Are you going to give me one of them?"

Josie felt herself begin to blush. "Sure. It's from a jug—from California." She didn't add that it had cost about the same as the diet soda she had bought at the same time. She passed him a goblet of wine. "Don't say I didn't warn you."

"Do you usually steal things from the places where you work?"

"I didn't steal anything. These glasses were left in the trash pile behind the house. I asked the Firbanks about them. They said they didn't care what the crew took. They're not interested in old things. I think Mrs. Firbank refers to them as 'retro.' And we didn't take everything. You should see the window that Chris saved and used when she remodeled the bathroom on the first floor."

"About Chris. Tell me again how she met Noel Roberts." From his expression, Josie could tell that Sam wasn't overwhelmingly enthusiastic about the wine, but he drank it anyway.

"They met working on a Habitat for Humanity house. Noel stopped off to donate materials that Island Contracting couldn't use."

"Is that usual?"

"What?"

"Is that what Island Contracting usually does with over-runs?"

Josie thought for a moment before answering. "Actually, we rarely have problems like that. And when we do, we usually either send whatever it is back to the manufacturer or use it up on another job. But it's like Noel to think about a charity when faced with a problem—and it's even possible that he just ordered the materials, planning to give them away. He was like that."

"And that's where he met Chris." He put down his wine. "And she wasn't a carpenter at the time."

"No. She wasn't."

"But he encouraged her to go back to school and learn carpentry and then he hired her as a finishing carpenter."

"A finish carpenter," Josie corrected him. "And yes, that's true."

"In fact, he changed her life."

"He improved her life."

"Well, we don't know where her life would have gone otherwise, but I think we can agree that he changed her life from what it was at the time."

"So?" Josie put down her glass. For some reason, being with him made her drink too much too fast.

"So let's think about the other women on your crew."

"Are you trying to convince me that Noel Roberts had anything to do with the murder?"

"He is the common denominator," Sam stated flatly. "Every time we talk about the possible suspects, we come back to him."

"That's just because the suspects are the crew of Island Contracting. And they were all hired by Noel."

"It's not just that they were all hired by him, it's that their lives were changed by him."

"Improved."

"If you will, their lives were improved by him," Sam agreed with her. "But think about it. Most people are hired by a company and they are given a job. But in the case of Island Contracting, they were given more than that."

"In the case of Island Contracting, they were given a life," Josie insisted.

"No, only a chance for a life."

"What do you mean?"

"Let's take yourself. You had to pay back Noel for your education by working for him for a couple of years."

"True."

"But you had to make the job and your life work by yourself."

"Yes." But she answered more slowly this time.

"It's like Chris's new approach to her mother—one that Noel indirectly taught her. She is going to give her mother a chance to sink or swim on her own."

"That's true. And that is what Noel believed in. So how does this get us to the identity of the killer?"

"When Noel hired these people, he was giving them a new chance at life. Which would imply some sort of complication in their past, wouldn't it? Noel hired people who needed to make a change and he gave them a chance to do just that."

"So you think the answer to all this is in someone's past." Josie knew that she was reacting so strongly because she felt threatened by him snooping around in her past.

"Don't you?"

"It makes sense, but we're all bonded and insured. Everyone's gone through a background check." Besides, her instincts told her that he was missing something. "It's almost like you're blaming Noel for this murder!"

"I certainly am not."

"It sounds to me like you think he hired a murderer—gave her a second chance—to kill somebody!"

"I said nothing like that."

"You . . ."

They stopped arguing as a vision in black lace walked in the apartment door.

"*Carciofi alla Giudia.* The first artichokes of the season. They are very healing. And asparagus and prosciutto. The thinnest that can be bought." Risa held out a heavy earthenware platter piled high with food. Josie bit her lips so she didn't smile at the astounded expression on Sam's face. She had given up trying to figure out where Risa found the time or the ingredients for her lavish and impromptu meals.

"Eat," Risa insisted. "It is impossible to fight while you are digesting good food. Is gift from the gods, not to be denied." She put the food on the last unoccupied spot on the coffee table, passed out small plates and napkins, pulled up a chair, and sat down across from them. "Eat. Both of you eat."

They ate. They didn't talk. They ate and ate and no one said anything until Risa offered to get Sam some bread to sop up the liquid on the now-empty platter.

Josie was amused to see Sam's embarrassment. He had been eating as though starving and Risa's offer seemed to remind him of the fact. "I don't think we need anything else," Josie assured her.

"You are without a doubt the best cook I've ever had the privilege to know," Sam complimented her. "Everything you make is superb."

Risa smiled. "Then my little Josie told you that I prepared most of the meal the other day?"

"She said something about it."

Josie, who hadn't heard herself referred to as little since graduating from kindergarten, felt the color of her face begin to compete with her hair. "I—" she began.

"Did she tell you that I am going to be giving her cooking lessons? Passing down the traditions of my family?"

Josie didn't bother to argue. Risa would tell the story she wanted to tell and it would all be only flattering to her. She drained her wineglass and moved forward to put it back on the table. And missed.

"Your *bella* glasses!" Risa jumped up from her seat. "Ah, thank heavens. It did not break."

Sam picked up the glass he had been drinking from. "These really are wonderful, aren't they?"

"Risa thinks they are Venetian crystal."

"They *are* Venetian crystal. You talk about something that I know about," Risa said.

"You found them at the Firbank house, right?"

"Yes. When we were cleaning up before the initial demolition."

"Were they packaged?" Sam asked. "You know, wrapped in plastic or something so that they wouldn't break?"

"No. They were just lying on top of the pile of rubbish and junk. You know, old curtain rods and the curtains themselves. Boxes of odds and ends from the backs of kitchen cupboards. Bits of carpeting. Things like that." She saw how interested Sam had become. "Why?"

"It didn't strike you as strange that they hadn't broken?"

"Not really."

"Did the Firbanks clean out this debris by themselves?" he asked.

"Wow! You've never met the Firbanks, have you? I'll bet they don't pick up their own socks; they pay people to do that type of thing. There's not a chance in hell that they would ever sort through stuff that someone else left behind. That's probably why they could have cared less about the crew scavenging through the refuse pile. They believe in new and chic." She noticed that he wasn't paying attention anymore and she stopped talking.

"You know what I think, *cara*? I think we should leave this man alone to think."

"I can't do that. This is my problem, not his problem." Josie picked up the notebook that Sam had found earlier and began to draw.

"What are you doing?" Sam asked, after she had scribbled on the pad for a few minutes. "Is that a house?" he asked, looking at the result of her industry.

"It's the Firbank house. I've marked where—"

"Hmm. Pipes and stuff," he said absentmindedly. "Would you mind if I poke around in Island Contracting's computer again?"

"Not at all."

"I know how rude it is to eat and run. . . ." Sam began, standing up.

"No, a man must do his work," Risa insisted.

"In this case, I'm afraid a woman must, too," Josie said, getting up. "I have to go with Sam."

"Of course. Of course. I would think of nothing else. Go, my little angels. I will lock up for you." And Risa shooed them out the door.

"You have some landlady. I thought she was going to tell us that the night is still young," Sam said, grinning.

"She lived a very romantic life at one time."

"Where did she learn to cook like that?"

"I don't actually know," Josie answered. "Risa only talks about those parts of her past that she wants to talk about."

"Isn't that true of us all?" Sam asked, starting up his car now that they were both inside.

"What do you mean by that?"

"Hey! I didn't mean to offend you. After all, you're the one that spent part of the day checking on me."

Josie was silent the rest of the way to the office. It was true that she had gone to New York to check on him. Was he now heading to Island Contracting's computer to do the same to her? And had Noel treated her as kindly as Jinx had treated Sam?

THIRTY-ONE

A COUPLE OF hours later the tiny office looked like an argument for the computer information age. In the center of the room, Sam sat at Noel's old desk, peering into the glimmering monitor, pressing buttons with his right hand and petting a contented kitten with his left. Behind him, Josie knelt on the hardwood floor surrounded by sheets of notebook paper, some of which she had piled up neatly, some of which had been confiscated by three hyperactive kittens. She looked very unhappy.

But Sam was too busy to notice and, to Josie, seemed to be positively reveling in the words passing before him on the computer screen. She frowned, got up, and went out the back door to the tiny deck behind the building. There, as the rays of the setting sun reflected off the bay, she pulled up and checked the contents of her crab trap.

She was tossing females back into the brine when she realized that Sam Richardson had joined her.

"I think I know who did it," he said softly.

She didn't look at him. "I do, too." She fastened the top of the metal trap and dropped it back into the sea. Then she leaned against the wall.

Sam perched up on the rail and, together, they watched the sun sink into the water and marsh grass. Egrets and snowy ibis flew overhead. For a while neither of them spoke. Then Sam pointed out the head of a large turtle that broke the surface tension of the bay.

"I've never spent much time on this side of a barrier island," he said, his voice almost a whisper. "The bay is different, isn't it?"

"It's wonderful. Much more peaceful than the ocean, of course."

"And more pungent," Sam added, taking a deep breath of the salty air.

"The smell of the estuary. Things rot here. And then life comes from that rot." She brushed her hair off her face. "That's what Noel used to say and I never understood it. Until now."

"Sounds like it was almost his philosophy of life," Sam muttered.

"That's what you've been reading about in the computer, isn't it?"

"I should have seen it before," he answered. "Your Noel Roberts was some guy. He hired people to save their lives."

"But when you create a new life, you have to make sure that your past doesn't reappear and destroy what you've created."

He just nodded. "But we need proof."

"We have it. In fact, it's probably decorating someone's home at this very minute."

He gave her a puzzled look. "Like that beautiful crystal?"

"Exactly like the beautiful crystal. And that's why I should have seen this earlier. That crystal doesn't fit my lifestyle. It stands out. The answer was standing out as well."

Sam shook his head. "I don't understand what you're getting at. I found the answer because Noel was also a remarkable judge of character. He knew the person whose past could catch up with them and cause problems. But I don't have any proof. And we can't let her get away with murder. Who knows what else might happen that will threaten the life she's created?"

"But it will never happen again! If we hadn't been hired to work on this house . . ." Josie realized the stupidity of what she was saying. "I know. She can't get away with killing him, no matter what her reason was." She stood up. "I guess we'd better get going."

"Where to?"

"To the Firbank house. To get you the proof you need." She snatched up the paper on which she'd been doodling and started for the door. "Aren't you coming?"

"You don't think it's awfully late?"

"Betty's still there," Josie answered, and continued on her way. She noticed that Sam didn't hesitate to join her.

They drove the familiar road between the office and the Firbank home slowly. Josie wondered if Sam was now also unwilling to attract any unnecessary police attention. Sure enough, Betty's car was still standing in the street before the house.

"Have you given her permission to spend the night?" Sam asked, putting on the brake.

"No. She's working late. She's volunteered to lay ceramic tiles in the downstairs bathroom. It could take all night, though," Josie admitted. "This is something new for her and she wants to prove herself. And it's possible that she doesn't want to be home alone tonight. Maybe staying busy is good therapy for her."

"How did she take the news of Mike Rodney's death?"

"She was sad, but I got the impression that she was going to live. She knew damn well that he was taking advantage of her. I guess some people don't learn their lesson unless they're hit over the head more than once."

"I gather you're talking about me." Betty appeared in the hallway. There were traces of mastic in her curly hair.

Josie began to feel a familiar blush of embarrassment and started to speak, but Betty cut her off.

"Don't worry about it. I know the truth when I hear it." Betty turned to Sam. "How are you tonight?"

"Fine, thanks. But I have a few questions."

"I'll answer anything that you ask—as long as I can do

it while I lay tile. This is taking longer than I thought it would. And you're going to have to stand in the doorway while I work. It's a pretty small room."

"How's it going?" Josie asked, peeking around the corner into the bathroom.

"Fine. It was a lot of fun laying out the pattern, but it's been slow going from then on. But I'll get faster. Remember how long I used to take to frame in a window or do other simple jobs."

"Yeah."

"Noel always said that practice was the only way to increase competence and speed—and he sure was right," Betty said, returning to her task.

"I was wondering if you would answer some questions that I have about Noel," Sam asked, squatting down on the floor to speak to Betty more easily. "And about you and your coworkers," he added. "You see, we're trying to find out who murdered Mike Rodney."

It was a statement that attracted Betty's attention. "That's why you both have been spending so much time together?" she asked, tears staining her cheeks. "Everyone was thinking that you two had fallen in love." She looked up at Josie. "We were all happy for you—even Chris."

"Chris? Why wouldn't Chris be happy for us?" Sam asked Josie.

"It doesn't make any difference," Josie insisted. "And we're not in love," she added to Betty. "Are you okay?"

"I'm fine. It's just been a horrible day." She looked down at the floor. "But I'm going to get this done. Don't worry."

"That's not import—" Sam began.

"I can't tell you how much I appreciate that," Josie interrupted. "But it's not really as important as solving this murder. And there are some questions. . . ." She was reluctant to ask Betty for help right now and it could be heard in her voice.

"Go ahead and ask," Betty insisted, taking a deep breath. "I hate to admit it, but I'm not as miserable about his death as I should be. I guess I didn't really love him—just his lifestyle," she said, looking at Josie.

Josie nodded her understanding.

Sam just looked confused. "You wanted to ask her some questions," he reminded Josie.

"They're going to sound strange. Some don't have anything to do with Mike Rodney."

"What can I tell you about Mike Rodney, anyway?" Betty muttered almost to herself. "That he's married, that he has children, that he's rich enough to own a second home at the beach which provides him with a place to have affairs with stupid local girls."

"Girls? Were there more than one?" Sam interrupted to ask. "Maybe other members of the crew?"

"He sure knows how to make a girl feel special, doesn't he?" Betty asked, with a glance at Josie.

"Men." Josie offered the standard response.

"Yeah. Men."

Sam just bit his lip, shook his head, and glanced up at the ceiling.

"I'd like to think that Mike thought I was special," Betty insisted. "And he certainly wasn't stupid enough to tell me if he was having an affair with anyone else on the crew. Not that I think anyone else on the crew was stupid enough to get involved with him."

"Why do you say that? Was there something wrong with him? I mean . . ." Sam seemed to realize that perhaps he was asking the wrong person to criticize.

"You mean do I know anything about him that would make someone want to kill him," Betty said.

"Exactly," Sam agreed.

"Well, I can't say that I do. I loved him—well, I thought I loved him and he was nice to me." Betty looked down at the pattern of tiles laid out on the floor. "I guess the truth was that I didn't know anything at all about him, did I?"

"You've been in his house. Did you learn anything about him from his house?" Josie knew the clue they were looking for didn't lie in the house next door, but she had a feeling Sam was not getting the answers he wanted.

"His house is wonderful," Betty said wistfully. She looked up at Josie. "You said you'd been in it. You know what I mean."

"I do. It's certainly one of the most interesting places I've ever seen. All those different kinds of stone."

"Mike's father is a famous geologist. Some of those rocks are very rare specimens that come from exotic places. There were lamps made from chunks of agate next to the bed in the master bedroom that you wouldn't believe!"

"Rocks? Stones?" Sam looked like the discussion had gotten beyond him.

"Mike Rodney's house is decorated in a rather unusual fashion," Josie explained. "You know how decorators can be. Go on," she added to Betty, ignoring Sam's suspicious look.

"He was very successful in his business—of course, he couldn't afford a house like that unless he was."

"He must have been a jock. There's quite a bit of sporting equipment in the shed at the back of his property," Sam suggested another topic.

"That's true. He was in wonderful shape," Betty agreed.

"Did you ever go fishing with him?"

"Fishing? No, never." Betty seemed surprised by the question.

"You haven't actually been with him during the fishing season, have you?" Josie asked, trying to clear up details for Sam.

"Not really."

"Wait a second," Sam ordered. "This isn't a long-term relationship? When did you meet Mike Rodney?"

"Just a few months ago."

"But when exactly?"

Betty thought for a moment. "It must have been eight—no, nine weeks ago." She looked up at Josie. "We began on this project when? Ten weeks ago?"

"Exactly ten weeks on Monday."

"So you met Mike Rodney at the same time as you began working here?" he asked Betty.

"Sure," she agreed. "I was jogging on the beach nearby because I was working here. It was before work."

"You do the work you do after an early-morning jog?" Sam sounded incredulous.

Josie suspected that Betty's jogging had been designed to provide an opportunity to meet the man next door, but she wasn't going to betray the secrets of her sex to Sam.

"Well . . ." Betty began her answer slowly, "Yes. I always gain a few pounds over the winter and it was warming up, so I was anxious to work them off."

"I'm sorry. I didn't mean to interrupt you. It's just that I know a woman you should meet."

Josie knew he was thinking of Jinx Jones, but she didn't say anything. Betty continued her story.

"Well, we met on the beach and we . . ." She hesitated. "We started seeing each other almost immediately. We had a lot in common," she added rather defensively, although no one had said anything.

"At my age you stop trying to understand what attracts each half of a couple to the other. It's enough that they've found each other, isn't it?" Sam asked gently.

"That's how Mike and I felt," Betty said, apparently grateful for the understanding. She stood up and stretched out. "I'm going to get some coffee. Anyone else want a cup?"

"No." Josie said.

Sam just moved out of the way so that Betty could go into the large kitchen.

"Weren't you a little suspicious about how quickly he became interested in you?" Josie asked. "I mean, I know how attractive you are and everything, but . . ."

"I know what you mean and it was strange, but Mike was like that."

"Like what?" Sam asked, wanting specifics.

"Impulsive." She poured coffee in a stained mug and stared out the window at the side of the Rodney house.

Josie looked up at Betty suddenly. "How old was Mike Rodney?" she asked, remembering that Chris had said Betty was involved with an older man.

"I don't know . . . thirty . . . thirty-one. . . ."

"Son of a gun," Josie said, nodding. It was beginning to make sense—finally.

"He didn't seem that old, though—my God!" Betty splashed coffee across the counter and leaped into the air. "He's there! That's Mike!" she cried out, and charged out the back door.

THIRTY-TWO

"WHAT . . . ?" SAM STARTED after her.

"No, it's okay," Josie insisted, grabbing his arm. "That's her Mike Rodney. Not the man who was murdered." She would have continued to explain, but the smooth muscle under her fingers was a slight distraction.

"Then who was murdered?"

"Mike Rodney, Senior—the family man, fisherman, and famous geologist. I didn't realize it until she started talking about him just now. See, Chris described the man Betty was dating as older. I just didn't realize that what seems older to someone in her early twenties might not seem older to someone my age."

"Or mine," Sam agreed.

"But it makes sense." She frowned. "Well, it almost makes sense. Certainly a man in his thirties is too young to have anything to do with the first murder."

"There was another murder?"

"Oh, yes. I'm sure of it," Josie said. "This house has quite a history, when it comes right down to it."

Sam sighed. "I know who did it, but only because Noel specifically singled out only one person on your crew as a possible danger."

"Let's go up to the third floor." Josie started searching in the pockets of her overalls.

"Is this what you're looking for?" Sam asked, plucking a sheet of paper from a back pocket and handing it to her.

"Yes. Thanks." She started toward the stairs. "Are you coming?"

He glanced out the window in time to see Betty make a

fist and land a left on Mike Rodney, Junior's handsome jaw. "Sure," he agreed, grinning.

Josie unfolded the sheet of paper as she walked up the stairs.

"I know this job is important to you, but do you have to think about it right now?" Sam asked, lifting the yellow police tape for her to climb under as they arrived at the stairwell.

"Huh? Oh, I'm not thinking about work. I'm thinking about the murder. See." She turned and handed him the sheet of paper.

Sam stared at the diagram for a few moments. "I'm sorry, but I don't see it. I'm not even sure which floor that depicts."

"Sorry. That's my fault." She pulled the paper from his hands and laid it out on the floor. "See, I started to diagram the second floor because I was focusing on the closet—because that's where I found the body. But then I realized that it was the attic that I should be paying attention to. It's up here that all the unexplained work has been going on."

"Like what?"

"Well, first Betty spent all those extra hours on the roof and then Evelyn replaced all the wiring in the master-bedroom ceiling from up here."

"But isn't that the way it's normally done?" Sam asked as Josie wandered to the corner of the room.

"It can be. We do usually prefer to tear up an unfinished space, but that wouldn't explain why Evelyn spent so much time in this corner. Look at the diagram," she added. "I superimposed the third floor over the second. And that's when I realized what was going on. The master bedroom isn't below this." She knelt down and, taking the appropriate tools from her toolbox, began to pull up the floorboards. "Besides, Evelyn was complaining about all the time Betty spent up here—I wondered about that. We're all pretty good at just letting everyone go about their own business. I should have known that something was up then. Evelyn must have felt uncomfortable with the possibility of Betty looking in at what she was doing. I just hope she didn't have time to remove all the evidence."

"What are you looking for?"

"Well, it seems to me that the stash is probably long gone. I don't mean drugs or anything like that, but there must be something." She squinted down into the hole that she had just created. "Well, there *was* something here."

Sam peered down the hole and then sat back on his heels. "Look, I just don't get it. I know that Evelyn did it because, in fact, she is the only person on your crew that Noel had suspicions about."

"How do you know that?"

"He had an extensive background check done on her. The rest of you—and you all have pretty varied backgrounds—he seems to have trusted to have told the truth about your lives."

"Then Evelyn didn't tell him that she had been in prison?" Josie remembered that Evelyn had claimed to have done so.

"She did actually. But he checked her out. And his investigation included the fact that there had been a death involved in her arrest for drug dealing. A suspicion of death, I should say."

"The kid who went to the rock concert after meeting his friends here at the house." She nodded. "Yes, I figured that out."

"But there was no evidence that she had killed him. According to the records, this kid just vanished into the horde that travels with these concerts and Evelyn was arrested for dealing."

"But he didn't," Josie insisted. "That's the whole point. He didn't die at the concert. He came back here. And there must be evidence that he'd been here."

"What?"

"That's what I'm looking for. Look, I've marked the location of everything that was found in the house—that I know about—on the diagram."

"Wait a second."

She turned and took the paper from his hands. She had been proud of her unusual organization and was surprised by his confusion. "Look. My glasses were found on the refuse pile out back; that's why a list beginning with goblets is in the right-hand corner behind the house."

"Okay. That makes some sense. And you've also written

'wind'—no, it says 'two winds,' doesn't it? Were there wind socks found or—"

"Windows," Josie explained impatiently. "That means window. Stained glass, to be exact. Evelyn found one and took it home to hang on her wall."

"But there were two windows, weren't there? What about the one Chris found and installed in the downstairs bathroom?"

"Chris and Evelyn found it in the closet, but of course, it wasn't around when I put Mike Rodney, Senior in there and it certainly wasn't there after he was moved. After all, I found that tiny comb that someone had lost on the floor. I certainly would have noticed a large window, so she had to be lying. She must have moved it."

"Chris?"

"No! Evelyn!" Josie insisted, getting angry. "What could Chris have to do with all this?" And then she stopped and took a deep breath, all the blood draining from her face.

"Are you all right?" Sam leaped to his feet.

Josie tugged at a lock of hair and pursed her lips. "No. We were wrong—it wasn't Evelyn. It was Chris, wasn't it? She was the intermittent problem that has been coming up throughout the project."

"I don't think I understand," Sam admitted.

"Think about it. She was the first person to go through this house. She volunteered to come over while I was so bogged down in the paperwork."

"So?"

"Because the house was opened for Island Contracting that morning and Chris checked it out while I was working. Then, later the same day, the rest of the crew came through it with me and that's when we found the glasses—and the windows—and the vase that Evelyn took to make into the lamp. And those are all very, very fragile things. They couldn't possibly have been lying around very long or they would have been broken. And that other window must not have been there then—or either Evelyn would have taken it or it would have been carted away with the rest of the trash pile."

"That's true," Evelyn said, suddenly appearing at the top

of the stairway. "I thought of that when I saw the window in the bathroom downstairs."

"You know more about this than you told us," Josie said grimly.

"And now is the time to tell us everything," Sam added sternly.

"I gather you've heard that I used to travel with the Dead . . . the Grateful Dead," she added to Sam.

"I'm not all that old," he insisted, not bothering to add that some of the band members were celebrating birthdays in the same decade that he was.

"I didn't know if Josie had explained to you," Evelyn replied a little defensively.

"Just tell us the story yourself," Josie suggested.

"Well, this particular concert was like most of them. I was doing . . . well, what I did back in those days, and I met up with a nice group of kids. They were mostly college kids and they were on spring break and were partying. One of the group had invited friends to stay at his parents' vacation home on this island and a bunch of their friends had crashed their party and ended up flopping here." She looked around the attic. "This attic is a great location for a flop because there are windows on all four sides and you can see anyone coming.

"One of the kids showed me this hole in the floor. They stashed . . . uh, valuables there. At the time the wood boards just slipped on and off. In fact, they did that until a few weeks ago when I nailed them tightly shut."

"After Chris had taken out the contents and thrown them on the garbage pile out back."

"I guess so. It was empty when I found it. But of course, it wasn't empty the last time I saw it years ago. Then it was stuffed full of things that had been borrowed from the rest of the house and items brought back from the concert."

"Like what?" Sam asked.

"Well, like the handblown bong . . . which is what the vase was that I took and made into the lamp base. No one will ever know its original use and it's very attractive, if I do say so myself. One of my best efforts."

"You've been making vases from found objects for a long time, haven't you?" Josie asked.

"Yes. That was one of the ways I supported myself during my travels back then," Evelyn answered. "Not everything I did was illegal. And of course, it helped to get away with selling illegal things if I could show a profit from a more legit activity."

"Did you make lamps from chunks of quartz when you were here?" Josie asked, remembering Betty's description of the Rodneys' master bedroom.

Evelyn paused. "I could have. I did work in crystals and geodes—and I made stuff for some of the kids, but I don't really remember what specifically. In fact, that lamp making is what convinced me to train as an electrician when I was in prison and offered the chance."

"What do you remember about that night? It was only one night that you spent here?" Sam returned to what he considered the important questions.

"Definitely. I remember that, but not much else. The partying turned into fighting. I remember coming out of a blurry sleep and discovering that a young man had been killed. I remember that two people threw the dead . . . murdered . . . young man in the sea and then we all split as fast as we could and tried to forget what had happened.

"But in my case it didn't work. Drifters can get killed and no one looks too hard for them, but wealthy male college students get full-scale police investigations. I had been seen with the group that came here. The police could never pin anything about that night on me. And I was too high to know exactly what happened. I've never admitted to being here before now, in fact. But the police watched me long enough to see what I was doing. They caught me dealing and I ended up in jail."

"So what makes you think Chris had anything to do with this?" Sam asked Josie.

"I don't think she just had something to do with it all. I think she killed Mike Rodney."

"Is that the name of the man that was killed the night after the concert?" Evelyn asked.

"No, there's been another murder. I'll explain it all to you later," Josie insisted, and then turned all her attention on Sam.

"See, two other people knew what happened that night. Mike Rodney and the person who killed him."

"I don't get it," he insisted.

"Look, this house sat here and held its secrets for years and years. No one came in and no one looked around—not seriously. A few real-estate agents came through and they brought prospective buyers. But no one crawled around on the floors and there was no risk of anyone tearing up floor-boards until we started renovations. So the evidence that a murder had happened here was hidden until someone started to worry that someone in Island Contracting might find it—so it was disposed of. Probably tossed into the sea."

"And Mike Rodney?"

"Mike Rodney must have been here the night of the original killing. He may even have bought his house to keep an eye on this one. I suppose we may never know that now. But I guess when he found out that Island Contracting was going to renovate, he got nervous and sent his son to pick up Betty on the beach. Betty, of course, was supposed to be a spy—although she doesn't know anything about that. Mike Rodney, Senior didn't get to be so rich without knowing an opportunity when he saw one. But he left everything in his son's hands. Only the son wasn't so interested in spending his weekends in a cold, uninhabited summer community off-season and, after a short fling with Betty, stopped showing up without finding out what the father wanted to know. We can probably ask him about all this," she added.

"If he's still capable of speech after Betty vents her anger," Sam muttered.

Josie gave him a questioning look before she continued. "Whatever. Anyway, Mike Rodney, Senior came to the house at night and Chris, realizing that he was looking for something, killed him. It was probably a mistake, of course. He just wanted to keep the past buried, too," she said sadly.

"I don't recognize Chris," Evelyn said slowly. "It's been a lot of years, but I think I'd know if she had been there. There were only a half-dozen people. . . ."

"But I'll bet you'd recognize her mother," Josie said quietly. "And no matter what she said, Chris still hadn't stopped protecting her mother. Or maybe it was killing Mike Rodney that made her realize she had gone overboard, that she was overprotecting her mother."

Evelyn and Josie leaned together and put their arms around each other. Sam stood by silently. "She'll be arrested and . . . and go to prison, won't she?" Josie asked no one in particular.

"Probably," Sam answered quietly.

"But she's had such a difficult life," Josie protested, tearing up. "And she thought she had a good reason to do it. She thought she was protecting her mother."

"They always think they have a good reason to do what they do," Sam murmured, staring out the dormer window at the boiling surf. "That's what makes it so sad."

THIRTY-THREE

"YOU NEVER KNOW the way things will turn out, do you?" Sam asked, tossing the summer decorating issue of a famous newspaper across the table to Josie.

Risa's elegant, long silver fingernails reached it first. She opened it to the place he had been staring at and shook her head in disbelief. "You Americans have such strange standards. Graffiti done by an artist is one thing. This . . . this was done by a carpenter."

"One of the best carpenters I've ever known," Josie corrected Risa as she pulled a claw from a boiled crab and dipped the meat in melted butter. "Of course, it wasn't intended to be art. Chris thought that the police would keep everyone from entering a crime scene. That's why she painted the attic walls and then called nine-one-one to announce a break-in. She was worried about all the time

Evelyn and Betty were spending on the third floor and the roof, so she tried to keep them out of there."

"Still. You spent months renovating that house and it turned out beautifully. It is light. It is airy. It is everything a beach house should be. And then, *cara*, you were so excited about this newspaper doing an article about the renovation."

"No, they were doing it about the interior decoration, but I thought that maybe, just maybe, they would include some of our work," Josie corrected Risa.

"They did. They included this attic mess. Americans!" Risa left it at that and returned to her meal.

It was a beautiful summer evening. Josie had spent the day crabbing off the dock behind Island Contracting's office while Sam tried once again to organize her paperwork. In return for his efforts, she had promised him a meal he wouldn't forget. She had caught dozens of crabs and boiled them along with ears of corn over a small barbecue set up on the deck.

"Why did the Firbanks leave the graffiti in place?" Sam asked, trying to find some meat in the belly of the crustaceans.

"Let me do that," Josie suggested, taking his plate from him. "They didn't have to. We offered to repaint as soon as the evidence men were through, but the Firbanks had a friend who owns a gallery in the city down for the weekend and apparently the man thought that the idea of having a personal spa decorated in what he called 'slum motif' was terribly original. So they refused to let us change a thing." She picked through the shells and created a small mound of nice white meat, which she handed back to Sam. "I couldn't believe it. After all the time we spent trying to keep them from seeing that mess . . ." She sighed. The ways of the sophisticated were clearly beyond her.

"Well, maybe it's better that that newspaper reporter didn't put your name in the article," Risa said consolingly. "You will get other work, you know. After you finish this restaurant for Basil, all the summer people will see your beautiful work and will hire you to do the same things for their houses. Just you wait and see."

"Basil was in the store last week and he seemed very happy with the job," Sam added.

Josie knew that these two nice people had gotten together to keep her from thinking about Chris's trial, which was due to begin any day now, so she did her best to smile. "He turned out to be easy to work for."

"He thinks very highly of you," Sam said.

"Of Island Contracting, you mean," Josie said.

"No, of you. He told me that Noel always said all you needed was confidence and that Noel had turned out to be right." Sam got up and went over to the ice chest for beer as he spoke.

Josie flushed. It was true that she tended to think less of herself because she hadn't had any formal education and didn't know why everyone said Sam's name in such a knowing manner when they were introduced to him.

"Of course," Sam was continuing as he handed her another beer, "I, myself, appreciated that fact from the first time I met you. When you have a name like mine, people are always using it to prove that they have at least a passing acquaintance with English literature. You were modest enough not to bother with such silliness. I found it refreshing. So don't get overconfident. I don't need that."

"What you need is a nice man," Risa hissed in Josie's direction.

"What she needs is a competent accountant," Sam insisted. "I cannot believe the mess your records are in. Why, I couldn't tell whether or not you've purchased one hammer, two, or two dozen from the notes you wrote down."

"Two," Josie answered. "The murder weapon that vanished and the one that was found covered with blood on the public dock."

"What?" Risa cried. "When you told me this story, I thought you said the one at the pier was the murder weapon. Now you say there was another. What other? Where is it now?"

"I had the one from the pier tested. There was blood on it all right, blood from a fish. It had been used by someone doing some early-season fishing," Sam explained. "And the murder weapon—"

"Was thrown into the bay," Josie said sadly. "At least

that's what Chris said she would do with something she wanted to get rid of when I asked her about it."

Both Sam and Risa began talking at once, trying to keep Josie from breaking into tears. That's probably why they didn't hear the knock on the door.

"Miss Pigeon!"

No one had to look around to know that Chief McCorkle had entered the building.

"I have a bench warrant here for a Miss Josephine Clay Pigeon," he announced.

" 'Clay Pigeon'?" Sam repeated with a grin spreading over his face.

"It's a family name," Josie said, trying to resist those crinkles forming around Sam's eyes.

"I am Ms. Pigeon's attorney," Sam said. "Why was this bench warrant issued, Chief McCorkle?"

"Miss Pigeon has not been paying her speeding tickets—or her ticket for littering in a public space. She's received more than one summons. And there are still questions to be answered about that breaking and entering at the bait shop."

"Excuse me," Josie said to Sam and Risa. "I need to speak to Chief McCorkle alone for a few minutes. If you'll join me on the deck?" she indicated the back door of the office and followed the man out.

Risa and Sam exchanged looks, but there was little time for any lengthy conversation. In a few moments Chief McCorkle reappeared, a scowl on his face.

Sam leaped to his feet. "Ms. Pigeon is my client," he began.

"This is a small island," Chief McCorkle said. "And sometimes we're a little casual about our paperwork. There won't be any tickets."

"But—"

"Good day, Mr. Richardson." And the island's chief of police stormed out the front door.

"What is going on?" Sam asked when Josie reappeared. "What did you threaten him with to get him to drop the tickets?"

"Threaten him? How could I threaten him? He was wearing a gun and all I had was a crab claw in my hand."

"So, *cara*, what did you do?"

"I bribed him."

"You're rich?" Sam asked.

"All you have to have to bribe someone is to have something they want. And it doesn't have to be money."

"Oh, *cara*, not . . ."

"Yes." Josie nodded seriously.

"What are you going to give this man?" Sam asked indignantly.

"Not him. His son."

"His son? What is going on here?"

"I just promised that I would not enter the crabbing contest that is held over the Labor Day weekend," Josie explained calmly. "I know the best places to crab on the island. I always win."

"And Rick?" Sam looked as though he couldn't believe what he was hearing.

"And Rick usually comes in second. This year I won't enter. Rick will win. That's all." Josie shrugged sunburned shoulders.

"You're telling me that a fishing contest is so important that a policeman will ignore the law to make sure his son wins?" Sam brushed his sandy hair off his forehead in disbelief.

"Welcome to life on the island," Risa said, lifting her glass in a toast.

"Well, I came here to find something new and different." Sam ran his hand through his hair and grinned. "And I guess I found it."

Josie walked over to the window to pet the cat that was sleeping in the warm sun. "I hope so," she said quietly, a smile on her face.

More murder in the suburbs
with

SUSAN HENSHAW,

wife, mother, chauffeur, chef,
friend, and amateur sleuth.

Read all of
VALERIE WOLZIEN's
outrageously witty mysteries
featuring America's favorite
domestic detective,
Susan Henshaw.